FURNACE
FLAT

Center Point
Large Print

Also by Frank Bonham and available from
Center Point Large Print:

Trago
Dakota Man
Devil's Graze
The Dark Border

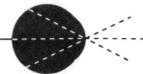

**This Large Print Book carries the
Seal of Approval of N.A.V.H.**

FURNACE FLAT

A Western Duo

Frank Bonham

CENTER POINT LARGE PRINT
THORNDIKE, MAINE

A Circle Ⓥ Western published by
Center Point Large Print in the year 2015 in
co-operation with Golden West Literary Agency.

First Edition October, 2015.
Printed in the United States of America on permanent paper.
Set in 16-point Times New Roman type.

ISBN: 978-1-62899-735-4 (hardcover)
ISBN: 978-1-62899-740-8 (paperback)

Library of Congress Cataloging-in-Publication Data

Bonham, Frank.
[Short stories. Selections]
Furnace flat : a western duo / Frank Bonham. — First edition.
pages cm
ISBN 978-1-62899-735-4 (hardcover : alk. paper)\
ISBN 978-1-62899-740-8 (pbk. : alk. paper)
1. Western stories. 2. Large type books.
   I. Bonham, Frank. Sergeant forson's dirty-shirt army.
   II. Bonham, Frank. Furnace flat. III. Title.
PS3503.O4315A6 2015c
813'.54—dc23

2015025190

Table of Contents

SERGEANT FORSON'S DIRTY-SHIRT ARMY

I

After the evening meal that September evening, Sergeant Forson mounted the guard. He arrived at the main gate with one sentry still to post. In the coolness the two of them climbed the sprung steps to the look-out, the sergeant climbing briskly, the guard lagging. It was a beautiful evening. The broad meadow of Cañon Creek drowsed in the dusk, and beyond the grass some small hills faded back to high mountains almost lost in smoky twilight.

Within the log-walled room the new guard relieved the old guard, who yawned and slouched away to dinner, and the sergeant lingered to peer through a rifle slot at the meadow.

"When do I get off, Sergeant?" asked the sentry as he loaded his gun.

"When your relief gets here."

"When's that gonna be?"

"At eleven, unless somebody falls asleep . . . it better not be you," added the sergeant. "There's just one crime nobody in this post has discovered yet, and that's sleeping on duty."

The sergeant had to stoop to gaze through the slot. He was a tall man with the whippy build of a horseman, dark-skinned and dark-haired, with a good-natured mouth that was becoming stern. His eyes traveled the big meadow curled like a cat in the lap of the hills. Fort Haney lay in a beautiful but vulnerable site. Because of the abundance of grass and water there was plenty of game, because of the game there were plenty of Indians, and because of a spineless commanding officer there was plenty of danger.

He heard the sentry lounge to a rifle slot to peer, trying to seem alert, at the small-timbered foothills. The horses that had grazed all day on Cañon Creek were being driven toward the water gate.

Studying the creek that looped like a snake down the meadow, the sentry said: "Them hydraulic fellers will be the death of us, hey? A horse has to have a tea strainer before he can drink crick water, after the mines've been working."

"That's a fact," agreed the sergeant. "Time to have another talk with Major King about Christianizing them."

"That'll fix it," said the trooper cynically.

From the stream, the sergeant saw a long smear of mud that trailed like war paint across the meadow, flattening the grass and creeping finally under the wall into the stable area. This was hydraulic mining country. Only a short distance above the post a big mining outfit had its main workings. When the great nozzles went rooting through a cliff like hogs going for turnips, the creek swelled with mud and water so that fifty miles downstream, riverside farmers and cowmen had to sprint for high ground.

The sergeant's eye cooled as he thought about his commanding officer, the only man this side of Applejack Mining Company who had the power to shut off those nozzles when the going got rough. But Major King disliked a ruckus. He was hardly a soldier's soldier. He had acquired his commission by paying the debts his predecessor had run up with local merchants when the state vouchers never came through, thus relieving Captain Poole for emergency service in Idaho. Sergeant Ward Forson was left behind, a cadre of one, to train the new troops.

Shortly Major Miles J. King, Oregon Volunteer Cavalry, had arrived in a tailor-made uniform, towing a collection of fifty-odd recruits dredged up in the coastal towns. He was said to have seen previous service somewhere. The sergeant often wondered about this. But out here in Oregon, with the Snake and Cayuse tribes growing meaner than a summer cold, and all the regular troops fighting in the South, the state was granting commissions to anyone who owned a uniform, spoke a little English, and would pay the debts of the outfit he wanted to command.

Naturally King's troop took the image of its commanding officer. It was the outyawningest, outscratchingest, most homesick, least promising gang of recruits the sergeant had ever trained. In three months he had succeeded in teaching them part of the manual of arms and the General Orders up to Number Three. But that was the result of having a shiftless commanding officer, whose conception of Indian fighting was to lock himself in his office and build ship models. And while he fashioned his little stern-wheelers, the Snakes were proving up on their ancestral claim to eastern Oregon, and in cabins where no lamp could risk being lit, farmers and ranchers were molding ball lead in bitter anticipation of having a bullet or two left for a hydraulic miner if they survived the next Indian raid.

"All right," said Sergeant Forson briskly, "it's your post, soldier."

"Say, thanks a lot," the sentry said, grinning widely,

Forson glanced sharply at him. He saw the face of a creature he had never met in this war before King crossed a civilian with a soldier and got a homesick trooper. It was difficult to recall that, with all its hand-me-down equipment, Fort Haney had been a place of proud horse soldiers a few months ago—horse soldiers who furnished their own horses, wore cast-off uniforms, fired anything they were able to buy that looked like a gun, but were dedicated to what they were doing. They fought nagging little engagements with the Snakes and Cayuses, and buried their dead hastily under small white crosses inscribed: AWAITING

THE LAST REVEILLE. Their credit had been defunct since the first year of the war. When they were in camp, the biggest tasks First Sergeant Forson handled were adjusting their bad debts, straightening out their love affairs, and keeping them from fighting with ungrateful civilians whose clotheslines, orchards, or daughters they had visited nocturnally. They were lean, tough, and homely. Nobody but the Indians had much respect for them. Nobody but the Indians was supposed to.

Crossing the floor, Forson said dryly: "Put your gun on safety, Trooper. You'll blow somebody's head off."

Outside, with the freshness of the late-summer evening against his face, he descended the lurching stairs and started up the street. The small gray barracks at either side were plain, each with a soot-streaked chimney and a mossy shake roof. The post would accommodate about two hundred men, and the fifty-seven volunteers now stationed here were insufficient even to keep the weeds down on the parade ground.

As he paced up the street, Forson glanced at his pocket watch. At once his stride quickened. Time to take a special detail down to Cañon City, two miles away. He was ten minutes late, and even in this post, haunted by ghosts who whispered wistfully of spit and polish, he tried to be punctual. Time for this and time for that; time for everything but loneliness. A codified system of life in which a man with something to forget had only one time of day in which to remember it—those five minutes between sprawling exhausted on his blankets and falling asleep. And if a bullet or an arrow found him and he fell asleep forever, even that might be welcome.

It was why Forson had joined up. He had been a rancher before he enlisted, but as the war continued the Indians made it increasingly hard to ranch in the high, dry country of eastern Oregon. Suddenly in the midst of the struggle Forson's wife died, and all at once there was no reason for him to stick it out, little reason for anything. They had been as much in love as it is possible for a man and woman to be, and he had enlisted out of pure misery. Things to do—that was how you held yourself together when life cracked you like a china cup. He sighed, and pressed the old loneliness back.

A lanky trooper with an old fatigue cap tipped down over one eye stepped into the street as Forson passed one of the barracks. He was a very tall man with yellow suspenders against his blue tunic and knee-length black boots. He gave the sergeant a surprised glance, and started up the street with his head down.

"Riggs," called the sergeant, "you're out of uniform!"

Riggs turned back, a stringy man with oily-black hair, pale eyes, and a long chin. He had been a trapper and prospector before he joined the Army. He spoke the Snake and Cayuse dialects and always had a few kinnikinnik leaves in his pocket for chewing or smoking. "See there?" he said with a bitter grin. "Man shovels mud all day, and then gits jumped for bein' out of uniform. I declare, Sergeant, there's no pleasin' you army folks."

"Don't blame me for the mud," said Forson. "The mines make it. We shovel it. Have you looked at the bulletin board today?"

Trooper Riggs maintained an amused contempt for Army ways. He colored a borderline insolence with tobacco-chewing humor. "No, sir, I been busy," he said. "What's on the bulletin board?"

"Your name, among others. You're on duty tonight in Cañon City. We're going to try to stop some election brawls before they start. Get into your blouse and clean your boots. Saddle up and fall in before the flagpole in fifteen minutes. Try to look like a soldier."

Riggs ran his thumbs along his suspenders. "I've plumb given up tryin' to look like a soldier, Sergeant," he said solemnly. "Reckon I'm more of a shootin' soldier than a fall-to-in-blouses soldier. I joined up to fight Injuns. I've scouted and told the major where the Snakes be, but that's just about as far as it's gone."

Forson agreed with him completely, yet he had

to be cautious. If this troop still had any morale at all, it was important not to destroy it by admitting that Major King was a fool. So the sergeant punched Riggs's shoulder and said: "Buck up! I've got information that we'll be in the field within two weeks."

"Not this 'coon," said Riggs. "I'm on my way right now to tell the major I'm buyin' out. If we ever do go to war with the Snakes, I don't want King doin' the thinkin' for me. Well, Sergeant, if I've took any Army towels, just send me a bill care of General Delivery."

He hitched at his pants and started up the muddy street. The sergeant spoke sharply: "As you were, Trooper! Get your equipment and fall out. You've got two years and some months to go."

Riggs sauntered back. "That's what I know. But it's down there in that book in the orderly room about how much it costs to buy out. Corporal Collins ciphered it up for me."

"Sometime," suggested the sergeant, "get Corporal Collins to cipher out how a man buys out in wartime. Can't be done. I need your kind of man, Riggs. You can outtrack an Indian, and you even talk a little Snake. I'm going to make a soldier out of you if I age ten years doing it."

Riggs's bony horse face hardened. "Ten years would be about the least you'd age." He spoke in a drawl, but a sleety anger was in the gray eyes. After a moment he turned and went back into the barracks.

Sergeant Forson found the other men waiting on the parade. It would be a few minutes before Riggs appeared. There was time to get Major King's approval of the election detail—a formality, for King would approve anything short of making an effort—and he might also bring up the matter of the damage caused by the flooding of the creek. He left the detail in charge of Trooper Brough and walked up the stone-bordered path to the little rock headquarters building.

Just then an old man in dirty Angora chaps, a brown canvas coat, and a black Stetson came from the orderly room and banged the door shut. He stood there with his head tilted down, glaring at the sergeant as he approached. Forson saw that it was old Bob Davis, a horse and mule rancher down on the John Day.

"Everything fine, Bob?" Forson asked.

"If losing seventeen animals is fine," Davis said through his teeth, "then things couldn't be better." He had been ranching in Indian country so long that he had fleshed down like an Indian himself—erect, silent, sparing of smiles. His neck was stiff, and he wore his hat squarely on his head. Weathering had cracked his brown face full of lines.

"When'd this happen?" asked the sergeant.

"Last night. While you were frolicking at Mother Gilbert's Dancing Academy, the Snakes were running off the last of my stock."

Out on the parade the recruits were listening with amusement. Forson said: "Can we talk about it in town? I've got a formation waiting on me. I'll see you at the Hydraulic, Bob."

Davis seized his arm as he tried to pass. "Don't try to hide behind a regulation book like that offscouring in there. I can talk to you any time, savvy? You're my size."

Forson's mouth hardened. Yet he knew everything that was in Davis's heart because he had been through it, too. "Sure you can," he said quietly, "but you can't shout at me. Do you know whose bunch this was?"

"I couldn't read his card," said Davis seriously. "It was wrote in Snake. But I judged from the arrows they shot in my hogs that it was Rogue Buffalo. He's taken enough horses and long blond scalps to drag weight any place in Oregon."

Just now, the window of the commandant's office being open, Ward Forson could not remind Davis: *It was different under Captain Poole.* He tilted his head toward the window and asked: "Is the Army taking action?"

Davis turned his face toward the window at the corner of the building and gave a braying laugh. "Action?" he said. "What the hell is action? Ain't seen any in so long I wouldn't recognize it. Ain't seen anything but paint and feathers and hydraulic slickers since Cap'n Poole left."

The sergeant laid a hand on his arm and said quietly: "Why don't you go in town and have supper? I'll look you up later."

"Man, that'll help a heap," scoffed the rancher. "You can buy me a drink and find me a job. Nothing doing out in the country these days. All the cow outfits the Snakes ain't scared out are up to their eyeballs in mud."

Touched with irritation, Sergeant Forson spoke shortly. "Maybe you'd better join up, then. They say the fear of Indians is the beginning of patriotism."

"You ought to know," said Davis as he walked off.

The sergeant removed his slouch campaign hat as he entered the building. His boots on the desk, Corporal Collins, the troop clerk, was reading a newspaper. He glanced at Forson, grunted a greeting, and resumed his reading. The sergeant stood there, long-limbed and somber of eye. Bad temper was spreading through him. He was hungry for the old days of efficiency and self-respect.

He regarded the clerk steadily and said: "Sergeant Forson requests permission to talk to the troop commander."

Collins stared at him over his journal. "How's 'at? Oh. Go on in," he said.

19

As he passed, Forson's boot caught a leg of the clerk's chair and the chair flattened under Collins. His head hit the wall as he crashed down.

"Beg pardon, soldier," murmured the sergeant. He drifted on to knock at Major King's door.

"Come in!" called the major.

Ward entered, closed the door, and saluted. King was working on his miniature steamboat. There was a cold dinner plate on his desk and a glass of whiskey by the inkwell. His craftsmanship was at odds with the slovenly nature of the room. Shavings covered much of the desk and the floor about it. Casey's *Tactics* lay on the desk, a pocket Bible, and Byron's poems. King's back was to the door. He was a big, middle-aged man with curly gray hair and easy-going ways.

"Take me down, Major," suggested the sergeant.

King glanced around and made a flaccid salute. "How's she look?" he asked, tapping a saw-toothed smokestack with his penknife. The boat was about two feet long. Sometimes he worked all day on the model. He loafed through his days like a man with his mind on something else, reading letters from his daughter Jess, writing letters, and drinking. Meantime the Snakes were briskly at their trade of raiding horse ranches, farms, and stages.

"Looks very pretty," said Ward. "Naming it after your daughter, I see."

"Sergeant"—King smiled—"you *do* notice everything." On a little plaque slung between the stacks was lettered the name JESSAMIN.

"Yes, sir, and I noticed a little mud in the post after last night's hydraulics. I expect you know what happens when buildings like this get wet through?"

"The joints melt," said King. "I spoke to Jim Harris about it this morning. He says they'll be more careful."

Forson spaced his boots eighteen inches apart, clasped his hands behind him, and stared over the major's head. His leather-brown eyes were angry. "Major, I thought he was going to be more careful beginning two weeks ago."

King stood the penknife point-up on the desk and rocked it pensively. "His superintendent got a little ambitious. If it happens again, Harris will send a clean-up crew over." His voice had changed as he spoke, seeming to run out of conviction and force.

Coward, fool, or bungler? the sergeant wondered. King had laid a lot of money on the line for his commission. Yet he let a civilian push him around and he had not the faintest idea how many hostiles were in the area or where their camps were.

The sergeant did not comment, and King tipped back in his chair to gaze out the window. Before the flagpole, two soldiers lay on their backs Indian wrestling while the others shouted them on.

"Do you actually think this election detail is necessary?" asked the major.

Forson glanced down at him thoughtfully. "You heard Davis roasting us, Major. There are a lot of farmers and ranchers just like him in town tonight, and they've brought their cowhands and plow hands along. They can't do much about the Snakes. But some of them would put a shot in Jim Harris if they got a chance. He's washed out bridges and a lot of their good hay lands. This election's got them all heated up. Not that they've got a prayer to elect a ranch mayor."

King did not move. He was a big man, exceptionally broad-shouldered, but he was putting on too much weight sitting around this post. Yet with all his faults, he was curiously likable. "True," King said at last. "But of course the man who takes the blame for everything . . . the mines, the Indians, and the sad condition of Cañon Street . . . is Miles J. King, Major, First Oregon Cavalry. Isn't that so?" He turned quickly to glance at Ward.

Ward cleared his throat. "Well, sir, I . . ."

"Of course it is. With fifty-seven unseasoned recruits, I'm expected to police the stage roads, decimate the Indians, and make all the gravel miners in the area behave themselves. It can't be done, Sergeant. It simply can't be done!"

"Captain Poole did it with forty-odd, sir."

The remark fell like a pool ball on a wooden

22

floor. The sergeant stiffened as if waiting for a blow. After an instant King tossed the knife on his desk and rose. He brushed wood shavings from his blue tunic. A large, handsome man, his dissipations were just beginning to alter his face. Little deltas of broken veins reddened his cheeks, but there was a strong ledge of bone over his eyes and a hard military strength about his mouth, and his eyes were sad and friendly and cynical.

"You must miss Captain Poole terribly," King said. "No doubt I could get you transferred to Idaho with him, if you like."

"I'm needed here, sir," Ward said stiffly.

"How did my famous predecessor accomplish these miracles?"

"They weren't so much miracles," said Ward, "as a constant sort of drudgery. When Harris got his monitors roaring, we posted a guard on them. There are gravel mines on every creek in this area, but most of them are being run with some conscience. When it was time for Harris to turn his monitors off, his men turned them off or got the butt of a gun under the chin. So there wasn't much flooding downstream."

"I find no mention of this in his daybooks," argued King.

"No, sir. He was too busy to keep up his daybooks. You know what Harris is doing, don't you?"

King's big face was polite. "Tell me."

"He's racing. They've got laws to control hydraulics in California, now. Ours go into effect next year. He's trying to wash out all the gold he can before he has to build silt basins to catch the run-off."

King walked to the window and crossed his arms as he gazed out. All the coolness of the September evening was gathered into the breeze blowing over the parade ground. "Sergeant, don't you know what would happen if I tried to close up Applejack Mine? You and I would be at war with two hundred miners and the entire town of Cañon City in forty-eight hours. Jim Harris isn't Applejack. Cañon City is Applejack. Every bookkeeper and waitress and stonemason and teamster in town owns stock in the company. And any that don't are indirectly working for it. This town has to cater to it. Do you think they'd let me bankrupt Applejack Mining Company by locking up Harris?"

"I didn't mean to lock him up, Major. Just slow him down."

"Something else you seem to miss," argued King, "is that possibly Harris can't afford to be slowed down. He's got a big payroll, and maybe not much fat to live on."

"That's his look-out. He can't wash out the farmers and beef cattlemen to keep his stock-holders happy."

King faced him again, his jaw stubborn. "You

24

seem also to miss the point that Washington needs the gold that Cañon City produces."

"But Cañon City needs the beef and crops those ranch people produce."

Smiling ironically, King clasped his hands behind him. "Tell me," he said curiously, "just how would you run this outfit if you were wearing the leaves instead of me?"

Ward looked carefully at him.

"It's not a trap, Sergeant," King encouraged.

Holding King's gaze, the sergeant began to talk in a deep and thoughtful voice. "To begin with, I'd put a headlock on Harris. Then I'd make soldiers out of those horse-playing civilians out there. I'd drill the hell out of them. I'd teach them how to tell an Indian from a sage hen. Then I'd show them some real Indians. The ones that had listened and learned would probably come back. In a couple of months I might have the stages rolling again and put some beef ranchers back in business."

"In two months you're going to make soldiers . . . out of *those?*" His thumb indicated the men on the parade.

"It's happened before."

"No doubt. But to pay six hundred and fifty dollars as I did . . . and be given a troop of clodhoppers. God forbid I should be sitting on a camp full of citizen soldiers again. Excuse me," he added at once. "I forgot you're one."

"Excuse *me,* Major." The sergeant smiled. "I thought you were one yourself."

King frowned, tucked one hand in his blouse pocket, drew it out again, and, shrugged. "Some previous service, at least. Enough to know a farmer from a trooper. Ah, well, I'll go in with you tonight and have a talk with Harris. There's nothing we can't work out with him."

He donned his hat and blouse, pulled on high-fringed gauntlets, and when he approached the door Ward was holding open for him, he smiled— again the aimless, hard-drinking, easy-going officer.

"No hard feelings?"

"Only for Indians and hydraulickers," replied the sergeant.

"That's the spirit." King chuckled. He slapped him on the shoulder, and they left the room. Corporal Collins, who was on the list for election duty, had departed.

II

While Major King received his horse, Sergeant Forson called the roll from the slip of paper listing the guards.

"Brough!"

"Here, sir."

Brough was an earnest man with flat feet and

thick glasses, who would do what you told him, if he could. Because he had been an elder in a church, he read services for the troop.

"Collins!"

"Yeah," responded Collins, in the voice of a dog growling over a bone.

He glanced up at the camp clerk with a frown. Collins was a tall, tough-chinned man who had been a muleskinner in civilian life. His head was like a skull and his narrow face was dark and ugly. There were no sleeves in Fort Haney long enough for his arms, and his big hands seemed to be all knuckles and sinew. With them he did the finest penmanship Ward had ever seen. Collins was resentful about having been tipped over, and he returned the sergeant's stare doggedly. Ward smiled to himself and glanced down at his list.

"Viets!"

"Here."

Viets was about fifty. He was too small for his uniform, too short for his musket, and had no upper front teeth. He had been a printer. His skin was white and loose, like that of a dressed pullet; he looked as unsoldierly as a man could look, but the sergeant had made good troopers out of less promising material than Viets. He went on down the list, and the final name seemed to jump at him. He glanced up.

"Riggs!"

There was absolute silence in the ranks. Ward

27

slowly scanned the group, his mouth setting. His eyes trailed coldly down the double line of troopers holding their mounts. "Riggs?" he called again.

No reply. He shot a look at Trooper Brough, who bunked nearest Riggs. "Have you seen Riggs in the last fifteen minutes?"

Brough's hand rose to adjust his silver-rimmed spectacles. "Yes, sir."

"Where?"

"Going . . . going out the water gate."

"Were there packs on his saddle?"

All the other troopers were looking at the ground, smiling, except Collins, whose eyes traced a hawk through the sky. Brough looked frightened.

"Yes, sir."

Ward was breathless with anger and surprise. He about-faced and announced to the major: "All present or accounted for except Trooper Riggs, sir. Trooper Riggs absent without leave."

King sat his horse calmly, but his eyes were hard. Behind Ward the cavalrymen were waiting quietly, but distantly, in the kitchen, a man was trying to muffle laughter. Ward noted King's lips pressed together and it seemed that he was getting ready to pull all his anger together and spit it out in a curse.

"I think it's time the men of this post realized something," he said slowly. He drew his tasseled saber and began spanking his boot with it as he stared at the men. Impelled by some new respect, they drew themselves up. "It's damn' well time," continued King, his voice rising, "that you men understood you're in the Army! Not the big Army, maybe, but an arm of it! And the fact that Riggs volunteered won't take any of the heat out of that branding iron when I slap a D for Deserter on his rump! And that, gentlemen, is what will happen to any other soldier who leaves without permission or gives indication of intent to desert. Clear?"

Startled, two of the men saluted. A trooper's carbine clanged on the ground. A few nodded.

"If he isn't back by bed check, Sergeant, take six men and find him." Ward saluted. His hand cracked his thigh as he brought it down. "Column of twos, Sergeant," grunted King.

Ward's eyes shone. He felt wonderful. He had his hands on this gang at last. "Detail!" he shouted. "Stand to horse . . . ho! Prepare to mount."

He jogged along the hillside road beside the major. Cañon City was a two-mile ride down the creek from the fort. The early night was tender with fragrances of the meadow. Butterfly moths flicked across the road, and horses in pasture ranged up and down the snake fences as they passed, whickering urgently to the cavalry horses. It was dark overhead, but on the broken horizon the sky was bottle-green, with chips of stars settling out. He was pleased to find himself noticing these things. Nothing had seemed beautiful since his wife died. The pleasure of sharing was really all the pleasure there was when you were in love. And now suddenly, tonight, things were inexplicably pulling together for him. His satisfaction in seeing King take hold made him aware that he had crossed a threshold. He was capable of genuine pleasure once more.

Along the road, lamps burned with a mellow light in the small houses they passed. In the dusk he discerned beauty in the shacks, clothes-lines, sheds, and family orchards of Cañon City. King began speaking. His voice was low and brusque, and Ward had to thrust his horse over to hear him.

"What's wrong with Riggs? A man doesn't usually take off without good reason."

"He's sore because he was planning to buy his discharge and I turned him down."

King made a sound of disgust. "What's he think this is . . . a marching society?"

"They all do. Men go barn-sour just sitting around. They must have got all keyed up for Indian fighting, or they wouldn't have joined up. Then there was the big let-down."

Cañon City was located just where the banks of the stream squeezed in. The mining town lay like two halves of a walnut on either side of the gorge.

Cedar slopes climbed high over the city on both sides, and far above were bands of rimrock, where the pines started. Bridges, trussed and anchored with cables, tied the two halves of the town together. They passed a turn, and the business district was ahead, a solid looking alley of two-story buildings constructed of yellow volcanic tuff that was so narrow that a wagon team could not be turned around in it. There was a sprinkling of lights in the windows, yellow and diffused, and a view of turnouts and wagons on the gullied road. Carbide lights, hard and white as diamonds, illuminated the street.

The town was thronged with farm and ranch people in for the election. Banners flapped lazily above the street and distantly the wheeze and thump of a band, like a steam engine, pulsed in the air. A big flannel-shirted man on the walk before the Hydraulic Saloon shouted at the cavalrymen: "Hey, soldiers! I hear you're all being transferred to the Navy. How about that?"

It was John Champie, superintendent of Applejack Mine's gravel operations. He was standing on the walk by a wagon from which a load of miners was dismounting. As they jumped down, they went jostling into the saloon. He stood half a head above most of the miners, a strapping man of forty with a strength like oak, his hair black and cut short, a bantering smile on his mouth, his eyes grained with squint lines. Ward glanced at the major, expecting him to say something, but King peered straight ahead. So the sergeant, too, was silent.

Now, on the right, he saw a big gas-lit banner before a print shop:

End the Shame of Cañon City!
Plummer for Mayor!

Roy Plummer was editor and publisher of the *Courier*. The old man was up on a saw-horsed platform, making a speech to a little crowd of out-of-towners and local citizens brave enough to take the derision that came from being on the wrong side. He was lean as a saber, wore an iron-gray mustache and goatee that they said he darkened with printer's ink, and his jeering sense of humor kept even his partisans from liking him very much. As the troopers passed, Plummer ceased speaking suddenly, removed his hat, and placed it over his heart, his head bowed.

Champie's voice called from downstreet: "Old Plummer'll do anything for a vote, boys! There's respect for the flag!"

Plummer raised his head and gazed at Champie across the street. He did not shout, but his voice went through the racket like a file. "No, no, Champie, not for the flag. Respect for the dead!"

Ward saw King's face flush. King's horse stepped out a little and the major brought it back with the bit, but he had given himself away by that involuntary squeeze of the spurs.

As they reached the stage depot, the noise of the band expanded, became a ragged gather of individual noises, and the band of the Cañon City Union Guard marched from the yard. King pulled to the edge of the boardwalk to let them pass. Stepping high behind the bass drum, the marching society moved down the street. A wagon banked with baled hay rumbled behind, with some of the town dignitaries seated on the tiers in silk hats. There were posters on the sides of the wagon, carrying the name of Mayor William T. Blair—Big Bill—who operated the stage line to The Dalles and was up for reëlection as mayor. Having Jim Harris behind him, his only concern was the size of the plurality. Election was assured.

The noise of the band was making the horses nervous. A landau decorated with red, white, and blue bunting rolled into the street. Except for the driver, Big Bill Blair and Jim Harris were the only men in this vehicle. Blair was just tucking a bottle inside the buffalo greatcoat he wore whenever the weather permitted. He was a huge, pink-faced man with the voice of a bear and the emotions of a child. Jim Harris was smiling faintly as they came into the gaslit twilight of the street. Drawn by the concussions of the band, spectators were beginning to line the walks. Harris's head turned, and he was looking squarely at Major King. Ward saw his brows pull with displeasure for an instant. He was a large man with a quiet power, smooth, fast on his feet, a match for anyone in this town. He wore a wide-striped brown suit, a tan silk hat, and was smoking a cigar. His features were regular and strong, the chin broad, and his eyes keen and good-humored. Ward had seen him in work clothes. Then he had a look of sledge-hammer solidness. He had been a mucker and a hard-rock man in his time, and he still had the trim frame of a man who could swing a sixteen-pound maul hour after hour. His expression changed quickly to one of amiable recognition and he tapped the driver's shoulder. The landau stopped.

"What's this, Major?" he called to King. "Electioneering? I didn't know the Army had a candidate."

"Keeping the peace," said King.

Harris winked at Big Bill Blair and smiled. "You mean there's some upstart running against Bill?"

"Not runnin' . . . crawlin'," said Blair with a grin. His face was richly veined and shining.

"However you like it." King shrugged. "But we're going to try to keep the riots down to a series of quiet brawls."

Harris spoke suddenly to the mayor: "Bill, what do you say to a military escort? Some anonymous ill-wisher might throw something at you. That way we could have him executed on the spot."

"That's an idea, Jim!" exclaimed Blair, standing shaggily in his coat. His immense shoulders made his head look small. He glanced at the troopers and pointed his finger at Ward. "Couple of you fellers ride in front and a couple more in back," he directed.

Harris watched the major with a taunting smile. "Do us the honor of riding beside the carriage, Major."

Fury ran like syrup through Ward. *Ah,* he thought, *now we break this ambitious clothes-horse down to a bank clerk fourth class.* He waited for King's bitten-out retort. King had a nice sense of irony with which he could cut any man in this town to pieces.

"We're here on business," King told Harris. "Some of these farm and ranch people . . . even a few of Blair's own parishioners . . . might be just sore enough tonight to start a fight."

"Now, now, Major," reproved Harris. "It wouldn't cost the government a nickel for you to ride around town with us for a half hour. And look at the tone it would give our parade!"

"Also the Army's tacit approval of your candidate," retorted King.

Harris smiled and settled back. "Give the men to the sergeant and let's go. We'll never catch up with that hay wagon."

Gazing at King, Ward saw the long, hard line of his jaw ripple. King's hand dropped to his saber and he rubbed the polished metal for a moment. He seemed to bristle like a fighting cock. Harris kept watching him, his long, squarish face confident. In a way he looked as military as King. Blended with his quiet force, yet hidden by it, was a core of strength like that of one of his huge brass monitors that shaped the water it threw into a deceptive, glistening smoothness.

"All right . . . a half hour," King grunted finally. "Take over, Sergeant. I'll meet you at the Hydraulic in a half hour."

He did not meet Ward's eyes as he picked four men and rode off beside the carriage. Ward watched him ride away. He glanced at the troopers. They had felt it, all right. They sat their horses awkwardly, sheepishly, a little resentfully. He cleared his throat, wiped his mouth, and tried to decide what was best. After all, what could you say when your commanding officer had just shown himself publicly to be a coward?

Suddenly he turned in the saddle. "Collins, button your blouse! What are you chawing on, Selaya . . . Navy plug? This is the Army . . . spit it out. Column of twos . . . ho!"

They rode into the stage yard, where they customarily left their horses while in town. *This cooks us,* Ward realized. *This really cooks us!* A troop had no more prestige than its commanding officer, and King had none.

In the stage yard, while they tended the horses,

Ward made enough noise to try to offset the impression King had left. A few men working there listened with good-natured amusement as he assigned the men—two to this saloon, three to that, four to the Hydraulic Saloon, of which he himself made one. He was preparing to leave with his own detail, mounted so that he could make his rounds more quickly, when a girl in the door of the waiting room spoke.

"I'd like to talk to you a moment, Sergeant . . . if you'll promise not to make me dress up my line."

Ward stopped with his boot in the stirrup, looking across the horse at her. It was Jamie Harris, the mining man's daughter. She stood with one hand on the doorknob and her other hand on her hip, looking right at him with a laugh in her eyes. She was a brown-eyed, succulent little morsel who was often on John Champie's arm. Her brown silk gown was lightly hooped and very snug at the waist, gleaming in the folds like metal, and sparkling with a row of glass buttons down the bodice. She looked small and attractive and very, very expensive.

Ward set his boot down. He said boldly: "I wouldn't want your lines dressed any other way, Miss Jamie." She was close enough to Jim Harris that he felt he could reach Harris a little by showing disrespect to her.

"Why, Sergeant," said Jamie, but she continued

smiling at him, "I would like to talk to you, though. Please?"

Ward told troop clerk Collins to take the men to the Hydraulic. Pulling off his gauntlets, he walked to the door, put his foot up on the sill, and said: "At your service, miss."

"If you'll just walk me around the corner," she said, "there's something in our buggy that I was to give you."

III

The side street pitched steeply away from Cañon Street and a block below ended in a barricade. The high branches of poplar and willow rose from the cañon. Lost in dark greenery, the creek sounded heavy and full. A pungent odor of leaves filled the air. Ward saw the buggy parked under a big mountain ash with a *morral* of grain over the horse's muzzle. Jamie Harris's hand rested lightly on his arm. Reaching the buggy, she turned back a blanket in the carry-all to expose a small crate.

"What's this?" Ward leaned over to scrutinize the box.

Jamie giggled. "Do you like wine? It's a case of Spanish sherry for the officers and non-commissioned officers of Fort Haney."

Ward slowly straightened, turning a glance of disapproval on her. "What's the occasion?"

"It's the occasion of our nearly drowning you," said the girl. "Father wanted you to have it. He was terribly angry at John Champie for letting it happen. But he thought it would be better, perhaps, if it came from me than from him."

"Why was that, I wonder? He wasn't bashful about drafting King to his colors just now."

"Oh," she said, "what's a parade without uniforms? But honestly . . . we feel so guilty about flooding you. We want to make up for it a little. Please take it, Ward."

Ward rubbed his nose, squinting at her. Something in her humility rang as false as a cracked church bell. "As I get it, we save the wine until the next time we get flooded, and then we sit in rowboats and drink it. That right?"

"You're a wicked and hard man," pouted Jamie.

"I'm a tired and disgusted cavalryman," he said.

"Disgusted? Why? Wishing you were in civilian life again?"

"That's the long-term disgust. The short-term one is serving under an officer who licks the hand of anyone with enough money and position to flag him off."

Frowning, Jamie crossed her arms, studied him for a few moments before she spoke. "That isn't very nice, Ward."

"Whereas it's very, very nice to see your outfit made ridiculous by a poodle like King. I'm not saying he's taken money to leave Applejack alone. But you might remember it was different under Captain Poole. The mines worked just so long when he was around." He flipped the blanket back over the case of wine. "Why don't you present this to King yourself? If there's any apology accepted, it won't be by me."

It was quite dark now. Her face was pale and only half seen. He could hear her light breathing. Finally he offered the girl his arm. She hesitated an instant, then took it without looking at him, and they walked up the steep walk.

"You take things so seriously," she said finally.

"That's what the major says."

"And, you're so sure you're right."

"About this, yes. It's the original one-sided argument."

She smiled archly. "Now I'll tell you the other side. You're forgetting that miners built Cañon City. It was built by and for miners. And you can't get gold out of gravel with a magnet. You have to wash it, and with a good head of water." She was talking rapidly and a little angrily. It was her voice, but the words were her father's.

Ward smiled. "That's upstream talk, Miss Harris."

"All right. But it won't go on very long. Then they'll be through here and moving on somewhere else." She sounded breathless and impatient, quite furious with this man who could not tolerate a little corruption even when he was being cut in on it.

"Ah," said Ward, stopping. "I wish you'd make a little speech to that effect on Roy Plummer's platform. Most of the people in this town aren't voting your ticket at all . . . they're voting their own meal ticket. If they thought there was any chance of the mines closing, they'd start nailing together some sort of economy that didn't float on Applejack."

"I didn't say that," Jamie protested. "You turn my words around! When the big deposits are washed out, then they'll settle down to reworking the old bars."

"So that nothing but willows will ever grow along the rivers again. I've seen that, too, and some of the corruption from the cement mining. I'll tell you what I'd do with that wine, Miss Jamie," he said seriously, patting her hand. "I'd pour it in the creek so the folks downstream would feel better about being washed out because Jim Harris won't build silt basins. What do you think about that?"

The girl drew her hand away. "I think you're as unreasonable and short-sighted as most of the Army people I've known."

"Known a lot of them?" asked Ward.

"Sometimes a very few can seem like quite a lot." The girl smiled.

"In fact," Ward told her, "your father seems to

think that one sergeant can be an oversupply. But you'd better tell him for me that if I had a price, it wouldn't be as cheap as a smile and a case of sherry."

"You'll take less before you get more," Jamie Harris told him quietly. In the dusk her face was small, neat, and as threatening as a knife. With a whirl of her skirts, she turned and started away.

Ward began to chuckle. But it was not at all funny, when you thought about it. It indicated that Jim Harris thought he could buy anybody in Fort Haney, including trouble-making sergeants. A case of Spanish wine. For a dozen bottles of good wine, First Sergeant Forson was expected to withdraw his opposition to Applejack's operations. Probably John Champie had suggested a bottle of whiskey, and Harris, being more imaginative, had countered with a case of imported wine. He thought about it as he walked to the Hydraulic Saloon. Somewhere he could hear the band. He thought of King with his bought commission and his tailor-made uniform, riding beside Harris's carriage. What the devil ailed the man? Maybe he was drunk when he decided to become a soldier, and now all of Troop F had to share his hangover.

The Hydraulic was a prosperous saloon in a two-story structure of yellow volcanic blocks. From its ornamental cornices a cable dipped across the road to the top of the City House Hotel, a Big Bill Blair banner flapping from it. Flanking the wide doors were a pair of brass nozzles fitted out as lamps to illuminate the shiny liquor shields displayed like coats-of-arms. Trooper Brough was standing beside one, looking ill at ease in his baggy uniform. He smiled nervously and said: "No trouble, Sergeant."

"The brawls," snapped Ward, "won't be out here. Get inside!"

He parted the doors with his knee and heard Brough hastily coming after him. The other troopers had posted themselves at either end of the tall bar, Collins, ugly and glowering, standing nearest the door. The ceiling was high, covered with stamped, metal wall covering. Behind the bar, sweating bartenders in vests, slicked-down hair, and aprons like tubes, desperately poured liquor, and rinsed glasses in buckets of murky water. Men crowded the bar six deep, shouting and trying to get a drink. The rest of the room was almost bare.

A bell rang. "That's all, boys!" a man shouted from a balcony at the end of the room. The sergeant looked up and saw John Champie, Harris's superintendent. The men at the bar began to grumble. Many of them drifted away to the tables. Champie, rugged in his red flannel shirt and stagged pants, shouted good-naturedly: "Five minutes of free liquor every hour . . . what more do you want?"

"Fifty-five minutes!" bawled a miner.

Laughing, Champie walked to the end of the balcony and passed through a door. In a moment he came from a stairway entrance into the room. Here he paused to light a cigar, his glance moving expertly over the crowd. He crossed the floor in Ward's direction, stopping to lay a hand on this shoulder and that among the tables, smiling, joking, buying votes for Big Bill Blair.

Ward watched him steadily, his jaw set. "Anything new?" he asked Collins out of the corner of his mouth.

"That clown, Champie," growled the trooper. "I wanted to buy a drink, and he wouldn't let them sell me one till I got a note from my mother."

"He was right for once. If I smell liquor on your breath tonight, you'll go back to latrine duty."

Collins glowered at Champie. "And old Davis is loaded and looking for trouble," he said. "Liable to find it, too, shooting off his mouth about the mines in *this* crowd."

"I'll ease him out," Ward said.

"Ease me over a half pint of cough medicine," suggested Collins. "I'm getting the quinsy from all that mucking in the mud today."

Ward saw the old rancher at the bar among some cowboys. He supposed the cowboys were showing their independence by drinking in the Hydraulic Saloon on election night; nevertheless all of them except Bob Davis were being mighty quiet. Still, a fuse was quiet, and Ward uneasily glanced along the bar. Davis was drunkenly pounding the bar, his Stetson on the back of his head. No one was paying him any attention. Then Davis saw Ward. His old Indian's face lit. He stepped back dramatically from the bar.

"Attenshun, you muckers! General Grant's a-comin' this way!"

A cowboy glanced at Ward and turned back to his drink. "A.P. Hill," he said.

Davis clutched Ward's arm and held himself steady. "Hey, General," he said. "Make contact with the enemy tonight?"

"What enemy?" asked Ward.

"That Snake squaw they say you went scouting with. She invite you up to the big chief's teepee tonight?"

"Both of us," said Ward. "She asked me to bring you along for dinner. They're going to barbecue a hydraulicker with an apple in his mouth. We've just got time to make it. Come on, old-timer."

"Oh, hell, I ain't going to eat for a week," said Davis, brushing Ward's hand off. "I got stuff to celebrate. Here comes my friend, Champie. Want you to meet him, Sergeant. Champie, this here is . . . whud you say your name was, General?"

"Longstreet," said Ward.

Champie took his cigar from his mouth. "I'm Lee," he said seriously with a wink at Ward. "Pleased to make your acquaintance, sir."

Champie had a voice like a trumpet and an overbearing manner with which he dominated everything and everyone who crossed his path. There were shadows of uneasiness in his eyes. "I hear," he said, "you were with Brown at Harper's Ferry, General. That a fact?"

"Well, no," said Ward, "but I was with King at Fort Haney. I got a medal for distinguished pick-and-shovel work."

Champie laughed heartily. "And now you're going to get some more decorations for beating up miners on election day, eh?"

"Only if they ask for it."

"You know," Champie said, still grinning, but with vindictiveness in his eyes, "if you worried about the Snakes a little more, I bet we'd bother you less. I don't know what use Indians have got for bullion, but they've knocked over two of our shipments since King took command. How about that?"

"That's something you'll have to take up with Major King," Ward told Champie.

"Is Rogue Buffalo a brother-in-law of King's, or something?" asked Champie. "Way things are going, they'll be calling you the White Flag Troop in the history books."

Ward turned abruptly to Bob Davis. "Bob, that dinner's not going to keep forever." He took the old rancher's arm, but now it was John Champie who disengaged his hand.

"Let him alone," Champie said. "He's my guest tonight."

Ward started to speak, but Davis suddenly put his hand on Champie's shoulder and pushed his face close to Champie's. He made his eyes small and mean. "You know what you are?" he said, weaving his head sarcastically.

"Tell me." Champie's hand slowly took his cigar to his mouth. Around them, his miners were turning to listen.

"Come on, Bob," Ward said gruffly.

"You're yella!" snarled Davis. "You got a yella streak that laps clean around from your backbone."

Champie's arm came between Ward and the rancher as Ward tried to take Davis in charge. He laid his big hand on the bar and his arm was like an oak scantling. He had sloughed off his tinplating of good nature. "There's just about one thing a man can do after a remark like that," he said.

"Yeah, and you ain't man enough to do it." Davis crowded him with drunken courage. Champie was under forty, as tough as any man in his crews, and could have broken Davis's jaw with a six-inch swing. "You ain't even man enough," persisted the drunken rancher, "to match me drink for drink."

Champie's teeth shone and his eyes glinted. "Name your poison," he invited.

Davis's faded eyes flicked to Ward's. Deep in them was a spark of sense. "Think he's man enough to down an Oregon Trail boiler-maker?" he asked Ward.

A laugh formed in Ward. Maybe Champie didn't know about Davis's famous drink. "No, I don't reckon he is," he said soberly. "I don't reckon any man in this room is, Bob." He glanced at Champie.

The superintendent's arrogance had been reached. A boss hydraulicker had to be God and straw boss to his men. Champie struck a match, relit his cigar, and dropped the burning match without taking his gaze from the tight face of the rancher. "Lots of wind, Davis," he said, "not much action."

"Two beers," Davis told a bartender. Along the counter, cowboys and ranchers were grinning. Davis had a special fame in the ranch country for this drink of his. The bartender drew two beers from a keg, whisked an ivory suds knife across them, and set both at Davis's elbow. Along the backbar was a row of cut-glass mirrors broken only by pyramids of bottles, trays of hard-boiled eggs and cold meats, and in the center an oil painting of a nude washing her feet in a creek. In one of the mirrors Ward could see the balcony spanning the back of the big room like a bridge. From one end of the balcony a hall ran toward some rent rooms. A man was standing at the entrance to this hallway, out of view except in the mirror, watching the action at the counter. He stood well back, as though he intended not to be seen, a lanky man with his hands on his hips.

Ward looked at Davis again. From the pocket of his canvas coat he was taking a handful of raisins. Lint and dust speckled them and there were what looked like pellets of clay among them. Davis put a few raisins in his mouth and began chewing them with his front teeth like a squirrel shelling piñon nuts. He laid the remainder on the counter and Champie glowered at them.

"If this bet involves eating any crumby raisins you've been carrying around . . ."

With his little finger, Davis flipped the raisins away until only the earthen pellets remained. "Know what them is?" he asked Champie.

"Dirt," suggested Champie.

"Strychnine," said Davis.

He dropped one of the pellets in his beer. He dropped another in Champie's schooner, and stirred both with a suds knife. His elbow slid a little on the mahogany; he caught himself, and grinned at the superintendent as he emptied a chamois poke on the counter. There were a $50 gold bar, a double eagle and a few pennies. "Seventy dollars says you ain't got the intestines to drink with me," he said.

IV

Champie glanced at a cowboy behind Davis. "What is that stuff?"

"Strychnine," said the cowpuncher.

Champie's eyes scoffed. He put $70 on the counter. "OK, you drink first," he said to the rancher.

Davis raised his glass, toasted—"To the gophers of Oregon, gentlemen, for I've poisoned a-many!"—and drank the entire glass without stopping. Wiping his mouth on his sleeve, he pushed Champie's glass to him.

Champie took the glass in his hand, started to raise it, and hesitated. Ward saw sweat on his brow. Champie turned quickly to ask Ward: "What the hell is that stuff?"

"Strychnine," Ward said. "A rancher in this country practically has to carry it and some raisins to keep the gophers down. I suppose after twenty years of eating raisins with strychnine dust you get used to the stuff."

Champie set the glass down suddenly and recovered his money. "You go to hell," he told Davis. "You rigged that bet."

Davis smiled and belched. "Worth seventy dollars to see the color of your backbone. Oscar," he told the bartender, "bring a glass of milk for Mister Champie. Not too rich."

The cowboys and ranchers in the room shouted their laughter. Ward laughed, too, but just then he looked into the backbar mirror and saw that the man on the balcony had come forward a little farther, drawn by the laughter that had shattered the tension. For an instant the light from a wall lamp sifted yellow over the side of his face. The face was long and bony, the man's hair was oily and black, and the shirt he wore was a faded Army blue. Instantly he moved back from the light. But Ward had recognized Trooper Riggs.

He turned quickly from the bar and pushed between Champie and Bob Davis. As he started through the crowd, Champie's big hand casually captured his arm. "What's the hurry, General?"

Ward tried to yank loose, but Champie held on. Upstairs a man was striding down the hall. "I'm getting serious about that barbecued hydraulicker," he snapped. "Cut loose, mister!"

Champie did not look at the balcony, but he showed that he knew what was going on. "Hell, let the poor jughead go," he said. "He'll be back after he gets fixed up. Bet he don't do it again till next time."

"I said cut loose!"

Champie's fingers bit into his arm like fence pliers, and without warning Ward raised his boot and stamped on the man's instep. As Champie let go with a gasp, Ward raked his knuckles down on the bridge of his nose. Champie fell back with his hand over his face. Ward started past him, but just then two miners moved in on him. One of them threw a long, loose swing at his head while the other drove at his belly, head down. Ward blocked the first man's swing, but the other man hit him like a boar hog. He was carried back against the bar.

Bob Davis uttered a roar. "Three against one, hey?" he shouted. And he lunged in with his beer schooner cocked. He hit the man who had tackled Ward, just as the other man met him with a punch on the side of the head. Old Davis staggered away, but he came up against several of the men he had been drinking with, who now came forward in a flushed and eager fury. An instant later, Champie, his nose bleeding, waved his arm to marshal his own troops to meet them.

Ward turned his head. "Collins! Brough! See to it!"

Then he skirted Champie and lunged through the crowd toward the staircase. Just before he went up, he glanced back and to his great surprise saw Corporal Collins standing on the bar with his rifle held like a club, kicking bottles and glasses out of his way as he came to rescue Davis and break up the fight.

Ward took the steps three at a time and emerged onto the balcony. Below him was the smoky, surging crowd, the flash of mirror and polished oak. Champie had left the brawl and was working toward the stairs. At Ward's left was the doorway, and he went through it and was in a hall. The hall ran toward the back and was lined with small sleeping rooms. A lamp halfway down the hall furnished a shadowy illumination.

As he stood there, he heard a lock click. He drew his Navy pistol and started down the hall. He could hear John Champie's heavy boots ascending the stairs. He heard a window scrape up and turned quickly to the door through which the sound had come. He twisted the brown porcelain knob; the door was locked. Ward struck it with his fist.

"Open up!"

A woman said irritably: "Go away. I'm busy."

"You're going to be busier, honey," rapped Ward, "if you don't unlock this door."

There was no answer. Ward hit the door with one booted foot. The girl cried shrilly: "Stop that!" Then he could hear whispering and a commotion. He gathered his weight and lunged against the lock. The cast-iron hardware cracked and the door whipped open. On the edge of a bed sat a woman in a green dressing gown. She was trimming her nails with a pair of scissors, and, as Ward came in, she rose angrily with the scissors held like a knife. "Get out of here!" she yelled.

Ward went toward her and she threw the scissors at him and ran toward a night stand as if to pick up the ironware pitcher standing there in a basin.

Ward reached it first and slid it out of her reach in a corner. He looked around. The woman kept screaming at him. A soldier's blouse lay over the back of a chair. The room was stuffy with tobacco smoke and perfume. A window opening on an alley was open, and as Champie came down the hall, Ward stepped to it and leaned out. Below him was a littered darkness. Then he saw a man limping toward the rear of the saloon.

"Halt!" he shouted. The man leaned into a broken run.

"No, you halt," said John Champie's voice.

Riggs disappeared. Ward turned. Champie was unarmed but was coming at him with blood on his face and his head down. His head was as curly and square as that of a polled bull. Champie's shoulders were huge and his fists were like stones, and his mouth pulled savagely as he waded in.

The woman began to curse them. "Get out of here! Get out in the hall and kill each other!"

Champie lunged at Ward as if to pin him against the wall, but Ward brought a short, hard left to the superintendent's ear and slid away. Champie whirled with him, fast and hard, slashing with both fists. He hit Ward's ribs, and Ward grunted. Ward kicked the chair into the miner's path, whipped the blouse from it, and swung it at Champie's head. There was something heavy in the pocket that thumped. He threw the blouse out the door and backed after it. When the big man in the flannel shirt drove after him, Ward stepped forward and smacked a left, a right, and a left to his face.

Blood was pouring from Champie's nose. His eyes looked insane with rage. He shouted at Ward and floundered into him. Champie's fist crashed against his temple. Ward staggered against the wall. Champie dived at him and grappled him about the waist. They crashed on the floor.

Champie held him down by his bulk, trying to get one hand free to strike at his face. Ward got a foot clear and dug his spur into Champie's calf. Swearing, the superintendent writhed away, and Ward got his hands on his throat. He dug at the soft skin with the toughness beneath, their faces close together. He heaved him over and piled onto him, doubling his fists and smashing at Champie's face with the edge of his knuckles.

Somehow the hall had filled with men. They were all willing to stay back and shout at them. But a pair of black knee boots rising to blue trousers came into Ward's view while he rode Champie and continued firing at his face. A hand took him by the collar, and he was dragged back. He sprawled, came onto all fours, and lunged up. Then he saw that it was Major King. King was red with anger. His hat was on the side of his head and his teeth were set.

"So this is how you keep the peace," he snapped.

Ward glanced about and saw that Champie had risen and was standing with Jim Harris. Harris was talking, low and hard, to the bloody-faced superintendent. Ward slipped his yellow neckerchief off, wadded it, and pressed it below his nose that had begun bleeding. "Riggs was here, Major," he said. "Champie kept me from taking him."

King looked surprised. "How about it?" he said to Champie.

"He charged me," Champie said angrily. "How should I know what he was after? He just charged me and kept going. Who's going to take that laying down?"

"Standing up or lying down," said Ward, "you're a damned liar. You were helping Riggs escape."

Jim Harris spoke to his superintendent. His tan silk hat rested on the back of his head and his expression was one of hard command. "Go wash up, John. The sergeant was carried away, I expect. Let's all forget it now."

Champie pushed his thick hair back with his fingers, glowered a moment longer, and shouldered down the hall. Harris kept frowning at Ward.

"It doesn't seem to me, Major," he remarked, "that the sergeant is setting us much of an example for a peaceable election."

"If Champie was interfering with a soldier on duty . . . ," King began.

"Champie said he wasn't," Harris interrupted.

"Sir, I told you Champie's lying," Ward told King.

King hesitated, and after a moment Harris said good-naturedly: "Well, there's no great harm done. Suppose we each take a little disciplinary action? I'll tend to John. Just as a suggestion . . . doesn't the Army have something called confinement to quarters?"

King faltered, staring at Harris, then flicking a nervous glance at the miners. Ward saw him softening under Harris's pressure. He felt suddenly abandoned and desperate, his hopes for this troop completely scuttled. A commanding officer that would not back up his men was worthless; he made his command futile and ridiculous.

The sergeant frowned at his wadded handkerchief, while King muttered, something about seeing to it. Ward looked up with a sour smile and said: "Like Mister Harris says, Major, there's no great harm done. Riggs escaped, but what's that? This here is just a sort of marching society anyway."

Then he saw a quick satisfaction ease Jim Harris's face, and with disgust he realized that he had walked into a trap. Harris wanted this outfit degraded. He wanted to make a joke of it and encourage the troopers to regard it as a joke themselves. He was furious with himself.

"I'll bet," Harris said, winking at one of his men, "you could tell the major a thing or two about soldiering, eh? I never heard of the non-com who couldn't."

The sergeant tucked in his shirt tail. He spoke to King. "I'm sorry, Major. Withdraw the remark. I was just sore about Riggs. If a man can desert and get away with it, I don't know what'll keep the others in line."

Harris chuckled. "Meaning no disrespect, soldier," he said, "but how can you tell whether one of your men has deserted or whether he's just lost? Most of them would need a compass to cross the street."

The miners began to laugh. King turned suddenly away. "Lay off them," he said gruffly, when the laughing stopped. "They're all right. You don't make a soldier out of a civilian over-night. I'm going back to the fort, Sergeant," he said. "Bring the men back at midnight."

"Yes, sir." Ward started wearily down the hall. Troop F was finished, he realized numbly. It was a wooden-headed command under a whiskey-soaked bungler who, for a grand half hour, had actually looked and sounded like an officer. Then his knees had buckled, and down with him had crashed F Troop. And when you talked about F Troop, you talked about the ranchers, stage men, merchants, and farmers of a good piece of eastern Oregon. *I've only got six months to go on my enlistment,* he thought as he followed King downstairs. *Maybe I'll go down to San Francisco then and enlist with the regular Army.* He wished he had accepted that case of Spanish wine from Jamie Harris.

V

In hot weather, the sheet-metal office building of Applejack Mining Company heated up like a kiln. The morning after the fight, Jim Harris stood at a window with his sleeves rolled, his collar open, and a cigar in his mouth. Once out of town clothes, he looked blunt-chinned and rugged. Harris had started as a hard-rock miner, had swung a maul, set charges, mucked in poorly timbered tunnels, and come out of it tough and realistic. Harris had seen poverty and death up close. He was not afraid of death, but he had never gotten the granite dust of hard times out of his pants cuffs. This morning, having cast his vote for Big Bill Blair early, he was going over the books with Harry Wheeler. Wheeler headed the Cañon City Bank, was a director of the company and its biggest stockholder, aside from Harris himself. The little banker was displeased with what he read in the books, and Harris watched, firm-lipped, as he closed the ledger. Wheeler put him in mind of a little hawk with his bald head, brown and black suits, and keen eyes.

High and thin, Wheeler's voice rose from his boiled collar. "If we hadn't had those losses to the Snakes," he said, "we'd be ahead a little."

"So it goes," said Harris resignedly.

"It was too bad Captain Poole left," Wheeler mourned.

"But he did, Harry. And that damned fool, King, has let the Indians lock us up like prisoners."

Wheeler leaned back suddenly. "By the way," he said, "a couple of prospectors found the loot from the last raid. The Indians had scattered the mail around, but these men picked up what they could."

Harris's heart gave a single, hammer-head beat. He started to raise his hand and dropped it. "No," he said. "What about the Wells Fargo chests? Did they leave the bullion?"

"No. You know, sometimes I think those Indians must be Southern sympathizers! What the devil use have they got for bullion?"

"Good question," said Harris bitterly. "And a good answer might be that Roy Plummer is in it somewhere. I tell you, Harry, that old Plummer is probably as Reb as Jeff Davis. Maybe he's siphoning it off to some spy ring."

Wheeler lifted his shoulders. "I don't think he's steady enough to be one thing or another. My guess is that the Indians are trading the gold somewhere. Wherever it went"—he sighed—"we haven't got it."

He pulled a sheaf of papers to him and glanced over them. They were the reports on the last big washing of day before yesterday. Harris quietly smoked his cigar.

"It would take a lot of mining, in gravel like this," decided Wheeler, "to cause any dancing in the streets."

Harris waited for Wheeler to finish his speech. He smoked in silence, narrow-eyed. Wheeler got up, looking as dry and fragile as a leaf, and walked to the window. He gazed down on the cañon sprawling away from the hillside where the mine buildings were braced against a steep slope. Here, two miles above Fort Haney, the cañon was deep and narrow. Just below the office building and concentrate mill, a small log and earth dam was chocked into the cañon to pen the water for Applejack's hydraulic operations. From sluice gates in the dam, water could be sent down the cañon in a long, dripping flume on stilt-like legs. A few hundred yards below the dam, the water entered three huge nozzles called monitors. When they were working, these monitors hurled the water across the cañon in long, roaring plumes that crashed against the cliffs and pulled down tons of earth, rocks, and trees.

Downstream the money was made. Passing over blocks in a series of troughs, the mud was robbed of its flakes and nuggets of gold by the mercury in the troughs. At the concentrate mill, the two metals were re-separated.

Wheeler moved his shoulders uncomfortably. "The way those things go through a mountain makes me think of hogs in a corncrib. Isn't there a better way, Jim?"

"There's a different way," said Harris pointedly. "Build silt basins . . . check dams . . . take it slow and easy. Only we'd go broke. I expect your depositors would just about hang you, Harry."

"No argument there. But what I'm thinking about is next year. You'll be working under the new mining laws. How are we going to keep any black ink in these books after we have to step up costs and cut down the profits?"

Harris's face suddenly creased in a fury of impatience. He leveled his arm at the cliffs. "Damn it, Harry, the big nuggets are there. But I can't find them by pussyfooting around with a teaspoon of water and a garden trowel. I've got to turn the water on to find the big deposits. Then we can talk about slowing down."

"How do you know they're there?" asked Wheeler.

"Instinct, plus geologists' reports and what I see on those hillsides. They took three million dollars' worth of gold out of these hills in one year, Harry. There's another thirty in them still. I *know* it."

The little banker helped himself to a cigar. "Not that I mistrust your professional opinion, Jim . . . but you haven't had much actual experience in gravel mining, have you?"

Harris's mouth went dry with anger. Lately he had been so sure they were about to strike the golden heart of the mountain that talk like Wheeler's made him want to hit someone. These were not Wheeler's questions. They came from the mouths of Wheeler's depositors. They were prodding Wheeler to explain why the bank was aisle-deep in Applejack stock. It was as if he almost had his hands on the gold and they were trying to block him from it.

"Listen, Harry," Jim Harris said. "I've got the best engineers in the business. I've got a hundred thousand of my own cash sunk in this mine. Maybe," he said sarcastically, "you'd better decide what you *do* want. You talk about spoiling the scenery with our methods, but you also talk about making money fast. You can't be a Nature lover and a miner all at once. Which is it going to be?"

With a wry smile, Wheeler said: "Putting it that way, Jim, there's just one answer."

Harris pointed his finger at him. "You bet there is. We've got a lot of gravel to move, and we've got to move it before the snow flies."

Wheeler squinted. "Another thing we may have to move is Troop F and its headquarters. Have you thought about that?"

"Yes, but it's not going to worry me." Harris smiled. "Major King's been fairly agreeable."

"So damned agreeable," remarked Wheeler, "that it makes me wonder whose body you found in his back yard. He looked ready to die of apoplexy, riding in Bill's parade last night."

Harris smiled again, puffed his cigar, and did not comment.

A wagon loaded with miners stopped outside the building. John Champie jumped from the seat beside the muleskinner. He started for the building in his headlong, serious manner, some papers flapping in his hand. He and Wheeler did not hit it off, and Wheeler said shortly: "I'll be getting back. Election signs look pretty good." He lit the cigar he had been chewing, and went out just as John Champie came in.

Champie's nose was skinned and his mouth was cut from the fight. He slapped the papers on Harris's desk. "What's the matter with Happy Jack?" he asked.

"A little bruised from the pressure. His depositors are pounding his desk."

"Let 'em pound," Champie scoffed. "I'm taking another load of votes down. There's a hell of a slew of hayseeds in town to vote for old Plummer."

Harris scrutinized the wagon. "Am I wrong? Seems to me some of those lads have been in a scrap."

Champie snorted. He was a pent-up, driven man who could entertain only one mood at a time. He did not get ideas, like most men—he got obsessions. He told Harris angrily: "Old Bob Davis is roaming around with a gang of cow-punchers and farmhands. They've been trying to challenge some of our votes."

"From the skin off some of the noses out there, I'd say they'd been having pretty fair luck."

"About a stand-off." Champie shrugged. "Taking a few axe helves down this time in case there's any more trouble."

Harris frowned. Champie seemed to miss the point that time was growing short. Soon the pressure against them would grow so heavy that they would have to slow down, and in low-grade gravel a slow-down meant defeat. But by that time, unless his own directors stopped him, Jim Harris reflected that he would have sifted all the earth within reach of the dam. Now he lowered his voice and asked Champie: "What happened to Riggs?"

"He's hiding in my shack. Says he tried to buy out of the Army, and they turned him down. So **he deserted. I gave him a hundred bucks and he'll** take off tonight. Then if this ain't Desertion Week, I'm a pit-mule's grandfather."

Harris's mouth hardened. "That's fine. What if they find him in your cabin?"

Champie flushed. "I didn't invite him. He just

holed up there. He's got a bad ankle. He'll leave tonight and that's the last we'll see of him."

"We hope," Harris said bleakly.

He did not like having Riggs around. By trade, Riggs was a prospector who had done some scouting for the regular Army before it pulled out four years ago. He had tried to sell Harris a few claims. These being bad days for prospectors, Riggs had finally joined the volunteers. And then suddenly Harris had needed his services very badly. He had used him twice and paid him well, but Riggs was inclined to drink and talk at the same time, and Harris wanted him out of the way. So he suggested to Riggs, who was sick of the Army by now anyway, that he buy out and go over to Portland or somewhere.

Champie was looking at some papers on Harris's desk.

"Did you know they found the loot from the last raid?" Harris asked with meaning.

The big superintendent started. He let the papers fall back. "No," he said.

"A couple of prospectors brought the Wells Fargo boxes in."

Champie cleared his throat. "Did they . . . did they find anything I ought to know about?"

"The boxes were empty when they found them."

"Not even any old shell boxes around, eh?" Champie grinned.

Harris shrugged. "Not that I've heard of."

Of course, Champie knew that the gold the mine had lost in the two stage raids was pure fiction. To keep the stockholders happy, Harris had had to fake some paper profits the firm hadn't made. He had intended to absorb these entries by discounting when he entered later profits. But the later profits had not developed, either; finally they had had to wash out the fraudulent entries. The quickest way to do this was to lose the gold outright. They framed two shipments to the mint and got Riggs to inform Rogue Buffalo, a young, ambitious Snake chief. Each time, Rogue Buffalo knocked over the stage and took the express boxes—not for fictitious gold, but for actual metallic ammunition for his stolen rifles, packed in sand inside the boxes.

This was just after Major King arrived. *Good old King,* thought Harris with warm satisfaction. If Captain Poole had been still in command, Harris would not have dared use the stage-raid gambit. In fact, the one consolation to having Poole's spurs in his ribs had been that he did keep the roads open. But when things shook out so that only a couple of stage raids could save Applejack, it had been mighty helpful to have the major bumbling around Fort Haney. Then, with King's teeth drawn, the opportunity was there for some wide-open mining.

As he had done many times since King arrived, he wondered whether the man had come here hunting him. Or was it just his bad luck to blunder into someone who had known him back there in New Mexico? Back when the major was Captain King, U.S.A., trying to operate a mine the Army had taken over from a disloyal citizen. He was the second officer to tackle the job. He had signed for all the property involved when the first man left, and a few months later, when a syndicate Jim Harris was heading bought the mine, it was found that a quantity of money had left with the first officer. Or so King had claimed. Maybe he had really pocketed it himself. No one ever learned, because the first man had gone South and joined the Confederate Army. But the Union Army had to stick someone, so it stuck King, who drew a year in jail and a bobtail discharge. And here, by God, he was in uniform again—not a federal one, this time, but at least a uniform. Hoping the state of Oregon would not find out about him, which Jim Harris assured him it never would, so long as he confined himself to minor Army business— laundry lists, inspections, things like that. So there was nothing to worry about down at Fort Haney except Sergeant Forson. *Who would also get straightened out,* thought Harris with a setting of his jaw.

John Champie was looking at the ledger. "What's Happy Jack say about the books?"

"He's not happy," Harris said. He pushed his hands in his hip pockets and stood with his cigar in his teeth, scowling. "We've got to get a flush of health into this outfit, John. And quick. What is commonly known as gold . . . for the stockholders to run through their fingers."

Champie spoke impatiently. "We aren't going to mine much gold while the monitors are turned off. You know something? This outfit does less hydraulicking than any gravel outfit I ever worked for."

"You know something else? I'm just waiting for the votes to be counted to turn them on again. First I had Captain Poole on my back. Now I've got my own directors. If Big Bill gets reëlected, that'll be our cue to start full-scale sluicing. I don't think there's much doubt about Bill's getting in again. So all we've got to worry about is how to handle our friend, Forson."

Color flooded Champie's face. "I just hope that tall drink of tap water comes charging up here, Jim. I hope to God he does."

Thinking more deeply into it than Champie, Harris reflected: "I'd feel better if he were in Tennessee. Zealots like Forson and Roy Plummer are like a handful of quicksilver . . . a little tough to handle."

Champie's lips pulled tight. He rubbed his fist against his palm. "You let me handle him. Next time I won't fool around."

"Next time you'd better not," Harris said with a bitter grin, "or he'll kill you."

Soon Champie left with his wagon load of votes. But Harris kept thinking about Forson. Forson had been a rancher. So his sympathies were powerfully bound to the land and to the men who made their living from it. He had the single-minded ugliness, sometimes, of a cannon-ball. He would like him out of the way before they started full-scale operations.

At noon Harris rode home for lunch and to get the election reports. His home was a large white house set in a grove of mountain ash, with a gallery belting it like a steamboat. Harris employed a housekeeper and a yardman, but his daughter Jamie did most of the cooking. She was a superb cook. Big Bill Blair brought his red-faced, boring personality to lunch. The Harrises treated him like a peer and made jokes about him when he was not there.

"Jamie," Harris said to the girl after Blair had left, "exactly what did Forson say when you offered him the wine?"

"I've told you, Dad. I've never been so humili-ated. He knew exactly why we were offering it."

Jim Harris held his amusement at the anger in her eyes. "Do you know what would serve him right?" wondered Harris. "To be restricted to the guardhouse for a month."

"If *I* were sitting on his case . . . ," Jamie threatened. Hell had no fury, her father realized, seeing the way her fine, small features had changed since he mentioned Forson.

"Maybe you *can* sit on his case," said Harris. "I want you to drive down to the fort later. There won't be many troopers around. I think most of them are on liberty tonight."

He told her what to say, and Jamie's eyes opened in mock surprise. "Father, aren't you afraid for my . . . my purity? After all, I'm a grown woman, and I hope with some attraction for men."

"If you didn't have," Harris said, "I'd send John Champie instead."

VI

Ward's room was a very small cubicle at one end of an enlisted men's barracks. Partitioned from the rest of the building by a stone wall made of shale, it had a tiny fireplace, a cot, a clothes chest, and some rusty hooks on the wall for guns and clothing. On this election night it was exceptionally quiet, without the muted chorus of Collins's banjo, Viets's loud yawns and belching, and the endless petty bickering of bored men. King had given most of the men passes for the day.

It was almost dark now. Ward had not lit the candles. There being no chair, he sat on the cot with the wall for a backrest. He had one boot off, and was mending the sole with a length of waxed linen, frowning as he worked. He heard a sentry challenge someone at the sally port, and then a buggy drove in behind a briskly stepping horse. He glanced up, then down again at his work, and decided he would have to light the candles.

He had not realized why he balked at lighting them until the fragrance of the smoke, sweet with beeswax, rose about him, and with the fragrance there rose also a sweet-sad memory of lighting candles at Cross Hollows. He sagged onto the cot and gazed at the wall.

He was in the barn, forking hay into the manger, and in the dusk his wife's voice called: "Won't you come, dear? Things are getting cold!" Yes, he would come! God above, he would come! Immerse himself in that time until he drowned in it, and all this—Fort Haney, Major King, his sorrow and yearning—became the memory instead of Cross Hollows. He saw his wife brushing her hair and smiling at him. In the evenings he liked to brush and braid it. He would kiss the back of her neck, and she would shiver and laugh, and the end of that was always loving. He saw everything with a beautiful, diminished farawayness, like peering through the eyepiece of one of those sugar-frosted Easter eggs with a little German manger scene inside.

"Ward, are you trying to hide? You might as well open the door, because I can see your light."

He started. He had not heard the knocking. "Who is it?"

"Jamie. Who else?"

"Just a minute." He scowled at himself in the triangular sliver of looking-glass wired to the wall. He had not shaved, his hair was uncombed —what the devil, you had to be a slob to qualify for Major King's company anyway. He raised the latch. The candlelight showed her smiling there in the street. She wore a dotted cotton gown with a light shawl over her shoulders. Seeing his expression, her smile faded.

"Well, if you really don't want to talk to me . . ."

"No," he blurted. "No, no. I . . . I was working on something. That's my bookkeeping expression you saw." He grinned. He suddenly felt so relieved and happy he was afraid he might giggle.

"That's better." She pouted a little and he saw how plump her lower lip was. Her eyes were the deepest, glossiest brown, like a puppy's, and her tawny skin was smooth and clear. The bodice of her dress was low, and he could just see the cleft of her bosom.

Suddenly he sniffed. "I smell food." The Harris buggy loomed behind her; he was convinced the odors came from it. "What've you got there?" he asked.

"Some . . . some dinner for you," the girl said, glancing down with pretty confusion. But she looked up at once, frowning. "I was frightened,

Ward. Father was in town, and I was in the house alone, when all of a sudden someone threw a stone through a window."

"No," said Ward, clucking.

"I was cooking dinner when this stone . . . why, it was as big as . . . I suppose it was one of Roy Plummer's fanatics. I was afraid to stay there alone. I just put some things in a hamper and drove down to ask for a guard. Father will be late. So, since I was coming anyway, I thought you might enjoy some home-cooked victuals."

"Vittles!" Ward placed his hands on her shoulders and moved her aside. "Lady, I haven't eaten food worthy the name of vittles in so long. . . ."

"It's just some baked ham and sweet potatoes," said Jamie. "And some bread I baked and . . . do you like cream in your coffee? I brought a little jug of coffee with cream in it."

Ward turned back the blanket and found the hamper. He also discovered the wooden box with the Spanish words on it that had been there last night. When he glanced around at her, Jamie smiled and tossed her head.

"I never give up. I'm determined that you and the major shall have that sherry. So if you'll bring it in after the food . . ."

Ward looked up and down the street. All was dark, now, except for a light in the guard room at the end of the row. He carried the hamper in and set it on the cot. When he came back with the

74

wine, Jamie was setting out plates and utensils. He smiled faintly, feeling fine and masculine and knowing exactly what she was about. She was going to charm him right into leaving Applejack Mining Company alone. And he was going to accept her friendliness and home-cooked food, have a pleasant evening, and not be swayed one quarter of an inch.

"Is that the new summer uniform?" Jamie was looking down at his unshod foot.

Ward pulled on the other boot and cut the threads with a knife. The room filled with the odors of food. Speculating a moment, he began opening the case of wine. He pulled out a bottle in a straw cover. The bottle was long and thin and dusty, with shoulders like Corporal Collins, and it was sealed with red wax.

"Would you be offended," he asked formally, "if I had some wine with my dinner?"

She laughed. "Help yourself." As the cork popped, she placed a tumbler beside his plate. "My, that looks good!" she exclaimed, when he had poured an inch in the glass.

He sipped it and closed his eyes. "It *is* good." He tried the baked ham. "But *this,* now . . ."

Jamie was eating very little, sitting gracefully on the hard cot with one hand lying on her lap, smiling. To Ward, it was odd to see someone eating with one hand and making no noise whatever. He liked hearing a woman's voice, too;

it had a silken texture, where a man's was burlap.

"You're much nicer tonight," Jamie commented.

"I'm a chastened man. I decided to mend my wicked ways.

"But don't reform too much," said Jamie. "Then you wouldn't like me. Because I'm a terrible girl, Ward. Do you know what I do sometimes?"

"No, but my ears are at present arms."

"Sometimes I take a drink. Oh, just sherry. Sherry, with a little sugar and water. Isn't that wicked?"

Ward refilled his glass and wiped the lip with his sleeve. "I'm sorry to report, miss, that we have no sugar or water. Would you care to try it straight? With a ham chaser?"

Jamie's laugh tinkled like ice. She drank a full inch of the wine and patted her lips with a lacy handkerchief. "Why, it's good that way," she remarked.

Before long Ward felt a deep, snug warmth spreading through him. "The ones I feel sorry for," he said, "are the rest of the farmers in this outfit. Miss Jamie, this is purely a repast."

Her giggle sounded higher. He glanced up with a faint quirk of suspicion. Her face was rosy. She beamed at him as she threw her shawl back. "Isn't it warm tonight!"

"It's the candles," said Ward solemnly. "They really give off quite a bit of heat."

It seemed that he could not keep the wine glass

from going empty. He was drinking very little himself, but Jamie's sips were substantial. After they had eaten, she packed the hamper and Ward carried it to the buggy. He had expected her to follow him; it was silent in camp, though the bugle was blowing "Quarters". But she was seated on the cot with her legs drawn up under her when he went back.

"I can imagine what John would do if he saw me now," she said.

"Is he jealous?"

"He watches me like a hawk." Jamie took a sip of wine, and her moist lips glistened.

Ward squinted at her. "I can't see you married to that fellow. Are you really going to marry him?"

"John thinks I am. Perhaps I am. I'm twenty. Got to marry sometime."

"You don't have to marry a boar hog like Champie."

She reached over and slapped his wrist lightly. "Such a way to talk about him. I . . ." She blinked in surprise.

Ward chuckled. "Speaking of the Champie," he said, "I wonder what his tie-up is with Riggs, our deserter?"

"Tie-up? How should I know?" sniffed the girl. She seemed vexed at the change of subject.

"There must have been some reason why he swung on me to help Riggs get away. Is Riggs a friend of Champie's?"

"Oh, Riggs is a sort of friend of us all. We staked him once or twice. He was always trying to sell us a mining claim."

"I thought he was going to be quite a scout for F Troop," Ward said sadly. "He can track . . . speak a little Snake . . . and when he smokes kinnikinnik he even smells like an Indian. But he hasn't done anything but complain about the work since he enlisted."

"Do we have to talk about Riggs?" pouted Jamie.

"I was just curious."

"Well, you're too curious," said the girl petulantly.

He thought: *Well, well! So Champie is a friend of Riggs. Or she wouldn't be on the defensive. I've got more out of this than she has.*

Jamie sipped some more sherry, turned the glass, and made him drink from the same place on the rim. "That was the best yet," he told her. But as she started to drink again, he said: "You know, Jamie, that stuff's a little stronger when it hasn't been cut with sugar and water." It had occurred to him that she might really get intoxicated.

"I know," she agreed. "I think I'd better stop pretty soon. If I don't marry John, though, who would I marry?"

"It's a big world." He shrugged. "Half the people in it are men."

Jamie smiled into his eyes. "And this is a small

room, and half the people *here* are men." Her teeth sparkled, and she seemed to dress the word *men* with tingling significance.

"And the other half," commented Ward, "are engaged girls. Very pretty but very engaged."

Jamie drew the diamond ring from her finger, pulled out the bodice of her dress, and dropped the ring inside. "Not tonight," she said in a slow, reasonable voice. She let her dark hair touch the wall behind her.

Ward leaned forward. His shadow fell across her face. Her eyes closed as he pressed her lips. Then her slim arm slipped about his neck and he caught her with force, forcing his mouth against hers so that her lips parted. She murmured deep in her throat, small, cat-like sounds of contentment, as he kissed her until his breath ran out. Then she kissed him on the brow and throat and curled against him.

"Ward . . . darling," she whispered.

He reached to snuff out the candle, but some unshakable wisdom drew his hand back. He knew why she was doing this; he could take what she offered up to a certain point and not be in trouble. Beyond that he was derelict. When he sat back for a moment, she reached for the wine glass and sipped, regarding him over the brim.

"I'll bet you ought to be going back," suggested Ward.

"I'll bet I shouldn't have come," giggled Jamie.

"Aren't you glad I didn't pour this wine in the creek like you told me to?"

"The way you're going," said Ward, "you're going to wind up in the creek yourself before you get home. Come on. I'll drive you to the gate."

He rose, very rumpled, tucked in his shirt tail, and donned his limp, wide-brimmed campaign hat. But when he looked down, she had not stirred. She watched with an odd expression. Her eyes were large and moist. He reached down to her.

"Come on. Gotta go," he said briskly. *What if she fell asleep here?* he thought. *What if I can't get her out?* He was making a fine example for F Troop.

She raised her hands, and when he pulled, she was impelled straight into him, where she clung with her cheek against his tunic. "You're disappointed in me," she whimpered.

Ward softly laughed. "I think you're great. You saved me from the lowest night I've had since I joined the cavalry. You see, I was thinking about . . ."

She looked up when he halted. "What, dear?"

"I was just sitting here remembering a lot of things, when along came you. This is the finest time I've had in years."

She let him lead her to the buggy, and lift her limply to the seat. The wine had gathered its forces; she was succumbing completely. He gazed at her. No, she would wind up practically anywhere but home. He would have to drive her.

He got his horse from the stable, rode back, and tied it behind, and they set out. They passed through the gate unchallenged. The sentry was missing. *My Lord, where will this troop end?* Ward wondered dismally. Through the darkness they swept along the road that led to the Harris home in the ash grove above town. Jamie sat a little straighter in the cool air.

"My shawl!" she said suddenly. "I left it."

"I'll save it for you. Well, I hope your fiancé isn't waiting up for you."

The horse clopped along a side-hill street of scattered homes behind low picket fences. Few lights burned, but when the horse turned automatically into the horseshoe drive of the Harris home, Ward saw light against the panes and a pair of prismatic coach lights burning on the porch. The horse stopped under a vine growing across the trellised porte-cochère. The fragrance of honeysuckle dripped about them. There was a high lift of steps to a broad gallery with a steamboat railing. Ward dismounted and helped Jamie to the ground. He tried to get her to look at him, but she was looking everywhere but at his face. Suspicion dawned in him. He took her chin between his fingers.

"Jamie," he said. He knew at last that she was the bait in a very complex trap.

She looked at him with tears in her eyes. "Ward, go quickly."

"I aim to," he said. "But I doubt it will be quickly enough."

He had heard the door open and a man step onto the gallery. Jim Harris's voice demanded gruffly: "Jamie . . . what under the sun!"

"Daddy . . . Daddy, go in the house," Jamie pleaded.

Ward was untying his horse. He glanced at Harris as the miner walked to the top of the steps, a grim, compact-shouldered man in a pleated shirt and tight brown trousers. With his well-brushed brown hair, his heavy jaw, and incisive eyes, he had a look of weight and importance. Another man was coming from the door, and Harris's head turned quickly.

"Stay inside, John, if you will."

"What the hell!" Champie's rough baritone demanded. "Well, by the Lord," he blurted, seeing in one sweep the sergeant and Jamie unsteadily mounting the stairs.

"Would you care to assist the lady?" Harris asked Ward with deadly politeness. "Since you contrived to get her in this condition?"

"Daddy!" wailed Jamie, clinging to the railing. "It's not his . . . I won't go through with it. John!" she screamed.

Champie had pulled a pistol from his belt, and fierce as a bull, haggard with fury, he shouldered past Jim Harris. Ward stepped forward to catch Jamie as she seemed about to fall. Champie was distracted for an instant and now Ward was standing, not too obviously, behind the girl. He did not honestly know whether the trick was to get him in trouble, or to kill him.

"John, put that thing away!" roared Harris. He gripped his superintendent's wrist. Champie wrenched his hand away and came down the steps. As he reached them, Jamie threw herself on the big man and clung when he tried to shake her off. He gave a heave and she was propelled into her father's arms. Champie leveled the revolver quickly just as Ward dived at him. The roar and flash broke stunningly on him. The bullet passed above his head and he crashed against the superintendent.

"By the Lord," panted Champie as they wrestled. "By the . . ." He was gray as lead. It came to Ward that Jamie may have overplayed the part she had been assigned, by getting drunk and staying so late. The girl was wailing loudly and her father was commanding her to come inside.

Ward twisted the gun away from Champie and threw it into the shrubbery. Harris moved in behind Champie and hit him behind the ear. Champie's knees bent; he sagged onto Ward, and they crashed down the steps and rolled to the bottom. Then the voice of Jamie came faintly.

"Daddy, I . . . I'm going to . . ."

Ward saw Harris catch the girl. He twisted from under Champie just as the big superintendent began to stir.

Holding the girl in his arms, Harris panted: "Get out of here before one of us kills you. You tramp cavalryman. This country would be better off if more of you were at the front and fewer loafing around the towns."

"And if more miners behaved themselves instead of using their daughters to bait traps. Good night," said Ward stiffly.

Harris turned his back and helped carry his daughter into the house.

VII

It was the first time Fort Haney's guardhouse had been used in many months. Under Captain Poole, the command was usually in the field, too busy to get into the kind of trouble men got into when they went barn sour. Major King had sentenced Ward to a month in the guardhouse. Jim Harris had come to the post with Champie the next morning and talked with Major King for fifteen minutes. Afterward the major had sent for his first sergeant and asked him one question: "Did you have a girl in your quarters last night?"

"Yes, sir. She came to trick me, that's all."

"Naturally," the commandant had snarled,

digging his fingertips into his thick, iron-gray hair. "That's what makes me so damned disgusted with you. Take a month in the guardhouse to think about women, Sergeant."

"A month. Sir, in a month . . ."

"You're excused," said King.

It was now the afternoon of the second day, nearly dark, and Ward sat on a cot reading an old newspaper Brough had brought him. Corporal Collins had requested guard duty, and he was standing by the corner of the small building, singing to himself:

In the prison cell I sit,
Thinking, Mother dear, of you. . . .

Ward looked up at the bolt-studded door reflectively. Collins's voice called softly: "Sergeant Forson, sir?"

"Yeah."

"Everything all right, Sergeant?"

"Fine."

"That's good," drawled Collins, clattering his musket against the wall. Tobacco smoke wafted through the strap-iron grille. "We like our boys to be comfortable, Sergeant. Anything you need? Tobacco? Whiskey?"

Ward strolled to the window. "Come here, Collins."

Collins moved into view, his face as dark and

ugly as a monkey's, a skinny, gnarled, tough-eyed man. His blouse was unbuttoned and he wore his hat on the back of his head with his dark hair falling over his forehead. Behind him was the meadow, where the horses grazed, beyond the meadow the dark hills, above the hills the greenish sky, and winding through the meadow little rivulets of water that had crawled above the banks of Cañon Creek, each ribbon of water enameled light green like the sky.

"This troop is dead, Collins. Did you know that?" said Ward softly.

Collins looked awed despite himself. "Dead?"

"All that keeps any outfit alive is the men who believe in it. Do you believe in F Troop?"

"God!" Collins said.

"Then why did you join up?"

Rubbing his neck, the clerk pondered. "I think I was a little drunk. There was a parade in Portland that day, and some feller talked about the Injuns killing women and children and all that. I don't know . . . it made sense to me then."

"It would still, if we had a commanding officer who could do anything besides make ship models. How's the model coming?" he asked.

"Between you and me, not good. His hand ain't been very steady lately."

"I hope he cuts his wrist," growled Ward. "He's disgraced himself, the O.V.C. and us. I have an idea he'll either quit or be removed one of these days. All I was going to say was I hope you stick around until we get a new C.O. I've always figured you'd make a pretty good soldier."

Collins yawned. Then he chuckled. "Old Riggs. Bet he's safe in the arms of some lovely thing in Umatilla, by now."

"Maybe he'll be remembering her when we slap that branding iron on his hip. That's if some Snake warrior isn't wearing his scalp on his belt now. But I'm hoping we get him first."

Collins eyes jeered. "Listen, Sergeant," he advised. "You're just as close to Riggs right now as you're ever gonna be."

The steady tread of boots approached down the troop street. Collins put the stub of a cigar in his mouth and glanced curiously around the corner of the building. The footfalls came close, and halted.

"Corporal of the guard!" snapped Major King's voice.

"That's you," prompted Ward.

"Yes, sir," said Collins, moving to the mouth of the alley with his cigar in the corner of his mouth.

"What's your second General Order?"

"Sir?"

"Second General Order," repeated King. "For your information, it has to do with keeping on the alert. Where's your musket?"

Collins pulled his musket from the wall and shouldered it.

"No!" barked King. "Port arms! Oh, hell," he

said, seeing that Collins did not follow him. "Go to the orderly room. You're relieved."

Looking grave and a little dyspeptic, Major King came in view as Collins hurried off. He was buttoned to the throat and looked soldierly. His knee-high boots had been polished. "I thought you'd be interested in the election news," he told the sergeant. "Blair won by five-to-one yesterday."

"You'd better sandbag then," Ward replied.

"I suppose so. Here's a letter for you," the major said. He had two letters in his hand and he gave one to Ward.

Ward held it to the light. It was wrinkled and the address was blurred. "Thanks. It's nice to know a stage got through. It's from my brother." Mail, which had once meant so much, had meant nothing since his wife died. But he remembered how, when they were apart for a while, he could actually hear her voice when he read her letters, and see her smiling at him. And this letter in his hand was just a piece of wrinkled paper bringing news of relatives he had not seen in years.

King was watching him. "You'll find the news rather elderly. This was last month's mail! They found the pouch the Indians took in that last raid. Blair gave it to me this afternoon. I drew a letter, too."

"From your daughter?" inquired Ward. It was hard to be polite to this man, this sawdust officer who would not back up a trooper before a lying civilian.

"Yes. From Jess. It was written six weeks ago, or I could have done something about it." King frowned. He looked up, tight-mouthed with worry. "She's coming to Cañon City."

"Why?"

"Something in the tone of my letters," said King satirically, "seems to have upset her. I suppose she means to stuff me with proper food and a lot of such foolishness. The point is, she's coming tomorrow."

Ward hesitated, thinking of the twisting forty miles between Cañon City and Rock Creek, the cañon-side roads that looked as though they had been dug by a wildcat, the fords where a coach was helpless in an Indian raid. A pulse of interest began ticking in him. "You mean she's leaving the riverboat tomorrow, or getting in tomorrow?" he asked sharply. "If her stage was leaving tomorrow, an escort could make contact with it around Burnt Ranch Station the day after, and see it through the worst of the Indian country."

"She's getting *here* tomorrow," said King, clearing his throat and sounding angry. "What the hell can I do in twenty-four hours?"

"Not much. Of course, the big danger is from Cottonwood to Rock Creek. Maybe you could meet the stage the other side of Cottonwood and bring it through."

89

King filled his chest. "Do you reckon you could throw some sort of escort together?"

Ward was astonished. "Me? Why . . . why, sure! How soon?"

"Two hours," King said.

Ward rubbed his nose. "In two hours I'd expect to be at Rabbit Springs."

King said gratefully: "Sergeant, you'll do!" He unlocked the cell, and they strode up the street and crossed the small parade to the orderly room. Passing through, Ward told Viets, at the desk: "Have the bugler sound 'Assembly'. Double time."

In the small office, King stared around as though he had come into the wrong room. There was a pint whiskey bottle on the desk beside the ship model, papers sprawling from a bottom drawer, and a map on the desk with a Colt lying on it.

"Let's see," King figured. "Food for . . . how many, do you say? Ten?"

"Fifteen. Of these men."

"Powder and ball for the muskets. Metallic for the . . . God damn such equipment! . . . for the carbines. Sabers. Have they all got sabers?"

He was like a stage driver trying to pick up, at full tilt, the lines he had lost. For weeks he had done nothing but drink and spend his time like a well-heeled gambler tossing dollar chips into a boring game. Now he needed to be a soldier, but his brain was torpid with alcohol and confusion.

"That's my department," Ward told him. "Get your personal equipment ready, and I'll round up the rest. After all, there's only one chance in a hatful that the stage will be hit. This is a precautionary move . . . not a rescue."

"Of course that's true. It just seems more critical where your own daughter's concerned."

From the desk, King picked up the bottle, pulled the cork, and then said confidently, slipping unconsciously into his faintly bantering tone: "Sergeant, I want to relieve your overburdened mind. I actually have had a plan of battle all along. You see, we could have been chasing Indians all over Oregon in weather like this, and never bag a one. But when it begins to get cold . . . ah, that's my season, Sergeant. The old winter campaigner."

"That right?" said Ward pleasantly, his mouth fixed.

"They'll be concentrated in certain spots, you see . . . digging camas roots, drying jerky, getting into their crouch for winter. And that's when we'll split them up . . . knock over their chiefs, dump their food in the rivers. We'll make Christians of all the Snakes and half the Cayuses by spring."

He chortled with the jolly good humor of a man falling from a cliff.

"You bet," Ward said.

His whole face changed when he closed the

door on King. For an instant his hand lingered on the knob. Hell, the Snakes weren't root diggers. They wintered as thriftily on a handful of jerked venison and a few berries as a mountain horse on burro grass. The worst part of this expedition was going to be keeping King from losing his mind. The actual danger to the patrol was slight. But King would have them all in a nervous sweat before they made contact with the stage.

VIII

Just before nightfall, the patrol reached the confluence of Cañon Creek with the John Day River a few miles north. They strung west on the military road, which followed the John Day for forty miles. An old ambulance creaked along behind them. The valley was wide, curving between low, tawny hills as lumpy and brown as Irish potatoes. The flats were yellow and green, with rushes and cottonwoods tracing the river, and partly harvested hay fields where bolsters of hay lay like corpses. The farmers along here had had to quit and move into town a month ago. Up on the hillsides were snake-fenced corrals from which the stock had long since been stolen.

Corporal Collins pushed in beside the sergeant. "How far we going to ride tonight, Sarge?"

"Rock Creek. Can't risk the gorge tonight. I

haven't got enough hands to hold all you boys' hands and guide my horse, too."

Collins grunted. "Anybody ask you to?"

"Not yet. But you're all scared. Collins," he said frankly, "I'm counting on you. Don't let me down."

Collins rubbed his chin with his sleeve. "What do you mean?"

"What I said. Collins was the first name I wrote down when I made up the order. It's something about you, homely and ornery as you are."

"Oh, no," said Collins. "It's something about where C comes in the alphabet." He dropped back. Ward heard him trying to borrow tobacco from Trooper Selaya.

By midnight the men were shivering with cold and nervousness. They were now in the bottom of the dark sack called Indian country. There were no buildings, no friends to sustain them. They were on their own. It was a ferocious country, and none of the troopers in F Troop could stare it down. Its mountains were paint-streaked like warriors, its voices the cries of animals and the throaty warnings of rivers. Its silence was so utter that the howl of a wolf set it to shimmering like the oily surface of a deep well. Ward regretted intensely the softening weeks of indolence around the fort.

On the north, barely seen in the night, the country opened up to long, flat swells of range. There was the clean liniment odor of sagebrush.

On the south were black mesas capped with rimrock.

King said tiredly: "We'd better make camp here. Rock Creek's just ahead. And that's rough country. Where do you reckon the stage would have stopped tonight?"

"Maybe Mitchell, maybe Cottonwood. Any way you figure it, we'll get through Picture Gorge in the morning before they do."

At least they would get into the gorge. Fire a gun in the air and this patrol would scatter like quail.

King gave the order to pitch A-tents and outspan the ambulance team. He posted sentries and organized the camp with an efficiency that left Ward staring at him. He did these things so gruffly and expertly that Ward knew for certain King had done his share of soldiering somewhere.

Ward took the first watch after camp was made. King was shamblingly tired. Lying in his blankets as the sergeant prepared to make his first tour of the posts, he sighed deeply. "She's quite a girl, Jess," he murmured, apparently to the sergeant.

"Writes a nice letter," commented Ward. Kneeling, he was stitching up a broken rein. King had read parts of her letters to him. He looked up at the white rind of moon, squinting. "Blonde girl . . . taller than common . . . blue eyes. . . ."

King came to one elbow. "How'd you know that?"

Ward tapped his temple. "Figured it out."

"How could you?"

"Her letters. Likes to cook, probably. Good housekeeper. Does needlepoint."

King chuckled. "Man that marries her will be lucky. She's got a hope chest that must weigh a ton. How'd you know all this?" he queried. "She didn't mention it in her letters."

Ward dropped the awl and needles in a box and stood up. He grinned down at the officer. "Good top sergeant knows everything. If I couldn't figure out a woman I'd never seen, how could I keep ahead of a Snake Indian I'd never been within five miles of?"

He walked out to start a round of the posts. In the main, they were good guesses. It was helpful, however, to have seen an oil-tinted ambrotype in an open drawer of King's desk of a very pretty girl standing with one hand on her father's shoulder as he sat in his new tailor-made Oregon Volunteer Cavalry uniform. King being a widower, his daughter would have learned her housekeeping early. And he had brought with him a footstool done in needlepoint. Just guesses, but they gave King something to mull over besides the condition that blonde daughter of his might possibly be in now.

"Sergeant!"

King's hand jarred him awake. He had been sleeping after being relieved at 3:00 a.m. He came out of his blankets, scrambling for his hat and revolver, jammed his hat on his head, and began buckling the revolver on. "What's the matter?" He stared about. The John Day valley brimmed with dawn; a light fog rising from the river shrouded the cottonwoods and rushes. The military road ran due west into some sparsely timbered hills. The soldiers stood in small groups, staring down the road.

"Smoke," King said, pointing. Unshaven, with puffy eyes, he indicated the hills where the road disappeared. He was holding his saddle gun.

Far away, a pencil of smoke ascended into the dawn. Ward relaxed. "Probably Snakes, but they're beyond Cottonwood Station. If the stage isn't already on the road, the driver will see the smoke and stay at the station. If it is on the road, I don't think the Indians can catch them the other side of the gorge."

King was not comforted. His heavy features were grim. "You know them. What do you suggest?"

A canvas bucket hung from a hook on the side of the ambulance. Ward scrubbed his face, combed his hair back with his fingers, and replaced his hat. He had a good feeling about it all, even if there were action—a tingling sensation that he used to be sure would end in panic, but which experience had schooled him to expect something better of desperation and courage.

"Regular order of march for this kind of

country." He shrugged, trying King. He wanted him to give the order, if he knew it.

King turned. "Break camp!" he shouted. "Collins, Selaya . . . you'll ride as security guards. Collins up on the mesa to the south. Selaya across the river. Selaya, you're a Klamath, aren't you? You ought to be able to scout like a coyote."

"Got hell of a fine way to cook grasshopper feast." Selaya grinned. He was a chunky little half-blooded Klamath with brown features and a pointed nose. Ward had been happy to see him in the line-up that first morning, thinking they would have a top-notch tracker. But it seemed Joe Selaya had grown up in the towns, and all he had of Indian skill was a genius for catching fish, some hair-raising war cries, and a recipe for a baked grasshopper feast.

"That's fine," King said sarcastically. "After we finish our work, we'll all eat grasshoppers. In the meantime, it'll pay you to remember you're an Indian in the pay of whites. Those Snakes would love to get hold of you. Do you know what security guards do?"

Selaya explained what he thought they should do, and it was close enough. The fifteen men in the main body, including King and Ward, would proceed down the stage road, with Selaya and Collins flanking widely on the high ground. Collins and the half-breed rode off. The detail, led by King, continued.

The John Day brawled in among some craggy little hills. They began hearing water moving over rocks within a shadowy split in the hills. "Rock Creek hits the river here," Ward said. "Narrow going for a while. We follow Rock Creek, then."

In ten minutes they were at the entrance to the gorge. They waited for the scouts. Collins was on a high, black cliff on the south, a quarter mile ahead and five hundred feet above them. Selaya appeared on a crag to the north. King signaled them both to continue. They entered the gorge at a walk.

Dawn was still trapped between the black walls. The air was cool and moist and at their right the river boiled in a muddy torrent. Farther along Rock Creek joined its waters with those of the John Day. The single stream ran north in another gorge. The road clung to the south wall of Picture Gorge, and not far ahead the hills fell back somewhat on the far side of Rock Creek, and the wagon road began to climb. There was moss on some of the stones beside the road, the earth was moist, and serviceberry and sticky laurel grew thickly along the stream.

Suddenly Ward raised his hand, and the column halted. He glanced at Major King. "Smell any-thing?"

King sniffed. "Tobacco?" He frowned and turned on the saddle to glance at the troopers.

"Wind's from ahead, sir. It's tobacco, all right . . .

Indian tobacco. I'll take a look-see around the bend. Maybe you'd better deploy . . ."

The muffled snort of a horse came distinctly to his ears, and in the same instant he saw a flash of horsehide in a thicket just ahead at the bend. He drew his revolver and spurred toward the thicket. He heard King shout and the men began sprawling from their mounts. Ward stopped with the gun leveled at the man standing beside his horse in the thicket.

"All right, Riggs," he said. "I can't keep this from going off much longer."

Trooper Riggs stumbled out of the thicket. He had been holding his hat over the muzzle of his pony, but now he donned it clumsily and stood there staring at Ward, his long-chinned, hungry features rigid. He was wearing a brown coat, but between coat and knee-length black boots could be seen blue Army trousers.

He blurted: "Snakes, Sergeant! Must be a hundred of 'em!"

Ward's eye flicked up the narrow cañon. "Yonder?"

"About two mile. I was ridin' that-a-way, do you see, and I rode plumb into 'em. They had the road blocked with burnin' hay and the stage is stalled on a bridge. They're cuttin' the livin' daylights out of it, Sergeant!"

King spurred up and loomed above the deserter with his saber drawn. "And you rode out of it?"

Riggs swallowed. "What use to stay, Major? One horse is already down. Driver was tryin' to cut it out of the tugs. I cut back and then I heerd you fellers comin'. Didn't know but what you was Snakes, too."

"Did they see you?" rapped Ward.

In the morning quiet a gun popped distantly. High above the cañon, Corporal Collins was desperately waving his hat on the south ridge. Faintly his voice drifted to them. "Indians! Dead ahead!" Whipping his horse, Collins came in a sliding descent from the ridge.

King swerved his horse and began shouting orders at the men. "Viets . . . Morrissey . . . Logan . . . horse holders!"

He deployed the rest of the troopers among the rocks and thickets at either side of the road, as the horses were run back by the horse holders. Ward found a place on the side of the road above the cañon. He laid his pistol by him and spilled shells into the crown of his hat. He cocked his carbine and set himself. Soon there was a clatter of hoofs on the road, and Ward flinched, waiting for the first nervous, unordered salvo. He heard King bawl: "Hold your fire, now! This will be Collins."

Collins came past the bend into view, hatless and bent over the neck of his horse. Joseph Selaya followed him by a hundred feet. "Whole passel of 'em on our tail!" said Collins as he pulled up. "Their scouts must've seen us!"

"Turn your horses loose," ordered King. "Hole up in the rocks."

The ponies ran on as Collins and Selaya dug in. Ward could hear the Snake ponies running now. Rock Creek was as peaceful as a summer sky. The troopers were silent, and Ward was wondering whether they would hold together when it started or shatter like an Indian bowl. He set himself then and gazed across the gunsights at the bend, where a light haze of dust still hung in the air.

IX

The quivering in Ward's body increased. His mouth was dry as cotton and he could not swallow. Around the turn flashed a ragged file of riders. Bars of red and yellow glistened greasily on their brown faces. They wore deerskin breech-clouts, and their moccasins, quivers, and wrist bands were bright with porcupine quills. A few wore feather bonnets.

Ward picked a racing buck and fired. He rocked with the kick of the gun. An Indian began to gobble a nightmarish war cry. The brave Ward had shot landed on the road and his body rolled with flailing arms for twenty feet. The pony tore on past. Two more guns crashed. In the narrow cañon the concussions were shattering. The Snake horses piled up in a rearing cluster. The Indians shook lances and rifles in the air as they searched for targets in the rocks. A buck with yellow bars across his face suddenly saw Ward and drove his pony forward. He aimed his rifle with one hand. Ward flattened against a boulder. The gun blasted, and he felt the ball hit the rock. Chips of stone slashed his ear.

Now the troopers' guns began exploding like a string of firecrackers. The crackling salvo shook the cañon. It was a wild turmoil of smoke, yipping coyote cries, and stampeding horses. A brave brandishing a feathered lance raced into the rocks to where King was standing with a smoking pistol in his hand. The lance flew, King ducked, and it smashed into the slope. Crouching as the horse reared over him, King fired pointblank at the buck. The Snake reeled, lost control of the horse, and it went over backward.

Horses were running again, pulling out of the smoky cañon to lope back up the road. Ward tried to get a shot as the riders swerved out of sight at the bend. Then it seemed that in a few seconds nothing was left on the road but downed warriors and a single pony, buck-jumping in the smoke. King staggered into the road.

"Horse holders!" he bawled. "Get those horses up here!"

Ward counted seven Indians on the road. There was one who might live; most of them had taken several shots. The horse holders came up with the horses. The volunteers came crawling down out of the rocks and serviceberry thickets.

King was looking at Ward. "You're bleeding, Sergeant."

Ward touched his ear. His hand came away, wet and glistening. He bound his neckerchief across his forehead and over his ear. Brough, shaking and white, brought Ward's horse. King was throwing questions at Riggs like pistol shots as the men mounted and reloaded.

"Any passengers?"

"I reckon."

"Any women?"

"Mebbe. Don't know."

"How far?"

"Mile . . . mile and a half."

"Drag those bucks out of the road," King told the men. "We may be coming through here fast. Check your loads. Column of twos!" he bawled. "Ho!" F Troop rode to its first attack.

The road climbed steeply, leveling off high above Rock Creek. From here could be heard a popping of guns. Juniper and mountain mahogany spotted the slope climbing away on their left. Ward pulled in by the major.

"Request permission to scout ahead before proceeding."

"What's the use of scouting if we know we've got to go anyway?" King flared. Then he breathed deeply and said: "Some advice, Sergeant. Never get emotionally involved in your work. Ruins your judgment. Go on. But make it quick."

Ward worked up to a ridge and followed it a quarter mile. The sun was on the ridge, warm and golden, but below him the valley lay in shadow. He saw the stagecoach. A ravine creased the flank of the mountain and ran diagonally toward Rock Creek Cañon. It cut the wagon road on a narrow beach. Here a log bridge had been erected. The stagecoach was stopped on the bridge. The bridge was too narrow for Indians to ride past the stagecoach, and they were sniping at it from the flats. Two horses were down, and the driver and a passenger were struggling to cut them free. Two men lay among the baggage on top of the Concord coach, firing at the Snakes, while other guns fired from behind the leather curtains.

The sergeant counted about thirty bucks. There were three dead among them. He could see their ponies in the ravine. Among them were a few mounted warriors and two or three on foot. One of the standing men wore the big feather bonnet of a chief. The mounted men, Ward concluded, were the survivors of the ambush. They were reporting back.

Just then he saw the chief shake his rifle in the air. A buck ran up the bank of the ravine and from behind a juniper gave a gobbling war cry. The Indians on the hillside began pulling back to the ravine. Puzzled, Ward watched them mount. That must be Rogue Buffalo, the big one, he decided. The Snakes rode up the ravine, leaving two braves behind. They topped out where the stage passengers could not see them. Then he knew what they had in mind. They were planning to follow down the ridge in order to take the cavalry men from above, if they were still in the gorge. Ward rode back.

King was walking up and down when he got there, slapping his leg with his gauntlets. Seeing Ward, he mounted hastily. Ward pulled his horse up beside him.

"There's about forty-odd, Major. The ones we missed just reported back. All but two or three are coming along the ridge. Either they mean to hit us from above, or they're taking a short cut to hit the stage road farther up and trap us. Right now, there's only a couple of them pinning down the stage."

"Then let's go."

On the bridge, the dead animals had been cut from the harness, but the stage driver and the passengers could not roll the horses from the bridge to let the coach pass. When they saw the troopers, they began moving, and the men on top of the coach yelled. King opened the door of the coach while the sergeant deployed the men and opened a crackling fire on the three Snakes on the slope. The Indians fired steadily. They were equipped with breechloaders and brass shells. A soldier named Fowler suddenly groaned and fell on the bridge. Ward was beside him. Blood splattered Fowler's face. He toppled into the ravine before Ward could help him.

Along the road, forted up behind brush and rocks, the other men had stopped firing to stare down at Fowler. They had heard about death, and now they were seeing it, but King had put no boot leather on their souls to help them. Brough was lying on the road with his round spectacles beside him, looking very white and shaken. Ward saw him lay down his carbine and rest his head against his arm. Crouching, he left the bridge and ran to the trooper. Brough was praying. A bullet hit the earth near him and he flinched.

Ward pulled him up and hit him on the mouth. He shoved the rifle into his hands and pointed up the hill. "The enemy's up there, trooper. Fire that thing until it melts in your hands. Pray if you want, but if you stop firing again, I'll belt you over the head with it."

Brough nodded, swallowed, put on his glasses, and began firing again. Ward worked along the line, getting them straightened out. He had them making noise again, but he knew they'd never hit anything. This could go on all day, but the Snakes would not wait all day to come back.

He worked back to Corporal Collins. Collins was bitterly intent on his work, aiming, firing, swearing as he reloaded. "We're going up the ravine and get above those bucks," Ward told him. "If we can flush them into the open, the boys down here may knock them over."

Collins gathered his shells from his hat and followed him. On the way down the line, Ward collected little Joe Selaya, also, and the three of them ran on. Collins and Selaya slid into the ravine. Ward ran to the stage. King was standing beside it, leaning inside. He could hear a girl's voice speaking urgently.

"Father, I'm all right. Honestly. Now go back to the men."

Inside the coach he saw her—blonde with a small hat worn on the side of her head. In the smoky interior of the Concord, her earrings sparkled. Her eyes looked enormous. She looked like a very pretty and frightened young woman. King closed the olive-green door. A bullet hit the far side of the coach with a splintering impact. King started to turn back, but Ward caught his arm.

"Request permission to smoke them out, Major. We've lost one man. Can't work under fire, and the rest of the Snakes will soon be back."

"All right. We'll get this thing moving."

Ward joined the men in the ravine. "Stick with me," he snapped. "If we're lucky, we'll get above them."

They trotted up the ravine. Selaya ran with a

queer side-to-side swing, his head bobbing. Running silently on the sand, they had gone a couple of hundred yards when a gun cracked close by on the left. Ward halted. Another gun cracked. Suddenly a dark head and shoulders appeared in a cleft of the bank. Shouting a warning, Ward dived for the sand. A gunshot smashed down and the bullet troughed the sand beside him. He twisted over and fired. The Snake sagged back without a sound.

Ward whistled a signal to the others and scrambled from the ravine. The brave was lying huddled under a shrub. Ward slung his gun away and looked for the others. All at once Selaya made that terrifying war cry of his, and two breech-clouted Snake warriors sprang up fifty yards away. They had been hiding there, and at once one of them fired the short-barreled carbine he held. Selaya dropped to his knees, holding his upper arm. Ward snapped a shot at the Snake and saw him reel back. There was a crashing shot from Collins's rifle. The other warrior leaped into the ravine. Collins stepped to the bank and fired once. Then he lowered his rifle.

Ward turned his attention to the bridge. King was already driving the men from shelter to work with the stagecoach. The sergeant turned quickly to Selaya, who was sitting on the ground with a knife in his hand. The Indian had already torn the sleeve of his tunic away. He made a quick slash on the swell of his biceps where the bullet had gouged a trough. Ward knelt by him, wondering if Selaya knew the Snakes used the juice of cowbane to poison their bullets and arrows. Selaya did. He bent over and commenced sucking blood from the gash in his arm. After a moment he spat, wiped his mouth, and rose with a grin. "OK. Le's go. Snake medicine no damn' good anyhow."

X

Down at the bridge, Major King's gunny-sack soldiers were falling apart, it seemed to the sergeant. As they dragged the horses away, their faces were grimy with burned powder and their eyes stood out haggardly. They worked like men just awake from a long sleep. The trooper who had been wounded was dead. King had some men burying him and the passenger who had been killed. Every man who was able to talk at all was complaining. It was like the whining of old women at a wake.

Standing by the stage, Ward muttered to Collins: "Maybe this makes sense to somebody. I'd say it was a hell of a way to train troops."

A girl said behind him: "It certainly is. But you know what they say . . . a troop is no better than its first sergeant."

He turned and saw Jessamin King standing

there. She was a tall girl with a fine figure and clear skin, and with something commanding about her. He could see the major in her face, a suggestion of his broad jaw and strong mouth, yet she was entirely feminine. Just now her brow was drawn with severity.

"I'll bet the same folks who say that," he told her dryly, "would tell you a first sergeant is no better than his commanding officer. Will you get in, ma'am? We're going to roll."

He put his hand under her elbow to help her onto the step. She entered the coach, smoothed her dress under her, and sat down. Then she said, looking at him clearly and with calm dislike: "That may be true. But I happen to know the commanding officer very well. And from his letters I've deduced that he hasn't been getting very much co-operation from his first sergeant."

Ward was staggered. "Ma'am . . . !" he began fiercely. Then he turned savagely away. He walked to the major and said sharply: "Reckon we'd better move, sir. Don't you think?"

King gave him a curious glance. He seemed somehow refreshed, surer of himself. "Yes, I've been figuring. It's too far to Cottonwood station. I think we'll have to go back the way we came, Snakes or not. If we get through the gorge, we'll be able to make a running fight of it." He turned. "Driver, are you ready?" he called.

Fred Arthur, the driver, was on the box with his

lines in his hands. He was running four horses now. "Roll 'em," he said.

We've fooled around too long, thought Ward tensely, taking his place in front. There was a hollow clatter of hoofs on the bridge as the stage moved forward. He settled his hat over his bandaged ear and glanced up at the hills. King was riding with the rear guard. Someone would have to go up and scout, but he hated to send any of these club-footed soldiers, and he could scarcely leave Collins in command and go himself. Riggs—Riggs could do it, but he could not send a deserter on a scout. *Riggs could have helped this outfit,* he thought resentfully. Then he saw a sloping ridge due south begin to bristle with lances and rifles. He twisted in the saddle and groped for King's eye, caught it at last, and pointed. King's head turned. After an instant King looked back. He signaled full gallop. Ward gave the command, and they started at a run down the long winding grade to the gorge.

The Snakes were a mile away. Yet, it was a mile of rough travel before they hit the stage road, and the coach could be well through the gorge before they caught up. A few hundred yards short of where they had ambushed the Snakes, Ward heard in back a distant coyote yipping, and some shots. He looked back but could see nothing but the stage and the roiling dust behind it. He turned back as they leaned into the sharp turn around which the Snakes had come into their ambush. The road straightened out with the black ledges going up on the right, the rocks and brush on the left sliding down to the river, the stains of blood on the ground and the marks made when the dead men had been dragged from the road. It was a lonely, open aisle as beautiful as a new Colt, as clean and dangerous. He looked for pinpoints of metal or daubs of color. He saw nothing.

They swept on. The cliffs fell back and they were in low hills; the hills opened out to a long green and gold valley, and suddenly they were through. Just ahead was the ambulance, where they had left it at last night's camp.

Ward let the stagecoach pass and waited to join the major's group. He saw a trooper beckoning urgently and at once he saw that a man had been hurt. The soldiers were supporting another between them. It was Major King.

The sergeant stayed with him as they continued. *This is all we needed!* he thought. A mile farther on they came to the shell of a ranch house. It had been burned out long ago, and remained now as three blackened stone walls and a few gnarled fruit trees. The sergeant had the ambulance and stagecoach pulled up behind the cabin. He ordered the major moved inside the roofless frame. Then he deployed the men in a wide ring. He made a swift examination of the major and saw that his wound was in his hip. He told Riggs to get a fire going inside the cabin and heat some water. He started looking through a supply box for the surgical kit.

"What are you going to do, Sergeant?" King's daughter asked. Jessamin—King called her Jess —stood nervously by the wagon. Ward found the instruments and started for the cabin, but Jess placed herself before him. She was a very proud, determined girl, but she could not hide the fact that she was about to break down.

"I've got to try to stop his bleeding," he told her

"I've had some training," Jess said weakly. "I'm sure my father would rather I did it than you." As she spoke, her cheeks whitened and she put her hand out to steady herself. But when he started to help her, she pulled away. "I'm perfectly all right. If the Indians come, the men will need you. I can do it. I've done it before."

Ward frowningly studied her face. "I don't understand why a lady should be so glad to do surgery," he said.

"I . . . I simply believe that . . ."

Ward set her aside. "I believe that if they come back, we ought to be ready to travel. Meantime, I'm going to do what I can for your father."

Inside the cabin, Riggs was heating water on a crane in the old fireplace. There were some rusty Dutch ovens slung around, and a great vacant square of blue sky overhead.

King saw him and called from the corner where

he lay on a blanket: "She's a capable nurse, Sergeant. I'd rather she worked on me. She's an Army girl, you know."

Kneeling, Ward untied the roll. He heard Jess telling Riggs: "We won't need you, Trooper. I can help here and you should be on the line."

"Stay here," said Ward. "A fainting female won't be any help to me. How's the water coming?"

"Ready when you are." Riggs drifted over, his long jaw working on a chew of Indian tobacco, his gray eyes scrutinizing the major curiously.

"Let's get his boot off," Ward said. King tried to pull his leg away but groaned, and a slackness went through his body. Ward shot a look at his face. King had fainted. "Let's go," he snapped at Riggs. "We may have the bullet out before he comes to."

With his knife, he ripped the blue trouser leg from ankle to belt and laid it back from the thigh. He slit the cotton drawers and exposed the wound high on the thigh. He touched the flesh with the scalpel above a blue swelling.

"Not so bad. It's a musket ball, and not very deep."

Riggs squatted, unconcernedly chewing tobacco as Ward washed away the blood with a cloth. There was an old scar on King's hip. Riggs grunted. "Been through this before, he has. Lookee there."

"Almost like . . ." Ward had intended to say—
"a brand"—but he shut his mouth on it. It *was* a
brand, he suddenly realized. "Riggs, I'll need
some cord," he said quickly.

But the trooper had reached out to trace with
his finger the outline of the brand. "Well, by
God!" he exclaimed. Then he began to chuckle.
"By God, he *has* been branded, Sarge. That's as
purty a D as a man could want, ain't it? Whatcha
reckon that signifies?"

"I don't know, said Ward brusquely. "Get the
cord. It's not a D. I think it's an O."

"No, no," Riggs insisted. "O wouldn't stand for
nothing, would it? But in some outfits, D stands
for deserter."

"Get the cord, or I'll cut your filthy throat."

Riggs lounged away to the ambulance. By the
door, the major's daughter was standing with her
face to the wall. She turned and came to where
Ward was working the ball out with tweezers.

"It wasn't his fault," she said brokenly.

"What wasn't his fault?"

"That they did this to him. He wasn't deserting.
He was absent without leave, and they knew why,
but they were after him for something else."

"That's too bad," Ward said. He pulled the
musket ball out and looked at it. It was shiny,
newly molded, and he felt better. Apparently all
the Snakes hadn't got to dipping bullets in venom
as they did their arrowheads. King had a chance.

115

"You don't believe me," the girl said.

"I believe we're in pretty bad shape, Miss King, and anything but survival is going to have to wait."

"I suppose you'll report him and try to get yourself a commission, won't you?"

Ward dropped the ball on the floor and looked up. "I never thought of that. But it's a good idea. I'll think about it while you rattle on, if you keep it up. Here's Riggs."

He finished with the major's wound, taking care because he was fairly sure the Indians were through. He reassembled the detail, installed King in the ambulance, and in the warm morning they started back to Cañon City.

XI

At assembly early in the morning after the troop's return, Sergeant Forson read a notice requiring all arms and equipment to be cleaned and made ready for inspection. "Full dress parade tonight," he added. "Trooper Brough will read a service for Trooper Fowler."

Long-nosed and pale-eyed, Riggs rattled his carbine against his leg. He looked unshaven and sardonically happy. He had this troop in his two hands. "Sergeant," Riggs inquired, "how come inspection when we just got back from the war?"

116

Ward gazed steadily at him. "I want to see you after the formation. The rest of you fall out. Read the bulletin board."

He walked up to Riggs after the others left. "What've you got in mind for the old man?" he asked.

Scratching inside his shirt, Riggs groused: "Shore does make a man feel puny to be takin' orders from a fella like that, don't it?"

"Not half as puny as it would make me feel to be taking orders from you. Are you going to inform on King or let me handle it?"

"Purty hard to tell you anything," drawled Riggs, "seein' as you're always a-tellin' me. Reckon I'll grind on it a spell."

"Grind on this, too," suggested the sergeant. "Regardless of what we do about King, you're billed for desertion. The penalty for desertion in wartime is the firing squad. King's had his trouble and paid up. Yours is still ahead of you."

Riggs's face tensed, but he held the sergeant's eyes and said: "They's goin' to be a little more trouble ahead of King, if I tell Roy Plummer about him. Old Plummer would print it so big they'd come down here and hang King from the flagpole."

Craft, the reckoning of chances, was all that had kept Riggs alive in the Indian country, and Ward knew there was no use trying to fool him. "Why do you think you aren't in the guardhouse right now?" he countered. "I talked it over with the major last night. He was all for slapping you in the pokey right then, but I talked him into swapping you the freedom of the post for his reputation. The first time you drop a hint about him, you get the guardhouse."

Then, carrying the morning report, he walked to the major's cottage. He had an intense dislike for what was about to happen. Jess would want to explain why it was not her father's fault that he had been drummed out of the Army in disgrace. She, and probably the major, would probably plead with him to keep the major's secret. And there in his lap would be the problem—to expose King and perhaps get some action out of the troop, or to try somehow to save him.

He knocked at the door and waited. He cleared his throat, tilted his chin, squared his shoulders, trying to find matter-of-factness. It was too bad it had to involve the girl. She was intelligent and sensible—except about Sergeant Forson. He thought of the Kings leaving Fort Haney, the major without insignia, the girl probably in tears. Damn it. Here she came.

The door opened and the girl stood there with her quiet grace, smiling. Her eyes were expressive, with faint shadows under them. "Will you come in, Sergeant?" she asked. "My father's been waiting for you."

Her mind was somewhere else. She was

wondering how she was going to handle him. He went in, pulling off his gloves. She took his hat and gloves, and then he saw King sitting at a desk by the window with his leg stiffly stretched out. What Ward noticed first was the exceptional neatness of the room. The girl's broom had found all the dust and cobwebs King had ignored. He had a pang of yearning for woman things about, her tidiness everywhere in evidence, her clothing in the closet with his, and he repressed a sigh. A man widowed was forever a reluctant bachelor.

"How are you feeling this morning, sir?" Ward asked King.

"Old," said King. He signed the book and dropped the pen. "Older than God, Sergeant. Did I see you talking to Riggs?"

"Yes, sir. I think I shut his mouth for a day or two. But we've got to play the bulldog and badger game with him. If we jail him, he'll give the story to Plummer. And we can't hold him incommunicado because there isn't a guard we can trust not to carry a message for him."

King frowned. "Asking favors is a little out of my line. But if you can wait a day or so, I'll have my mind made up about what to do."

"All right, Major. In the meantime, I'd like to take a few men out after those horses of Davis's."

King grunted. "Sergeant, those horses are browsing in the Wallowas by now."

119

"Maybe so. One way to find out would be to look. Whether we find them or not, the effect on the men of such a patrol would be good. Not to mention the effect on Rogue Buffalo. To keep up with a chief like him, you've got to be a little bit unpredictable yourself."

"I'd say you were practically unaccountable sometimes." King smiled with meaning. He opened a desk drawer and handed Ward a small, rolled parcel.

Ward felt its lightness and softness and knew it was Jamie Harris's shawl. "No sir," he said, "that was probably the most accountable thing I ever did."

King chuckled.

Afterward it was suddenly quiet, and the quiet did not break easily. King glanced at a copy of the Cañon City paper on his desk. "Old Plummer," he murmured with another chuckle.

It's Blair Again! the boldface type read. **The Shame of Cañon City! He Wins on a Platform of Rob Rancher to Pay Miner!**

It was Jess who finally spoke. "Are you going to keep us in suspense forever, Sergeant? What are you going to do about the shame of F Troop?"

"I don't know. I thought about it all night."

She took a chair near him. "Then will you listen to what I was trying to say yesterday? Perhaps if you knew the rest of the story, it would help you with your problem."

She still blames me, Ward realized.

"I don't need to explain what the brand stands for, but he wasn't truly a deserter," she said. "It was all politics."

He waited. He had been trying to justify King's position relative to the deaths of Trooper Fowler and the stage passenger.

"I suppose you know," Jess went on, "that when an officer takes over a new post, he signs for all the property in his command. He is supposed to take inventory. Actually, it's seldom done. He simply takes the word of the retiring officer that everything is there. My father signed for a great deal of property at Camp Piedras, New Mexico Territory, three years ago. Two months later he was found to be fifty thousand dollars short."

"Fifty thousand?"

"In silver. Part of the government property was a mine confiscated from a Southern sympathizer. It was being operated for the government when he took over. A few months later, it was sold to a group of miners. That was when the shortage was discovered."

Floating in from the cool morning came the clop of hoofs and a nimble grind of buggy tires. Ward saw Roy Plummer's turnout entering the post, unchallenged by the sentry seated on a box beside the gate.

King's voice said tiredly: "To make an unpleasant recital short, I was placed under technical

121

arrest. I broke arrest and tried to find the man I'd relieved. I'd known him before. We used to argue politics. I never caught up with him, but they caught up with me. It looked as though I'd scampered away with my ill-gotten gains. I suppose I was lucky . . . a year in prison, a dishonorable discharge, and a brand on the hip. End of story. Good day, Sergeant. Thanks for your help. Show the man out, Jess."

"Just a minute," protested Ward. "This begins to involve me, too. Apparently I'm the man who's got to decide what to do about you. You might say it's unusual for an outfit to be run by a deserter. It'd help if I knew what you were doing in the O.V.C."

"Jim Harris could tell you that," said King stiffly. Ward watched the man's jaw harden. King did not continue.

"Why Harris?" asked Ward.

Shooting a glance at him, King said: "Because he headed the syndicate that bought the mine. He was the one who discovered the shortage. . . ."

It struck Ward like a stone. Then from his surprise some unrelated facts began to find one another and merge, like drops of oil on water—King being backed down at the parade—King agreeing to discipline Harris about the flood, and doing nothing—Jim Harris's self-confidence where the Army was concerned. What still stopped him was King's being here in Cañon City at all. "Then why did you put yourself under Harris's thumb again?" he asked.

King rubbed his neck. "Well, you see, I thought . . . I thought maybe I could force him to clear me, if I could just get something on him. This hydraulic mining outfit had the old Harris smell. I found him up to the eyeballs in it when I finally tracked him down. Harris didn't even know I was in Oregon. So I went to Portland and got a commission by paying the troop's debts. Maybe it's a poor man's army," he said, "but I needed it and it needed any man with military experience."

"And Harris needed you," said Ward, "to keep the Army off his back while he washed out half the farms and ranches in eastern Oregon."

King began to fill a pipe. "It was a pretty sadly botched campaign, Sergeant. I gave him a gun and dared him to use it on me. It's been at my head ever since . . . the fact that I had to falsify my Army experience to get into the war. But all the time I've been hanging on in the hope that he'd get into a scrape of some kind . . . tip his hand, and I'd have my chance." He stopped speaking, looking tired and defeated.

There it is, thought Ward. *The whole thing, right in my lap.*

Outside, old Roy Plummer said to his buggy horse: "Now, stay there, damn ye!" He came tramping up the path, muttering to himself.

To Ward, nothing was clearer than that King

123

should resign. The cost to King was slight, compared to the price to others of his staying in, a beaten officer, where a fighter was needed. A fist struck the door, and at once it opened.

Roy Plummer stood in it, a goateed Don Quixote with printer's ink in his beard. "Am I interrupting anything?" he asked. "Some high-level conference on the removal of mud from forts, or the conduct of Army officers in parades?"

"My father has been wounded," Jess King said, her chin lifting. "I don't know who you are, sir, but . . ."

"Roy Plummer, Miss King," Ward said quickly.

"Well, Major, I'll be . . ."

"No, no." Plummer smiled. "I'll just be a minute, and I want to ask you both some questions. Won't take a minute. Major, I'm grieved to see you in this condition. Naturally the people who buy my paper will want to know all about it. Would you care to give details?"

Plummer made himself comfortable on the desk. Shadows collected in the deep hollows of his face. *With a staff and a robe,* thought Ward, *he would look like an Old Testament prophet.*

"The sergeant can tell you all about it," King said wearily.

"Fine. But maybe you can tell me this . . . to what extent is the Indians' boldness attributable to the Army's recent lack of activity?"

Jess crossed the floor to place herself before the

editor. "I don't care if you're the commanding general of the Department of Columbia, Mister Plummer. I ask you to leave."

Plummer said with his fierce smile: "But I only want to have the story straight before I print it. Certainly I don't want to say that this attack couldn't have happened to a more deserving man, unless it's true."

Ward took Plummer's arm; it felt like a slightly padded birch rod. "You heard the lady, Plummer. You've got time before you need all this, anyway."

"Sure. Ah, well," said Plummer, "I only thought if the major can ride in Bill Blair's parade, he can at least talk to me. I should think, though, he ought to be bedded down on higher ground, now that the hydraulic candidate is back in office. Something to mull over while you're in bed," he added. "What use have Indians got for gold bullion?"

"I don't know," said King dully. "But they took it."

"Somebody took it. Maybe Harris or John Champie came along after the Snakes had left and took the bullion themselves."

"That's not our concern. It's the Army's concern to try to prevent such raids. The express side is Wells Fargo's."

"Priests and preachers and generals," snorted Plummer. "Too far removed from ordinary life to

125

be concerned with the problems of it. So it's left for men like me to ask questions and suggest answers. And all I get out of it is abuse."

Plummer left.

Ward felt Jess's eyes on him. He glanced at her and knew there was something she wanted to say. At last she asked: "Will you be going to town this morning?"

"In about a half hour," he told her.

He had intended driving a supply wagon in to stock provisions for the patrol.

"I'd like to go with you, if you don't mind."

"My pleasure." Ward smiled.

Feeling that nothing had been settled, he went to the orderly room, where Collins was at his interminable work of copying. "Add this to your general orders," he said. "Send a copy to each man involved . . . 'The following men will fall out after "Retreat" with saddles packed.'"

Collins looked up from his writing. "Is this a patrol?"

"That's the idea."

"Let me guess the first name that comes to your mind," Collins said, and wrote *Matthew R. Collins, Cpl.* on the page.

"Make that Acting Sergeant," said Ward. "I'm putting in for your sergeancy if you come through this one in good shape."

"Ah, Sergeant," said Collins with bitter gratitude, "won't it look handsome on a headboard?"

XII

In his office later that same morning, Jim Harris had set the stage for a meeting with Harry Wheeler, the banker, and Mayor Big Bill Blair. The men had requested it, and Harris knew what was in the wind. So he had John Champie bring from the concentrate mill a bar of gold. On the neat surface of the desk, the ingot compelled even Harris's gaze. Still rough from the crucible, it had a pure beauty that was partly sentiment, partly the old yearning for wealth.

Champie was slumped in an oaken armchair scowling at his boots. Fumes from the concentrate mill drifted through the room. The clean-up after the last washing was finished; the mercury had soaked up the ultimate grain of gold from the riffles, the mercury and gold had been re-separated, and Harris now knew exactly what the giant washing had been worth.

"Let me have that old John the Baptist for an hour and I'll baptize him for you," Champie growled suddenly.

Roy Plummer had visited the mine last evening, full of curiosity about who watched the gold loaded into the Wells Fargo boxes when a shipment was made, what possible use the Snakes and Cayuses had for it, and whether Harris thought anyone would trade them guns for the gold they stole? He speculated that he might concoct an editorial about it.

"Let him alone," said Harris, lighting a cigar. "If you want to attract attention to us, just raise a hand to Roy Plummer."

"Tell you who I will raise a hand to," growled Champie. "Forson." He had been obsessed with the matter of Forson's bringing Jamie home full of wine ever since that night. "Blast him," muttered the big man, "I wish I knew for sure. . . ."

"We'll never know for sure," Harris told him curtly, "whether we made a fool of him, or he made fools of us. Here's Wheeler and Blair," he added, seeing the dusty rig stop outside. He put his hands in his pockets, trying to feel casual. There was so much at stake, so little time. A hill of gold, and they wanted him to mine it with a teaspoon.

Blair tramped in first, immense in his buffalo-skin coat. He was red-faced with anger. He brought none of his old tin-plating of florid courtliness. He entered with the long skirts of the coat flapping and stopped to stare at the bar of gold on the desk. Behind him, Harry Wheeler entered with grim taciturnity and closed the door.

"What the hell's that setting there for?" demanded Blair. There was whiskey on his breath and talcum on his jaws. His face was choked with color and his eyeballs were yellow.

One of these days, thought Harris, *old Bill's going to fall over with a seizure.* Meantime Blair was looking for a fight, and Harris braced for it. He drew quietly on his cigar, and then drawled: "Will you take that damned coat off, Bill? If you had a hump, somebody'd shoot you for a buffalo. When you're wearing that thing, I'm always afraid you're going to charge me or break wind."

Blair threw his wide-brimmed hat on the floor. "Time I did charge somebody. Last month was the first month . . . *the first month* . . . that a stage line of mine has ever been in the red."

"Is that my fault?" asked Harris.

"It is when all of my cash is in Applejack, and Applejack ain't producing. And when you make such an ass out of King, he don't even have the guts to keep the stage line open."

Harris chuckled and his cigar bobbled. "Bill, that's practically mysterious, it's so complicated. It sounds like something a man would think of in the middle of the night just before the bottle ran dry."

"What Bill means," said Wheeler, "is that he could stand some losses on the stage line, if the cause of his losses were sweetening the profits on this end. Mysterious or not, it's approximately the same complaint I have. I've lost some good depositors in the last six months because they were swamped out or Injuned out of their farms and ranches."

"Maybe a little more astuteness on Bill's part would help," Harris stated.

His bulldog face darkening, Blair laid his palms on the desk and leaned over it to glare into Harris's face. His voice was like gravel rattling down a chute. "I've been driver, hostler, super, and owner in this business. No man this side of John Butterfield can outdicker me on a mail contract. I can pick horses by their shadows on the wall. I'll watch 'em roll and pay you fifty dollars a roll, and come out on it. I know to the pound how much I'll lose on a fat passenger, and I'll get it out of overage on his baggage nine times out of ten. I know the best rivers to dump junk mail in, and I know the week of every year when I'll hit my break-even point and start making money. And you stand there and tell me I don't know staging."

Harris took his cigar and with a quick movement of his body moved closer to Blair. His hand thrust the gray tip of the cigar almost into the stage man's eye. Blair fell back. "And I'll tell you something else, Bill," drawled Harris. "If you ever try to air your personal difficulties in my office again, you'll get that right in the eye."

Blair rubbed his watering eye. He was dumbfounded.

"If that's clear," Harris said decisively, "and you think you can both stand some good news, I'll speak my own piece now."

Wheeler, the dried-up little banker with the

good mind, smiled with his restaurant-china teeth. "Good news is what we need most today, Jim," he said. "What is it?"

Harris picked up the little ingot of gold. "I thought you'd be interested in knowing that while the monitors were running the other day, we were making fifteen hundred dollars an hour."

Wheeler did not blink. "Net," he asked, "or gross?"

Champie grunted. "Gross . . . but you can pay bills with it."

"And after you pay the bills," asked the banker, "what's the net?"

"Expenses are about fifteen hundred a week right now," Harris said. "I include leases, labor . . . everything."

"The whole trouble is"—Wheeler sighed—"there aren't many weeks in the year out here in eastern Oregon. As I recall, your prospectus prophesied richer washings than that."

"And do you know why we haven't had them? Because first I had Captain Poole sitting on me, and now you boys are trying to mine by a prayer book. Never have I been allowed to operate the way I'd have to in order to make money. The gold is there, damn it, but we've got to take it."

"How do you know it's there?" argued Bill Blair. "Is this your instinct again?"

Harris snatched some papers from his desk and flapped them in the mayor's face. "Take these home and read them. Our last operation was up thirty percent. Does that mean we're getting closer to what I promised was there?"

"How close did you get in New Mexico?" asked Blair sourly.

Harris took a deep breath. The hard fighter's jaw was beginning to show, the coldness in his eyes. *When I get this thing going,* he thought, *I'll ace this barn baron out so clean he'll never know he owned a share.* "That was hard-rock mining, the biggest gamble on earth. Even so, we were minting money until a workman let a submerged pump burn out. We were flooded in a week. Bill," he asked suddenly, "do you want out? Do you want my I.O.U. for every nickel you've got in Applejack?"

Startled, Blair pushed his hands in his pockets and lumbered to the window. After an instant, Harris walked to his side. They looked down on the cañon where workmen were replacing blocks in the sluices. The long wooden flume twisted on its spidery stilts to the bulkheads and distributors.

"Not yet," rumbled Blair. "If I sell out now, I know I'm whipped. I'm like all the rest . . . can't afford to quit while I'm behind. When do we wash again?"

"Tomorrow. The twelve-inch hose ought to be ready, and with a head of water like that . . ."

Harry Wheeler stood with his hands clasped

under his coattails and his clear, cold eyes on Harris. "With a head of water like that, the Army will be up here in an hour. I've told you that before, and gotten no good answer out of you. What are you going to do about Forson . . . or King, if he should come to life?"

"And I've told you before I can handle them. King . . . he'll never come to life, I promise you. Forson is a sergeant. There is no law . . . no law in this state . . . to prevent us from operating as we see fit."

"That still begs the issue. What if Forson comes up with a couple of dozen riflemen?"

Above the door was racked a Henry rifle. Glancing at it, Harris said: "I'll arm the workmen. Or stop them myself."

"Well . . ." Wheeler frowned.

Harris turned back to the window. "It'd be a nice change to be trusted in at least one part of the work sometime."

At that moment he saw a horseman riding up the cañon below the sluices. Harris's first conjecture was that it was Forson, for the man wore a uniform. Then he recognized the slouching form of Walter Riggs, the prospector turned soldier. *Damn Riggs and his daytime visits,* he thought.

Blair and Wheeler were silent now, and Harris turned quickly with a twist of humor on his mouth. "Maybe I'm crazy, boys. All I see is a company making money. We've nosed out the big deposit at last. Yet I have to coax you for permission to operate."

Wheeler smiled. "Still, I think we understand each other. Banks and stage lines go broke like anything else. We just want you to understand that we can't afford to have our own businesses suffer without remuneration up here in the form . . . say . . . of dividends."

Wheeler replaced his high, square-topped derby. Blair grunted as he picked his own hat up from the floor. They left. Harris said quickly to Champie: "Riggs is coming, damn him. What's he using for brains these days . . . peanuts? Better go down to the bulkheads. I can handle him better alone."

Trooper Riggs had been smoking Indian tobacco. Into the room with him came an odor of burning leaves and bark. He had a way of walking—putting his toes down an instant before his heels—that gave him a prowling aspect and made his walk utterly silent. The lanky man pushed his fatigue cap back on his long, oily, black hair and slumped into a chair. Harris distastefully regarded the gaunt face with the socketed, pale eyes and thick black brows. Riggs was one of those men who could eat a horse a day and never gain a pound, but he was tougher than a crab-apple wood bow.

"What are you trying to do, coming here by day?" Harris demanded. "Get me a bad name for the company I keep?"

"See there?" Riggs grinned. "You give me a bad name, and then jump me for it."

Harris kept staring at him. "The talk is they picked you up in Rock Creek Cañon. Roaming around mighty free for a deserter, aren't you?"

Riggs shrugged, a crafty half smile on his mouth. "That sergeant must like me, I reckon. He gave me the freedom of the post instead of the guardhouse."

"This isn't the post," Harris reminded him.

Riggs was gazing at the gold bar on the desk. "What's that there gimcrack? Something a feller could make money out of?"

Harris gave him a wry smile. "The joker is that it costs a dollar and ten cents for each dollar's worth you dig up. What have you got to say that's quick?"

"Found out something about King," Riggs said. In his long face glistened a deep and twisted pleasure.

"What's that?"

Riggs touched his knob-like jaws. "Jim, I'm a-gittin' lockjaw again. Reckon it would take about a hundred-dollar chaw off that gold plug yonder to ease it up."

Harris leaned on the desk to pencil a mark on the back of an envelope. He handed it to Riggs, who scowled at the letter he had drawn. Harris had printed a D in black pencil. He smiled at the trooper's astonishment.

135

"You are shore one early-risin' man," Riggs commented disappointedly.

"I thought you knew I had an arm lock on him."

"Well . . . hell." Riggs sighed.

"So I keep my hundred." Harris smiled. "Can you find your way back? And don't come again by daylight. In fact, the last money we gave you was to see you to Portland, wasn't it?"

"You know what happened." Riggs's temper had drawn up like a cat with a belly cramp. He had just missed out on $100 and lost face as well. "You know what they do to a deserter in wartime? Shoot 'im. Forson just told me."

"That's why the pay's so good for deserting."

"It ain't so good that every man in the firing squad is goin' to miss," growled Riggs. "I'm takin' off just as soon as I can."

"Now?" asked Harris in surprise.

"Tonight. I shouldn't have left the post, but I figured if you knew about King, things might begin to pop to where they'd forget about me until I was a hundred miles away."

"Good figuring," said Harris. "But after I tell them about King, somebody else will take over this command and things will be tighter for me than they are now. What else is new?"

"Forson's takin' a bunch of them barracks generals out on patrol tonight."

"So soon?" Harris felt a flush of pleasure.

"He's all excited now. Figures he can crowd

them right into fittin' their soldier suits if he works fast. They're goin' to hunt the stock old man Davis lost last week."

"Can he find them?"

Riggs stirred. "Purty fair tracker."

"Where is the stock?"

Riggs scratched his thick, dirty hair and looked at his fingernails. "Prob'ly at the main camp. These people figger their wealth in horses. Chief with the biggest horse herd is the biggest chief."

"What if the Army finds the main camp?"

Riggs smiled dryly. "Well, sir, I've got worries of my own, without frettin' over a passel of tenderfeet losin' their hair. They's about a hundred fightin' age bucks in Rogue Buffalo's tribe. Three, four hundred, countin' squaws and brats."

Conscience was one of those irrational, throwback mechanisms in a man, about as useful as a house dog circling to trample the jungle grass before he lay down. But it was part of the excess baggage in Jim Harris's mind. A stain of guilt spread through him when he thought: *It would be fine if the Snakes knew Forson was coming.* For all of his outward sureness with Wheeler and Blair, he could not be certain the workmen would fight the troopers. But with Forson awaiting the last "Reveille", as the Army headboards had it— he was chilled and exhilarated by a vision of those clumsy soldiers of Forson's clodhopping into an ambush. "Maybe," he speculated, "it would be best if the chief knew Forson was coming. . . ."

Riggs spoke nasally, his skimmed-milk eyes on the miner. "You go to perdition, brother. Forson and King are watchin' me. When I take off again, it'll be to California . . . for good."

"Then you'd better travel fast and lucky," said Harris. "As long as Forson's around, you won't be long gone before they're on your trail."

"What are you gettin' at?" asked Riggs narrowly.

"I'm getting at the fact that you'd better be making some plans. What if they're making up a manifest of charges right now? What if they slap you in a cell tonight and tomorrow you're sentenced to the firing squad?"

"If I am," said Riggs, "they'll be some talk about you, too."

"Talk," said Harris with a hard grin of emphasis. "But you're under military justice, Riggs, and I'm not. You deserted and got caught. That's a lot more serious than talk."

Riggs peered at him, chewing on it, his pale eyes growing more disturbed.

Harris spoke levelly. "Riggs, I'd be traveling, if I were you. And I'd make sure nobody was traveling behind me. And the way I'd be sure would be to stop by at Rogue Buffalo's camp on the way south."

Riggs hunched forward, his elbows on his thighs,

his long hands squeezing together. With bitter eyes, he looked down at his unbuttoned blouse and pale blue trousers. Harris held his breath.

"This contrary suit o' clothes," Riggs uttered suddenly. "They put you in it and you can't even spit with free men any more. Well, what," he asked Harris angrily, "do you want me to say to him? What's in it for me?"

"A hundred dollars ought to put you in business," said Harris. "I'll leave it at Champie's cabin. Just tell the chief to be on guard."

Silently Riggs rose and pondered it. "I tell you, Harris, all the Injun blood ain't wrapped up in paint and feathers," he said with a wry smile. "Tell you what. Get a hacksaw and we'll split that there gold doorstop. Easy to pack. Good any place."

"Split it?" Harris laughed. "You're looking at three thousand dollars, mister."

"Well, split off about three hundred dollars' worth for me. Else just leave three hundred in gold at the cabin. Or don't leave anything and see if some of that talk helps sell stock."

Harris did some quick figuring. He did not want trouble with Riggs, but he disliked being bested in the bargain. Had the ingot been a thousand parts pure, it would have weighed out at about $3,000. But the bullion was running heavy in copper and silver and he supposed the mint would value it at about $2,000. "Oh, hell," he said wearily. "Wait here. I'll get a saw."

Afterward, alone, the remainder of the ingot locked away, Jim Harris rubbed one fist against his palm as he stood at the window, gazing across the cañon. This time he was going after it—the big kernel of treasure in that cliff across the cañon. He was going to wash the earth down from the cliffs until the sluices gagged on it. He would exhibit to Harry Wheeler and Bill Blair a sheet that would show them, once and for all, that action was for miners and morality was for the clergy.

XIII

A strong wind was pushing a dingy froth of clouds across the mountains when Sergeant Ward and Jessamin King reached Cañon City. Ward studied the sky. "Those troopers are going to roast me if we get soaked tonight."

"Do you mind their roasting you?" she asked.

"Not if I can make soldiers out of them." He gazed at her, and she smiled and looked down.

He found her pretty and engaging company. He noticed the slenderness of her neck and the way the fine hair was brushed up to a chignon.

"I've heard Father say just that," she told him.

"I wish I'd heard him say it. It seems as if we've known two different men."

"Is that meant to sound ominous?"

Ward hunched over the lines, tormented by the

knowledge that there was really only one decision he could make. "If I thought there was any hope of getting him straightened out . . ." he began. "But he's stalled, Jess. I can understand it, but I can't let it happen to the troop, and the people we're supposed to be protecting. If he won't stand up to Harris, then the whole troop is helpless." Yet he was experienced enough to feel a bond with any man who had lost the edge of his manhood and was frightened at his new character. King had put everything into this attempt to prove himself, and then he had sat down and done nothing.

"Do you mean you're going to inform on him?" asked the girl quietly.

"I mean I'll probably have to ask him to resign."

Her voice became small and tight. "Don't you ever make mistakes?"

"All the time. But not this particular mistake."

"In fact, you must have made one recently, according to the daybook. I can understand a man having a girl in his room . . . but *not* a first sergeant."

She did not look at him; he knew she was embarrassed to bring it out, and he found himself unwontedly ashamed. Of course, that was why she had brought it up—to prove that he was no fit judge. He drove silently as they entered the deep, sun-shot little main street. "Knowing this fellow, Harris," he said finally, "you should understand how it happened."

"You mean he forced the girl on you?" Jess said with wide-eyed innocence.

"The girl was his daughter. He sent her."

"He sent her."

"As bait. I was the only man Harris really had to worry about with this flooding he's been doing. I suppose he figured, if I were out of the way, he could turn the monitors on and not have to worry about the Army."

"And you couldn't wait to take the bait he offered," she said sharply.

Apparently it was difficult to get across to a woman. "I mean she just moved in on me. There I was, confined to quarters . . . and there came Jamie with a baked ham dinner."

Jess laughed. "I've heard of men being trapped for a husband by the home-cooked meal snare, but I must say it's unusual as a weapon of war."

"You tell me a better one," retorted Ward. "When you've eaten your wife's cooking for years, and then go on a straight diet of hardtack and moldy bacon. That girl can bake a ham to make an angel's mouth water."

"With cloves, I suppose?"

In good feminine tradition, Ward perceived, she had lost sight of the defense of Major King, and was most concerned with what spices had gone into the downfall of Sergeant Forson. "Cloves?" he repeated. "What do you want cloves for?"

"To flavor it, of course. Anyone can throw a

ham in the oven and heat it. I just can't see Jamie as a cook, anyway. But of course she's always a girl to get carried away by whatever part she's playing. Her father put her on the stand to say that she'd heard Dad say he'd made a physical inventory when he took over the mine. She was marvelous in the rôle . . . like a young widow. The longer she talked, the more certain it was that he'd stolen the silver to blight her young happiness."

Ward gazed at the mixed traffic on the gullied road, the lank dogs in the sun, the red-berried mountain ash at the edge of the street. A cloud shadow passed over the road, the wind puffed dust from the cornices of Harry Wheeler's bank building. Fall was in the air. Ward made a decision. "I'm going up the road for a while. Is there some shopping you can do?"

"I suppose. Where are you going?"

"I've got to take back something Jamie left. Won't take long. I'll leave it at the mine office."

Jess brightened. "Fine. I'll go along. I'm awfully anxious to talk to Jim Harris again."

Ward cleared his throat. "You know, it might be better if . . ."

In the end she went along.

At the big sheet-metal building that housed the mine offices, Ward set the brake. "I'll tell Harris he's got a guest," he told Jess. He walked inside. But Harris was not in the building, and a bookkeeper with paper sleeve-protectors told Ward with a pokerface: "I don't expect he'll be back for a day or so. He was going up to look at a claim on Little Pine Creek."

Ward went back. "They say he's gone to Little Pine Creek. I doubt it. Let's take a look down below."

From the office building the road descended five hundred feet in a half mile. Upcañon was a log and earth dam from which a flume carried water to the monitors. Below, the great nozzles had gashed deep holes in the far cañon side, leaving stratified bluffs with brush and trees dangling over the edges. The bottom of the cañon glistened with mud, and among immense boulders men in hip boots waded about the sluices, resetting blocks and riffle bars.

"There's Harris," Ward said suddenly. On a platform at the foot of the grade stood Jim Harris, John Champie, and three other men. With one hand Harris was swinging the counter-balanced tiller of a giant monitor, one of three bolted like swivel guns to the floor of the platform. With his other hand he was pointing at the raw cliffs across the cañon.

Ward stopped near a bulkhead where the flume ended. "You'd better stay here," he told Jess.

"Indeed, I won't. There are things I want to ask Mister Harris myself."

Harris and Champie had seen them now. The

men with them jumped from the platform and walked toward the sluices in the middle of the cañon. Champie and Harris waited as the sergeant and Jess approached. Ward gazed up at Harris and at Champie, who stood in denim pants and a red shirt, rubbing his hands against his hip pockets.

"How're things at Little Pine Creek?" Ward asked.

Harris was coatless, his shoulders looking square and hard. His face was grim as his hand dropped from the tiller. Then he saw Jess. His expression changed as he looked at her.

Champie moved abruptly to the railing and stared angrily at the sergeant. "Get out of here," he said.

Ward hooked his thumbs under his belt. "This is a bread and butter call, Champie. I just wanted to return your fiancée's shawl and thank whoever was responsible for the ham dinner. I enjoyed every minute of it."

Champie's face flushed, and he swung one leg over the railing, but Harris gripped his wrist and stopped him. "Wait a minute," he said. Harris was looking at the girl. "Miss King," he said, "I'm sorry about your rough time in getting to Cañon City. If I can do anything to make you comfortable while you're here, I'd be pleased."

"You can do one thing. You can leave my father alone."

"I'm not a grudge bearer," Harris said. "Maybe

I've got reason to carry one. But I left all that in New Mexico."

"Did you?" Jess said. She let her gaze travel over the torn cliffs and boulder-strewn wash. "Do you mean they let you do all this willingly?"

"We're not landscape architects," Harris said. "We're miners."

Jim Harris swung over the railing, and jumped to the ground. He walked quickly up to Ward. Standing close, he was like a taller and larger man. He was put together like a wood chopper, broad across the shoulders, wedging down to a flat waist, a lithe and muscular man whose temper shaped his jaw. "Now, I'm telling you, mister," he said. "I've taken all I mean to from you. I won't take any more advice on how to run a mine. Take Miss King and get out of here."

Ward felt Jess's hand slip through his arm. He turned to her. "Will you wait at the wagon?" he said. "I'll be along directly." Jess walked away.

When Ward faced Harris again, he saw that his fists were placed on his hips. Harris said through his set teeth: "Now I can tell you something else. If ever I see you with my daughter again, I'll kill you."

"That's up to your daughter. She came to me."

"It's up to you now."

Ward grinned. "Then don't make it hard for me by sending her around with a case of wine. Was she really orry-eyed that night?"

146

Harris's mouth suddenly tightened, and he drove his fist at Ward's head. Ward slipped away and fired a blow at Harris as the miner came in. Big and lithe, Harris ducked and swerved after him. He hit Ward over the heart and threw a looping punch at his head. Half blocking it, Ward felt the stinging force of the swing. As Harris lunged in, he set himself and caught him with a straight, jolting punch to the jaw. Harris floundered back against the platform. Blood smeared his mouth. His face was white, his eyes stark with fury. He looked like any roughneck from his mucking crews slugging it out in a saloon.

Now he shook his head to clear it; he leaned back against the framing, breathing hard. At the sluices, men were shouting and several were stumbling through mud and rocks toward the fighters. Something got through to Harris. His face changed. Ward kept waiting, and now Harris's fists came down. He stood there haggard with anger.

"Mighty big chaw you've just taken, trooper," he said.

Ward was panting. "That's a fact. But you're through hog-troughing Cañon Creek. Law or not, you'll build silt basins before you turn those things on again."

Harris gave him a bloody grin. "Yes, sir, that's quite a mouthful for a lad like you. It'll be something to watch you chew it."

"Maybe. But you'll see me try."

Ward returned to the wagon, and he and Jess drove away.

Jamie Harris was coming from the Applejack offices when they passed. She called to Ward, and he stopped the wagon while the girl ran up. Then she saw Jess and looked surprised. Quickly she recovered and put out a lace-gloved hand.

"This is so nice," she said. "Daddy and I were most happy when we learned you'd come. Won't you come to dinner sometime?"

"We'd love to, Jamie." Jess smiled. "You know you're simply famous for your baked ham."

Jamie laughed, her eyes sparkling. "You're too nice. But I'm afraid soldiers are easy to cook for. They're so lonesome for anything home-like."

Sitting between them, Ward had the uneasy sensation that he might be cut by an invisible saber. Jamie laid her hand on Ward's arm.

"Ward, did you see anything of my shawl after I left? It's been missing, and the last few nights were just real cool."

"I left it in your father's office."

"Oh, thank you." Then she let her long lashes come down, and for an instant seemed abashed. "I . . . I *hope* I wasn't forward that night. I mean in coming unescorted to the camp . . . ?"

Jess smiled down at her. "Don't be embarrassed,

Jamie. I've lived in Army camps all my life. This sort of thing happens all the time."

Ward had the presence of mind to kick the brake off and cluck the horses on. He glanced at Jess after a moment. She looked composed, entirely lady-like, not in the least as though she had just taken a scalp. He had a dim conception of other forms of warfare more bloodthirsty than the clash of arms.

XIV

At Fort Haney, mounted drill was going on and from the rifle range came the steady hammer of gunfire. After leaving Jess at her father's quarters, Ward turned the wagon over to a stable hand and walked out on the parade. Mounted, Corporal Collins was directing drill. He had three squads working. Ward watched a moment.

"They're looking pretty fair," he commented.

Collins shot another order. He did not look at Ward.

"Is Riggs around?" Ward asked.

Collins turned on the saddle. "Nobody gave him leave to go anywhere."

"I don't see him here. I'll check with the sentries."

Trooper Viets was on duty at the sally port. "Riggs left before you did," Viets admitted. "I asked for his pass and he said you'd given him permission to leave on special duty."

"You'll take latrine duty for three days," said Ward. "A pass is a piece of paper . . . not an oral statement. Has he come back?"

Viets, at port arms, stared straight through him, masking his resentment. "Not through this gate," he said.

"If he does, hold him and send for me."

Ward walked to the stable and found Riggs's horse in its stall. A trooper in a baggy stable frock paused with his pitchfork. "When did Riggs come back?" he asked the trooper.

"Half hour ago."

"Where did he go then?"

"Can't say, Sergeant."

He found Riggs at rifle practice across the meadow. The targets were set against a raised bunker, and after a round, men would appear from the butts behind them and spot the hits. Because metallic ammunition was being saved, all the men were firing muskets. Riggs was getting nothing but bull's-eyes. As Ward watched, Riggs primed a linen cartridge with his teeth, dropped it in his musket, and rammed a ball home. His lazy eyes lifted as Ward approached.

"Come over to the shed," Ward ordered. "I want to talk to you."

There was a stone ammunition shed fifty yards away. Ward asked Riggs what he had been doing away from the fort. "Did you go to the Applejack diggings?"

"Not me, Sergeant. I just drifted up to town."

"You're a liar. You were at the Applejack diggings."

Leaning on the musket, Riggs threw him a sharp stare and held it in silence. "Well, now, any place but the Army," he said, "that would be something to fight over. But you're the sergeant and I'm the trooper."

"What's been your business with Harris?" Ward pursued.

"No business," Riggs replied stubbornly.

There was a sharp rattle of musketry from the firing line.

"Harris's daughter told me they'd staked you a couple of times."

"Still no business. I didn't find any color."

"Riggs, there's had to be a reason why Champie helped you get away that night," said Ward angrily. "There's a reason why you were absent without leave this morning. Were you informing on the major?"

Riggs's eyes were lazy-lidded but deadly. "Up to now I've kept my mouth shut about him."

Ward suddenly drew his revolver, pressed it into Riggs's belly, and knocked his musket from his hand. Riggs stood absolutely still, but he was tense as a trigger.

"This morning we had a treaty," Ward told him,

"but now we've got a war. Before we finish with you, we may have to execute you half a dozen times on different charges. Turn around."

Riggs turned and Ward called the corporal who was directing the fire. "I'm taking this man to the guardhouse," he said. "Go to the orderly room and get the keys, and bring a man to stand guard."

Afterward, as he walked back to the squad room, he thought stoically: *Well, King gets it now*. Right about now, Trooper Riggs would be calling the guard over to the window. "Hey, soldier!" And the guard would listen to Riggs, and he would report to the rest of the men when he got off duty. News like that traveled faster than a sharp-shinned hawk. In twenty-four hours, old Roy Plummer would be pasting the special edition in his front window.

He packed slowly and methodically in his room. In a way he was glad he would be out of the fort for a couple of days. He would not have to see the situation develop. He would come back and maybe King would be gone; maybe at least he would be packed. And of course the girl would go with him, and Ward was sorry for her and for King, and for himself. He had begun to like that girl.

At 4:00 p.m. the patrol was ready. Ward inspected equipment and issued ball ammunition. As he was explaining the purpose of the patrol, a message came that Major King wanted to see him.

He found King at his desk. King seemed in a better frame of mind.

"I want to put your mind at rest about something," he said. "I've written my letter of resignation."

Ward was shocked. It was what he had wanted, yet he had been hoping that King would miraculously come to life and make resignation unnecessary. To his surprise, he found himself arguing against it. "Why not wait until I bring the patrol back, Major?"

"What would that accomplish?"

"Who knows? Harris might fall in the reservoir."

King leaned back and gave his old cynical smile. "That would be less miraculous than my stopping him by charging his monitors, waving a saber."

Ward looked at him. "As a matter of fact," he said, "you may have to make your charge while I'm gone. They were setting sluice blocks when I was up there today. That probably means they'll be back at work tomorrow."

King looked startled. "Are you sure?"

"First the blocks, then the mercury, then the water. Maybe you ought to sketch out a plan of defense," Ward suggested.

King's eyes stared out the window into the dusk. "What the hell can I do now, tied to this chair?"

"You weren't tied to it last week."

King looked at him. In his face was the gaunt

despair of a man seeing himself in the mirror after weeks of illness. "We might as well not fool ourselves," he said. "Whatever I do, I'm finished as a soldier. In this or any other army. In all conscience, could you ask a man with a gun at his back and a knife at his throat to storm a battery? What would he have to gain?"

"Self-respect," the sergeant said. "Isn't that what you joined for?"

King scowled, tried to stand, and slumped back as his injured leg gave out. "Yes, but . . . hell, Sergeant, heroics are for men with a stake in them."

"In that case," the sergeant said crisply, "you might as well send that letter."

He left.

Just before it was time to pull out, he told Corporal Collins to stay. "Just in case the old man needs help," he said. "Which I expect he will."

An hour before sundown, he led the troopers through the water gate and down Cañon Creek toward Davis's horse and mule ranch.

XV

Always dusk was the worst time for King, recalling long twilights in Wyoming or New Mexico when the whole camp took a breath and let down, and supper fragrances came with the breath of sage, and newly mounted guards turned their heads to watch the sunset. When duty was taken from you, and you pulled off your boots with a sigh. Tonight, using a cane, he walked painfully along the border of the parade ground, trying to pull the old nostalgia over his shoulders like a mantle. But it tore apart in his fingers.

For three years there had been this pressure on him. There was the corroding memory of having been wronged—disgraced—because they took another man's word over his own. And the man who took the silver had later deserted to join the Confederacy. But only lately was there this dead weight of lost confidence. He thought: *Whatever it was I had, I've lost it now. Maybe it's age,* the thought came. *I'm not thinking things through any more. Maybe the old sword's fallen asleep.*

Two troopers approached. They peered curiously at him in the light of near dusk, then recognized him, and one saluted, and both said: "'Evening, Major." The second man forgot to salute, and King half turned to call him back. He shrugged and let it go. Whose fault was it if the men were ignorant of military courtesy? The bind, always the bind. The things you were able to do, and the things you were supposed to do. They never balanced out. Obligations to this person and that group, but the eternal obligation to yourself— what Forson had called self-respect.

King cut at a weed growing by the path. He was

sick of self-examination. He had gone barn sour like a horse—sick of being pent up, yet unwilling to go out and work. There was Harris, if he wanted to work. He could try something tonight to put the hydraulics out of action. But what if he got caught? They'd throw the book at him this time. For this town was mortgaged to the mines. It could not conceive of existence without the mine payroll, the profitable mine outfitting.

King thought of Sergeant Forson with a twist of resentment. Too young to know there were traps with jaws that never opened, ten dead-end alleys for every through street. He thought of Harris, snug in his stronghold. The humiliating recollection of the Big Bill Blair parade made him shiver. Three years ago he'd have trounced the man for such a suggestion.

King found himself near the small stone guardhouse where Riggs was being held. In the deep shadows, he could see the guard slouched against the wall with his rifle propped against the wall beside him. For some reason the man's slackness annoyed him; it set the tone of the whole troop. King went toward him.

"Guard," he rapped.

The man moved but did not straighten up. Standing beside the window, his back securely planted against the wall, he was, King suddenly observed, dozing. His hat lay on the ground. King limped toward him, a hot flush of anger in him.

"Guard," he said again, and the man moved slightly and his hands went to his throat. The major saw with a shock the belt around his neck. King pulled a knife from his pocket and shot a look into the dark cell, but he could see nothing there. He wondered how long Riggs had been gone. He sliced the heavy belt and the man began making terrible, hoarse noises in his throat as he fell. King bent over him. He pulled his collar open. He pressed against his chest with both hands to make him breathe, but already the guard was pulling deep drafts of air into his lungs.

King heard boots on the earth behind him. Rising quickly, he turned and braced himself as a shape drove, tall and silent, from the alley. A fist struck heavily against his face, and a bright burst of pain exploded in King's head. He clung to the man, dived desperately to the side of his head, and as the man fell aside he recognized the gaunt features of Riggs. The deserter went to his knees, but came up like a puma. He drove in low, and the major, trying to step aside, put all his weight on his injured leg and stumbled. Riggs struck him and was on top when they hit the ground.

King began to fight with fury and loathing. He was a big man, but very soon he knew he was rotten as a swamp log. He had forgotten how to breathe and soon he was gasping and his eyes saw fire falls of tiny glowing pinpoints. Riggs fought with his knees, his fingers, his elbows. He snorted like a stallion and the instant King broke one attack, he struck with another. Once his hands were on the major's throat and King's face was swollen purple before he got his thumbs in Riggs's eyes and pushed him back.

Finally they were both on their knees. The charcoal dusk shadowed the long-nosed, crooked features of the deserter. There was a kind of wilderness ferocity in him. He was like an animal that did not understand merely fighting to win— the purpose of fighting was to kill. King began striking at his face, but all the time he was conscious of the feebleness of his swings. Riggs hunched his shoulders and began pumping his fists into King's belly. The major gasped and bent over. He did not see the last blow coming, but it took him on the jaw like an axe and he fell straight forward.

Corporal Collins and the revived guard were trying to carry him. He heard them muttering at each other as they struggled along. Collins was attempting to carry a hurricane lamp in the same hand that was clinging to the major's arm. King came fuzzily awake and groaned: "Let me down."

They crouched beside him. Collins's ugly face was tense. King let the world reassemble itself. "Help me to my feet," he demanded. Then, between them, he swayed along the path to the headquarters area. He could feel blood oozing from the wound in his thigh. He was sick with the pain at the base of his skull. His body ached as though he had been beaten with an axe helve. "What time is it?" he asked.

"About eight-fifteen, sir."

"Thought you were going with Forson's detail?"

"He changed his mind."

Decent of him, King thought. Forson had left Collins because he was the nearest thing to a soldier in camp. They reached the commanding officer's cottage at the head of the little officers' row. The door opened and Jess stepped out, then, seeing the three men coming slowly up the walk, she hastened to meet them. She looked at his battered face and dirty tunic, and King told her gruffly: "Lay out a change for me and make some coffee. Collins, have my horse saddled and bring it around. Saddle your own while you're at it."

The corporal's homely features squinted. "Major, you ain't going to try to follow him? Me and Selaya maybe, but not you."

"Time I made myself useful," King said. "No, I'm not going to follow Riggs, but I'm going up to town. And I want you and Selaya, if he's able, to follow Forson and take him a message I'll write. Can you find him?"

Collins smiled. "That Selaya can track like a panther on a venison trail."

"That's not what he told me the other day."

"No, sir, he just didn't want to work. But he's a pretty good feller when he feels like working."

"He'd better feel like it tonight, or I'll have him skinned."

Jess had a pot of coffee waiting when he emerged from his room. He had written a message to Forson, bandaged his leg, and dressed in fresh clothing, and by these simple acts he had pulled on a few shreds of his old confidence. He sat down, eased his leg out before him, and drank some coffee, pondering. All the time Jess stood tensely by the fireplace where a small fire burned, watching him with disapproving eyes.

"I'm afraid Forson's walking into something," he said at last.

Jess's eyes went over his face. "When you're quite ready to tell me," she said at last. "So far I don't even know what you walked into."

"Riggs," King said. He recounted his fight with the trooper. "He's like an animal," he said. "And he's got all the pity of an animal when it comes to protecting himself. Forson told me he'd restricted Riggs to the post while he was on patrol. Now I believe I understand why."

She looked at him with a little of the expression she had worn the other day when they were under attack by the Snakes. She hid her emotion well, but it was in her eyes as she waited.

"No doubt Riggs knows about this horse hunt

of Forson's, and he's going ahead to warn Chief Rogue Buffalo."

"How can you think that?" asked the girl. "Why would any white man turn against his own kind?"

"Riggs is only about half white," argued King. "And even that half seemed to be mortgaged to Jim Harris. I don't quite understand what Harris is up to, but I think old Plummer's on the right track in figuring there was something wrong with those stage raids." He drank the rest of the coffee. "Forson thinks Riggs is in some kind of game with Harris," he continued. "So do I. Forson had him pretty edgy about a firing squad. Riggs has left us for good. Since he's on good terms with the Snakes, it might make sense for him to let them set an ambush for Forson and keep us from following him."

Jess linked her hands. Then she turned abruptly to listen for horses, but they were not coming yet. Her face pallid, she looked at her father again. "Shouldn't Collins hurry?" she suggested. "He's been hours, it seems to me."

King rose painfully. He walked to her and put his arms around her. "The Army's a hard life for a woman," he said.

"Much too hard," she agreed. She was whispering, not trusting her voice. "I think I'll have to marry a rancher or something when this is all through. Why did you ask for your horse? Isn't it enough for me to worry about the others?"

King smiled. "You probably mean *the other*. No, I'm not going with Collins. I'm going up to see Roy Plummer."

Collins came with the horses. King went out and gave him his instructions. "Ride all night, if you have to. Don't stop until you find them. You're riding to save those men's lives."

XVI

As he rode, King pondered the mistakes he had made. *If I had to do it over again,* he reflected, *I'd level first with Jim Harris. If the town didn't tar and feather me after Harris spread the news about me, I'd give the men some training that would put leather on their souls. I'd buy up every mule in eastern Oregon and get rid of the horses.* Sentiment aside, a mule can't be matched for toughness and intelligence in the mountains. But, instead, he had played Harris's kind of checkers and been whipped soundly for it.

The rain that had been gathering this morning began to patter down as he rode into Cañon City. It was a quiet night. The miners had spent their pay from the last big session of work. Old Roy Plummer was rolling up his awnings as King reined in before the *Courier* office. Glistening barbs of rain streaked past the lamp-lit windows. Rake-thin and goateed, the old man confronted him over the tops of his spectacles, grunting finally in recognition. "Wet night for pleasure riding, Major," he commented.

"It's no pleasure, riding with a leg like mine," said King.

"Then why didn't you stay at the fort?" Plummer stepped back into the alcoved doorway out of the rain. He removed his spectacles and began wiping them on his shirt tail.

"I came to give you some news."

Plummer affected astonishment. "Don't tell me infection's set in?" he wondered.

King dismounted in pain, leaned against the saddle a moment with his eyes shut and his teeth clenched. He tied the horse and stepped up on the high walk.

"I haven't much time," he said wearily. "Do you know if that old horse rancher . . . what's his name, Davis . . . is in town?"

"He was getting boiled out over at the hot springs this afternoon," Plummer said, "but he may be back. Been on a bender that's of almost historical significance. Last night he threw eleven beer schooners through the front windows of the Hydraulic Bar, and only hit two miners. Ripped the felt off the pool tables to make himself a pair of drawers for the long winter that's ahead, he said. Took a pair of fetlock clippers to one of the bookkeepers from the Applejack Mine and shaved off half his mustache. He told him if he caught him with the other half shaved off to match, he'd kill him. He goes absolutely crazy when he's had a little strychnine."

King leaned against the rough, volcanic bricks of the building. "Well, if he's around and halfway sober, I'd like him present when I talk to you."

"You're talking to me now," said Plummer disrespectfully.

"You just think I'm talking. Go and look for him, will you?"

Plummer reëntered the shop. King walked into the dusky cave of the newspaper office. The fragrance of it was the biography of Roy Plummer, the odors of which his life was compounded—printer's ink, tobacco, dust, steam, oil, and benzine. It was somehow a wonderfully stable smell. It was the breath of the rebel, yet the fragrance of the conservative. It was the odor of honesty.

Plummer had donned his hat. He wore a gray shirt many times repaired and trousers stuffed into his boots. "I'll look for Davis," he drawled. Then, for the first time, he saw King in the full light of the lamp, and he clucked at the sight of his face. "You have been having it, haven't you, old fellow?" he said softly. "There's coffee on the stove. Pour yourself some while I get Bob Davis."

In fifteen minutes by Plummer's brass alarm clock, he was back with the rancher, Bob Davis. King rose, but Davis did not offer his hand. He leaned silently against a type case and waited. Except for his dirty Angora chaps, he looked exceptionally neat—pallid, clean-shaven, and faintly fragile, like a man just out of the hospital. He had been shaved and had his hair cut and there was a small razor nick with talcum over it on his chin. The odor of witch hazel was strong on him. With Davis were three other men King remembered from the brawl in the Hydraulic Bar on election night. They were terse, emotionless-appearing men with thin-fleshed faces. They had country haircuts, collars buttoned but no ties, and looked hard, capable, and about as sympathetic, thought King, as a fox in a hen house. He glanced at Davis, and the old rancher said: "These is friends of mine, Major. You can talk just as free to them as you can to me."

"Which may not be saying a hell of a lot." Roy Plummer chuckled. The printer rattled around in a box and produced three of the dirtiest cups King had ever seen, barnacled with old coffee stains. He poured coffee as black as printer's ink and set out some wet-looking brown sugar. To break the ice, he began talking as he swirled the coffee dregs. "Let me tell you something, boys . . . the reason most folks can't make a decent cup of coffee. They throw out the grounds. Don't *ever* throw out the grounds. They're the mother. Throw out half and add fresh to bring it up. When you can float a quarter in each cup, it's been properly brewed. Bob," he asked, "has Harry Bailey cleaned up those tubs of his over at the hot springs?"

"Filthy as ever," said Davis, terse and quick-spoken as an Indian.

"He'd have a gold mine there, if he ever swamped out. There's minerals in that water to throw half the gravediggers in this state out of work. But you've got to drink the water as you sit in the tub and get cured up from both sides, Harry says. So most folks look at the tubs and decide they'd rather be dead anyhow. Major," he said "you said something about a story."

King was looking at the rancher. "Davis . . . all of you . . . I want to say that I'm sorry for the spot I've put you in. I'm going to do all I can to get your stock back, or at least part of it."

"Thanks," Davis said. "Now I'm in business again."

"Maybe closer to it than you realize," said King. "If it weren't for propriety, I could show you something that would make you sit up straight. Have you ever seen a man with a brand on his hide?"

"There was a cowboy over on the Columbia we called J-Bar-S Billy," said Davis soberly. "He was a little bit given to drink. He was drinking near a branding fire one time and plumb set down on it."

"They didn't call me anything so friendly as

that," the major told them. He was conscious of Plummer's eyes glittering like ice. "They just branded me, turned me back into the herd, and called me a deserter."

Davis, accustomed to hiding his emotions, did not change expression, but he glanced down suddenly. The men with him stared. Plummer leaned forward. "That's for sure?"

"It's for so sure," King told him, "that Jim Harris, who knows about it, used it to keep me from doing any of the things I came out here to do. I put every cent I could raise into this job, and then I sat down and did nothing but drink." He talked about it, trying to make them understand the futility, the savage desperation he had been living with. "It was going to do so much for me. Put a decent end to things. Maybe I'd be killed in action. Maybe I'd distinguish myself somehow. Maybe I'd get the courage to ask that my case be reopened after the war. Well, the only distinctive thing I've done is to get myself shot with a bullet I probably put into the hands of the brave who shot me."

Plummer strolled to a roll-top desk and picked up a yardstick. Thoughtfully he began slapping his thigh with it. Davis still leaned against the type case, looking embarrassed.

Plummer was puzzled. "That's what you want me to print about you?" he asked.

King brought out the idea that had taken him to Cañon City tonight. "Sooner or later Harris was going to tell the story anyway. That would be when I tried to lock his mine up. I'd like people to have the story straight, so they can make up their minds about whether I came here to make trouble for them or to try to straighten myself out. I read your paper right along, even the parts that make me wad it up and throw it in the waste basket. I know you're worried about this one-crop economy of Cañon City's and what I thought was maybe you could tie up the story about me with some editorializing about how the town could exist without the mines."

Plummer's crooked grin made him look like an ink-stained satyr. "The day of the optimist is not over," he marveled, "if you think I can save your bacon by scaring the town witless with talk of existence without the hydraulics."

"I'm not talking about saving my bacon," retorted King. "I'd like to see Bob Davis back in business, and straighten out the Snakes so that you other men, and all the ranchers in eastern Oregon, can begin to spend more time working cattle and less watching out for Indians."

"Uhn-huh," one of the men said, with a glance at Davis.

Temper flashed in King's eyes. He was silent a moment. "Forson's left to try to find your stock," he said to Davis. "He's sticking his neck out to do it. Not for pleasure, but through a sense of duty. But in the process he's thrown the lock off

168

Applejack, because Forson has been the only leverage against unprincipled hydraulicking, and now he's gone for perhaps a week." *A week?* he thought. *If Collins and that half-breed don't find him in time, it will be for good.* And the cold grip on him tightened.

"I rode down Cañon Creek today," said Davis, "coming back from the hot springs. Champie seems to be getting ready for another big run. Does Harris know Forson's gone?"

"Yes. It doesn't matter much, now that Big Bill Blair's back in office. Harris is going straight ahead anyway."

"You looked mighty trim in that parade of his," reminded Davis.

King felt himself heating up. He rose. "If I've been talking to myself, then I'm sorry I came. I thought you understood that I wanted to make good on my debts."

Davis rubbed his nose, reached in his pocket, and drew out some raisins, which he began to munch. "How are you going to square for Harris?"

King looked at the ranchmen, then at Plummer, and smiled. "What a story it would make for your paper. Parties unknown boring a hole in the main distributor at Applejack Mine, pouring in black powder, and blowing it so high the pieces wouldn't come down for a week."

Davis began to heave with silent laughter, and finally tears came to his eyes. "Oh, glory!" he said. "Roy, where can we git powder this time o' night?"

Plummer wiped his glasses on his shirt tail. "Murchison sleeps upstairs over his hardware. Reckon he might be glad to contribute it. He's done some ciphering lately on which side of his bread the butter's on. The ranch people have quit buying, now that ranching's about done. And he never did sell much to the mines. They go around him and buy direct. Yes, I think he'd be able to find us some powder."

Davis's friends had finally melted. They were beginning to make suggestions about how to handle the night watchman at the mine. But King interrupted.

"Boys, I don't want to spoil anybody's fun. But I never did like to take a whole battalion along for a surprise raid. The three of us can handle that end of it. What we need from you is some diversionary activity."

"What the hell's that?" one of the ranchers asked.

"Well, like a grass fire behind the bank. Or somebody letting out all the stage stock and starting them through the saloon. Rocks might even get thrown through Jim Harris's windows. That sort of thing. So that while we were at work, there'd be enough activity down here to keep anyone from getting bored and drifting up the cañon to see the dam in the moonlight."

• • •

As they left town, the weather leveled off to a mountain fog, dripping with a small rain. Davis's arthritic wagon creaked along Cañon Creek road, while wet branches of alder and willow slapped their faces. Davis had begun to open up a little with the major.

"And I'll tell you something else about gravel mining," he declared. "All this mud they're swamping us with ain't a patch on the run-off from the placers. That's where they rework the old diggings with chemicals. I seen it down in California last year when I visited my married daughter."

"Look yonder!" exclaimed Roy Plummer. Sitting between the major and Bob Davis, he pointed at a stretch of bosque just ahead of them. Here the streambed was several hundred yards wide. Darkly shining rivulets of water twisted over wet sand and gravel. In the center of the stream were the blocks and sluices where during a run flakes of gold were trapped from the mud. Invisible to them were the bluffs and dam a little farther on.

"Better leave the wagon here," said the rancher. They had tied King's horse behind the wagon.

They stopped, and Davis turned the team and left the wagon headed downcañon. King mounted and the others handed up to him a small keg of black powder, which he balanced on the saddle.

He gazed up the creek. The gray, damp night hid everything. They seemed to be enclosed in a hollowed-out morsel of night.

They started quietly up the road. "Remember," Plummer growled, "if anybody jumps us, we were just going to dynamite some bass in the water."

The hoofs of the horse clacked loudly against the cobbled ground. All the soil had been scoured from the streambed and carried miles downstream. They kept close to the fringe of willows along the bank. Up a little farther they climbed the bank and were on a narrow shelf running along the base of the hillside. The mine buildings were somewhere in the mist high above them. Suddenly King saw a dark, skeletal shape ahead of them.

"There it is," he said.

Fifty feet ahead was the platform from which the monitors were operated. The great brass nozzles gleamed in the mist. King thought of the shouting tons of water hurtling across the cañon to pull down boulders as big as a wagon, to blast the foundation from under a tall cliff and bring it thundering down.

Davis reached up to take the powder keg. He set it on the platform. Above them, at the edge of the mine road, a clatter of small stones made them all start. For a moment they listened.

"Just some rocks the rain's loosened," whispered Roy Plummer. "You were thinking the best place to put the powder is in the distributor, eh?"

The distributor was a long, watertight box behind the platform. Out of it grew three twenty-ply twine hoses that ended at the monitors on the platform. King said: "Yes, but now that I look it over, I'm inclined to favor the bulkhead. The force of the explosion would travel down the pipe to the distributor and blow it apart, too."

He felt a thrill of glee and fear. For an Army man to be caught destroying private property would be the ultimate shame. Civilians—particularly Cañon City civilians—had the impression that Army people were all parasites anyway. But he was going to take a lick at Jim Harris tonight, and he was glad of it.

Davis began fitting a bit to the brace he carried. He regarded the thick iron pipe emanating, like a great naval cannon, from the strap-ironed shape of the bulkhead.

"My God," he exulted, "them monitors will travel clean to The Dalles."

"Not if we don't get some powder lit," Plummer complained.

The major sat on the edge of the platform, the coil of fuse in his lap, resting while the other men drilled several holes close together and began pouring the powder into the bulkhead. While Davis poured, Plummer held a scrap of tarpaulin he had found over the powder. King was cold and his head reverberated with a surging headache. The smell of wet earth and a taint of sulphur

173

from the concentrate mill came in the mist. Davis turned suddenly.

"Fuse?" he whispered.

King tossed him the coil of Black Dot fuse. They were figuring on a full minute's head start. That would get them back to the wagon, and King would head straight down Cougar Creek to the post. Davis fed the fuse into the big reinforced box. *It would make an interesting explosion,* thought King with a ripple of gooseflesh. *All that space to expand in, the black powder merely burning until the space was filled with gases and the compression suddenly began.* Again he heard a trickle of earth from the road slanting up the hillside beyond the flume. He listened. He thought perhaps he had heard a man clear his throat. "Hurry up," he said quickly. "Here's a match."

"Git back to your horse," chortled Plummer. He took the small match safe from King and extracted one. "Ready?" he asked.

King slipped to the ground. The sudden flare of the match scooped a yellow-white hole in the night. The face of the old man roasting the tip of the fuse in the flame was comical. He looked like a goat with a malevolent sense of humor. There was a fizzing sputter as the fuse caught.

"Let 'er rip!" Plummer cackled.

They ran a few yards. Davis stopped short. "Hey! Got that brace and bit? God, we can't leave *that* here . . . got your initials burned in it."

Plummer sprinted back and snatched the tool from the ground. A man called gruffly from somewhere beneath the flume: "What the hell's going on?"

A sick surprise rotted King's knees. Trying to toe into the stirrup, he nearly fell. "Let's go," hissed Plummer.

"No," whispered King. "He'll be blown apart."

They stood in the fine rain, staring at the sparkling fuse beside the bulkhead.

King looked around and saw a crooked branch. He picked it up. Beyond the distributor the watchman was running toward them. He passed the bulkhead and came on. Davis and Plummer watched the major numbly. King whispered hurriedly: "We'll have to lay him out and carry him downcañon. I'll get behind something. You two stay out where he can see you. I'll get him when he goes after you."

But there was little to hide behind. Seeing a large boulder, he crouched behind it. The watchman was coming along, flashing a bull's-eye lantern. He passed King and saw Plummer and Davis running, and a pistol glinted as he pulled it from under his coat.

"Halt!" he shouted. He stopped to train the lantern on them and take aim. King lurched after him. He saw the watchman turn and begin to swing the gun around. Then he hit him with the branch. The man's knees buckled, he slumped and fell forward on his face. His lantern struck the ground with a splintering of glass. Oil spilled from it and flames began to run blue and yellow over the gravel. Plummer and Davis came running back. Turning, King saw the sparks from the fuse crawling up the side of the bulkhead. Plummer seized the watchman's ankles and told Davis to take his wrists. They started at a staggering trot down the streambed.

After a time the major panted: "Lay him there behind that log."

Dropping the man behind a tree lying uprooted among the cobbles, they ran on, and just then a low-pitched whistle caused them to look back. It rose quickly to a thin wail, and there was a sound like steam escaping from a pipe. King saw the big crate-like shape of the bulkhead illuminated by cracks of light like a distant cabin, then it was one violent flash springing from the ground, illuminating trees, rocks, and flume. An instant later the distributor blew apart and flame rolled from the thick iron pipe like the flash of a cannon. Then the force of the explosion hit them. It hit the eyeballs and the belly, and it was like being in a cylinder when the piston drove in, one numbing concussion and then an end-of-everything silence. King felt as though he were floating. His pony stumbled. He heard in the black sky something like a far-off chuckling, deep and faint and diminishing. Across the cañon in the mist something crashed against a cliff. Boards and rocks began to rain down. Heavy objects thudded to earth. Then smaller objects began peppering them.

At last silence came, one astounding ache of vacancy. King floated in that vacant darkness, but it was moving under him now; he realized his horse was crow-hopping. He curbed it.

"Any casualties?" he called. He saw the spectral forms of the printer and the rancher ten yards away.

"All present," said Roy Plummer. "Do you reckon the dam will give way?" he asked in awe.

"In case it does, I'm getting back to the fort to start bailing. Gentleman, we'll do it again sometime, eh?"

"That's a promise," said Davis.

"I'll bet it shook my damned type cases all over the shop," Plummer said grimly.

"I hope it shakes the hell out of Jim Harris, that's all," said Davis.

King started off. He was suddenly weary. But he also felt absolutely wonderful—purified, clean as a top-sergeant's gun!

XVII

Even though the horse trail was nearly a week old, it was easy to follow while there was light. Ward took his fifteen cavalrymen down to the Davis Ranch and picked up the trail. From here the Snakes had herded the horses and mules east over the foothills to Little Pine Creek.

When they reached Little Pine Creek, it was almost dark, and it was apparent that it was going to rain. They stopped in a clearing where a log had been pawed to pieces by a bear, and Ward gave the order to camp.

"That fire's going to feel good," Trooper Brough said nervously as he dismounted.

"No fire," Ward said. "The next fire you warm your hands over will be the one when we get back to the fort."

He wished he had brought Collins along. He laid out his ground sheet and then he walked upstream along the small, sullen creek, taking four men with him. The water was muddy. It had been raining in the mountains. The air was pungent and the silence almost complete. He posted the men in a ring about the camp and went back. Coyotes were howling on a ridge a mile away. He saw the troopers looking at each other nervously as they remembered the yipping of the Snake warriors.

"Hit the hay," he told them gruffly. "Brough, pull on your boots. This isn't a training maneuver. Anybody that feels like he might sleep too soundly lay some sticks under your bed."

While the others dozed or lay in uneasy wakefulness, he sat hunched on his bed. The mist had lifted, the silent cold squeezed in, the utter silence made him hold his breath and wait for the tiniest crack to open in it. A trooper groaned in his sleep and turned over. The men lay together, and he sat here, apart from them, wakeful while they slept. This had to be, so that even in his work there was a loneliness and separation.

He was sorry for the men. They were disappointed in soldiering and lonesome for the old times. He thought back to the period before he was married, when he was first ranching. He was so full of foolish plans. He could scarcely believe, now, that he had really partaken of them so greedily. He was going to be the cattle king of Oregon, or something. But he had lost that dream imperceptibly and not missed it. He had lost other things as imperceptibly, but his first sudden loss was his wife, and it had nearly killed him. What made life bearable was that most things came gradually. When it hit you suddenly, you were either knocked out or staggered, but the blows kept coming.

That was what he had seen in King that had made him like him—the fact that King had had some losses himself and kept from whining. They had made him tolerant, too tolerant undoubtedly, but at least at the base of his suffering was compassion.

A night bird uttered its cry. Ward's hands closed on the rifle across his lap. Hawk or Indian? He waited.

His thoughts moved on. And maybe some of the same tempering in Jess was what he liked in her. You thought of Jamie as a girl, but of Jess as a woman. He liked the way she held herself, alert and graceful, the way her long skirts swayed as she walked, the sweetness of her mouth. The way she smiled to herself and you wondered what she was thinking. *Wonder how the Old Man's making out?* he reflected. *I sure left it in his lap. But if he can't handle Harris while I'm away, then he's hopeless. You might as well bury a man like that. If he lived another thirty years, he would still have died three years ago in New Mexico.*

In the dark woods a rifle banged and filled the night with wild reverberations. A man shouted: "Sergeant! Sergeant! We're surrounded!" Downstream the rifle crashed again, and upstream where he had left Trooper Viets a gun blasted now. The troopers rolled blindly out of their blankets, yelling in terror. Ward lurched up with a shout.

He ran to where a group of them had clotted like scared quail, and taking one man by the collar, he threw him to his knees. "Get down . . . all of you! Get back of something!"

Downstream the sentry, Krebs, was whanging away and yelling for the sergeant. Someone more distant was shouting, also. Everywhere the sentries' guns were firing and the reports and echoes shook the woods. Ward got the troopers forted up in a ring.

"Now, stay here! I'm going down to Krebs."

He moved swiftly through the trees. The horses were rearing wildly on the ropes. There was much underbrush, and as he waded through it, he tried to see what was ahead. His heart had come up in his throat so big it choked him. Now he saw the flash of Krebs's gun and heard the bullet go by twenty yards below.

"Krebs!" he shouted. "Hold your fire!"

"Sergeant Forson!" a man bawled in rage. "Tell that damned fool to stop shooting! This is Collins!"

Ward swore and closed his eyes while he took a long breath. "Where are you, Collins?"

"Me and Selaya are down here in the crick. We was trying to follow you."

Ward called to Krebs, who understood at last. He was already excusing himself, even before he could see anyone. Ward found him standing in the middle of a serviceberry thicket. Collins and Selaya were coming through the wet brush. "I kept hearing 'em, Sergeant! I said . . . 'Who goes there?' . . . but they didn't answer me, so . . ."

Krebs was a tall, thin ex-cowboy with freckled skin and staring blue eyes.

"If you said anything, you were talking to yourself!" retorted Corporal Collins as he led his horse up from the creek. He dragged wearily to a halt. His face looked irritable, unshaven, and hungry.

Selaya came in behind him, cheerful and brown-faced. "Hell of a time tracking," he said. "Purty soon she rain and we never find you."

"Now all I need to know is why you had to find me in the first place."

"Riggs took off again," Collins grunted. He wiped his nose on his sleeve. "Knocked hell out of the Old Man and left with all the gear that wasn't nailed down. Brough's Bible was about all he left. The Old Man thinks Riggs is heading for the Snake camp."

"Why?"

Collins handed him a damp, wrinkled envelope. "Here's the message."

King had written his belief that Trooper Riggs had deserted for good and might inform Chief Rogue Buffalo of Forson's patrol.

This could be purely for revenge, or more probably on order from Harris. I believe Riggs has been in his pay from the start. There would be danger in your taking the men any farther, and I direct that the patrol be terminated and you return to the fort at once.

Ward turned and walked back to the bivouac. King was thinking with just half his mind—the fat, cautious half. Leaving Riggs to run loose and unpunished was nothing but cloth-headedness. At the same time there was danger in the situation.

"Break camp," he growled. "Krebs, round up the rest of the sentries."

Cold and miserable, the cavalry rolled packs and saddled. Collins lined them up. Ward gave the order to mount. Mounted, he told them: "Collins will take you back. I'm going after Riggs."

The corporal's Adam's apple dipped. His tired, wizened face wrinkled. "Sergeant, the old man said you was to come back with us. Ain't that what he wrote?"

"I couldn't make it out. Next time you carry a message, wrap it in an oilcloth case. The supply room will provide one at no charge. Detail . . . column of troopers!"

Now he was alone and on his own again, the way he had been so often under Captain Poole. With the recruits off his back, he stood lighter. He had a great sense of freedom—he could stretch without knocking over somebody who was standing close for safety. He and Riggs had been tossed into the pit together, bulldog and badger, and this time the thing was going to be settled. He was leery of tracking in the dark, but afraid not to. If Riggs had already reached the Snake camp, Ward would be walking into a sack; if the deserter had not, then he might blunder into him. So Riggs had the leverage.

He traveled up Little Pine Creek until the cañon opened out into a meadow rimmed with dark hills. Here, at the edge of it, he halted. He discerned a ruined cabin a few hundred yards up the creek; he made out some tottering pole corrals, a mile of lumpy meadow fading back into blackness. The horse trail, a path of trampled grass, disappeared in the meadow. Suddenly a voice in his mind, with the clear urgency of a bugle, told him not to go any farther. He sat his saddle with the tired horse breathing frostily in the damp air. It was a big expanse of openness to cross. Of course he could skirt it. Nevertheless there might be important signs here that he might miss. The meadow appeared to have been grazed over extensively. That meant the Indian camp might be close.

He dismounted, unsaddled but left the horse bridled, and sat on his saddle pad with his back to a pine tree to wait for daylight. He dozed.

The loud whickering of his horse roused him. He found himself sitting, cross-legged, in a frosty dawn with his carbine in his hands. He watched the horse and sat perfectly still. He was behind a bristled cover of buckthorn through which he could see the meadow, white and crystalline with frost. The horse's ears pointed like prongs straight up the middle of the meadow. Now a horse at some distance answered it.

On all fours, he peered out over the meadow. In a wet half light a flock of quail bustled like chickens about the ruined cabin. A quarter mile farther, a mule deer stood with its head turned toward him. The meadow sloped for a mile up to a fringe of timber, and beyond that the trees mounted a thousand feet to the timberline. The sun was just beyond the ridge. His horse nickered again, and he heard the other horse start to answer and break off. The call was far away and he knew suddenly that someone had camped at the upper end of the meadow.

Rising stiffly, he girthed up and started through the trees along the west edge of the meadow. The mule deer went away with stiff-legged bounds. It took him ten minutes to reach the upper end of the meadow. He slowed and went on with great care, cocked like a spring. In some tamarack, he found where a man had camped. There was horse sign and a scoop in the earth where someone had lain in the tamarack needles. He dismounted to examine a little cone of blackened ash. It was no more than a teaspoon, and he broke it with his fingers. The smell was of Trooper Riggs's Indian tobacco. He mounted quickly without the stirrup.

He needed to ride fast, but he needed, also, to be careful. He watched the hoof marks in the soft ground and there were small, dislodged cups of earth among them, so he knew Riggs had been running here, but Riggs could cut back fast and drop him from ambush.

Ward took a line on where Riggs was probably heading. He rode east a few hundred feet before he started up the hill again. His horse quivered suddenly and turned its head. Ward swung off fast and had one foot on the ground when the bullet struck a tree beyond him and the big, booming report of the gun hit him. The horse started but held steady as Ward darted to a tree.

A hundred yards away he saw a horse running through the brush. He aimed hurriedly and fired. He heard a commotion and knew he had hit something. Riggs had fallen from his horse and was afoot. Ward started on, dodging through the trees. Another shot shook the woods, and he heard the bullet ricochet off a rock. Up the hill he could hear the man stumbling.

Gray and chilly light filtered over the ridges. Ward's boots were wet from the grass. He broke from some tamarack and suddenly saw Riggs a hundred yards above him, plunging into a gray jungle of serviceberry. Riggs was dragging a bad leg, and he turned swiftly in a crouch with only a revolver in his hand. He fired three shots, and Ward threw himself on the ground. Riggs turned and waded into the serviceberry tangle. Ward got off a quick shot, but when the smoke drifted off, the trooper was out of sight.

Well, he was in the thicket now, probably crawling fast. But he could not leave without crossing open ground. And he had that injured leg. Ward looked at his watch. *I'll give him fifteen minutes,* he thought. *If he's wounded, he'll begin to feel it and make some noise.* But there was another game Riggs might be playing. The Snake camp might be close. He could be waiting for some bucks to come over to investigate the shooting.

Ward laid the watch down. His gaze ran along the black, sun-silhouetted ridge above him, looking for signs of Indians. He could see Riggs's horse, standing now on the ground below. After a time, the horse began to graze. Blue jays slipped back and forth through the trees; a chipmunk's shoe-button eyes peered at him from a boulder, its striped tail working like a pump handle. Then it was gone. But no bird and no animal entered the thicket where Riggs was.

The sun came over the ridge. The minute hand of his watch seemed to have stopped. There had not been a sound from the thicket. Riggs might be dead by now. Or he might be lying on his belly with his Colt laid out before him and his eyes sharp as skinning knives.

Ward got to his knees. Earth and needles shed

from his shirt. He came to his feet, trembling, ready to dive again, searching intently through the red-berried branches. There was no sound, he saw nothing, and at last he crossed the open ground to the thicket. Where he had last seen Riggs, there were drops of blood on the ground, small splotches on the dead leaves and earth. A ripple of uneasiness went through him.

He walked a few feet into the brush, which came nearly to his armpits. He could hear movements now, but he thought they were made by birds. He went a little farther and his foot struck something hard. Looking down, he saw a Colt on the earth. Ward picked it up. It was unloaded. He looked up. His eyes searched through the brush. He parted the branches with his rifle barrel to look into a small den-like clearing in the thicket, the ground littered with small bones. Again he went forward, and a branch snapped behind him as a man sobbed a curse and lunged into him.

Ward wheeled, swinging the butt of the rifle. It hit the man in the shoulder. Riggs's features were those of a fox, long and narrow, and the sweat of agony was on them. As he reeled back, Ward saw that he was armed with a long case knife. The deserter caught his balance and drove with a full overhand sweep at the side of Ward's neck. There was no room to maneuver the rifle; Ward dropped it and tried to catch Riggs's arm. He caught the lean forearm, but the downward force of the swing drove the point of the knife into Ward's shoulder. The wound was cold and almost painless. Riggs ripped the blade out and his hand dropped swiftly as he shoved the knife at Ward's bowels. Ward was holding Riggs's wrist as the man's steel-wire strength forced him backward. Their faces were close together, and in Riggs's eyes was the acid of a long-distilled hatred. A root caught Ward's heel. He was toppling backward with Riggs uttering a grunt of exertion as he drove in with all his force.

Falling, Ward saw the treetops and the reddening dawn sky, and then Riggs's face obscured them. He heaved furiously and moved the trooper's hands a few inches to the side. The sharp spines of the brush stabbed his back as they landed. He heard the rasp of the knife going through his shirt and into the ground. He held on so that Riggs could not withdraw it. They struggled viciously for an instant. Riggs arched his back and pulled back onto his knees. He drew the knife again. Ward suddenly brought his shoulders from the ground and drove his head into the deserter's face. Riggs grunted. With the collected power of his back muscles, Ward hurled him aside. Falling away, Riggs suddenly got to his knees and began looking wildly for his knife. Ward saw it; bright and clean, it lay on the ground between them. Riggs crouched on all fours, staring at it, and Ward dived. His hand closed on the shaft just as Riggs moved. Riggs's sprawling dive was short, but he scrambled past before Ward could rise. As he passed, he ripped the Colt from Ward's holster. Ward twisted, following fast, trying to stay with him as Riggs turned. Still on his knees, the deserter cocked the gun. Ward swerved out of line. The Colt roared hugely in the woods. Stunned, Ward collided with Riggs, who was about to fire again. He felt the knife point come up against the deserter's belt, halt, and break through with cold eagerness. Riggs cried out. His body convulsed and the gun went off into the ground. Ward tore the gun from Riggs's hand and got up swiftly, obscurely shocked.

Standing above him, he watched grimly. Riggs lay on his back, taking quick, shallow breaths as he lay on the earth. He was dying; there was no question about that. Ward thought of Riggs's friends, the Snakes, and turned quickly to leave the thicket.

XVIII

Jim Harris had been at the hydraulic diggings with John Champie all morning. It was now 11:00 a.m. The brief rain had cleared, everything smelled fresh, and there was pine resin in the air. Harris, in work clothes, grimly watched the workmen begin to bolt one of the large brass monitors to the operating platform. The bulkhead was being rebuilt and the work on the distributor would be undertaken soon.

Champie came tramping down the road from the headquarters building. He had been to Cañon City to order supplies. Harris was leaving when he encountered the big superintendent at the foot of the road. The churning force of Champie's anger reminded Harris of live steam seeking to blow the end out of a boiler. His sleeves were rolled and he had not unknotted his fists all morning. His hard-fleshed face was stiff. He had worked all night, had not taken time to shave or eat, and he looked like a roughneck hunting trouble.

"Murchison held me up on the new hose," he told Harris hotly. "Up two-bits a foot . . . and we'll have to pick it up ourselves."

"Don't get heated," Harris advised him. "We'll fix his clock by pulling some of the other hydraulic mines off his list. Of course we haven't traded much with him, so . . ."

He began walking up the road. Champie came with him. Riggs was on Harris's mind, and Forson's patrol into the Snake country. He was almost grateful that someone had vandalized the mine. Now he could lay his conscience light-heartedly away. But he would feel better when the report came and he knew it was all over.

Champie was still, with single-minded ugliness, thinking of the work down below in the cañon. He stopped and gazed at the scene, his face sour.

"That's a hell of a looking outfit if I ever saw one," he told Harris. "Spikes instead of bolts . . . that bulkhead will come apart like an apple box the first time the pressure gets up. But she'll hold as long as we need her for *this* washing. By God, Jim, them troopers will be eating mud for the next month."

"You ought to be grateful to those troopers." Harris smiled dryly. "If anything ever put the town on our side for sure, it was dynamiting us. Did you give Blair the letter?"

He had sent down with Champie a letter to the mayor and the city council regarding Major King: *. . . and whereas I had hoped to remain silent about the major's bad-conduct discharge, it is now apparent that to do so would jeopardize the welfare and safety . . .*

"Old Bill turned about seven shades of purple," Champie recalled. "He sent a man to ring the fire bell and announce a special meeting of the town council at the Odd Fellows' hall . . . public invited. That'll shake this town." Suddenly he snapped his fingers. "Say, Forson's patrol came back last night. Out a few hours, and they were back again."

Harris snapped a look at him. He flushed hot and then cold. "What happened?"

Champie showed his teeth in a grin. "They weren't talking. Collins brought them into the Hydraulic Bar for a couple of drinks last night on the way in."

"Collins brought them?" Harris repeated.

"That's what the man said."

Harris hated to keep asking questions, but a long-swinging pendulum was moving in him and he had to know. "What happened to Forson? Where was he?"

Champie's eyes pinched a little when he looked at Jim Harris, as though he heard something in his voice that puzzled him. "All I know is they came dragging back."

"Was Riggs with them?" He had not told Champie about the arrangements with Walter Riggs. Better for only one man to have to keep that secret. Now he was wondering if Riggs had been captured and had started talking.

"Not as I know. Wasn't he restricted to the post?"

"Maybe. But the way he gets around, he might have deserted again and gotten caught. We've got to get that fellow out of here."

Champie's dry chuckle came. "Listen, they'll be so busy swimming to high ground that Riggs could leave in a general's uniform and they'd never notice him."

Harris tried to laugh, but it sounded as mechanical, he thought, as the call of a wooden cuckoo. "As far as that goes," he remarked, "after the council meeting, we'll have no more trouble with King. Suppose you sit on the workmen while I go down. I want to be there when they come out of the meeting hall."

"Don't get run down," advised Champie. "They'll come out of there looking for trouble."

But all the way down, Harris's brain was going like a pump. This was a time of crisis, and it called for action, but until he knew about Riggs and Forson, he hardly dared act on anything. If Forson had caught up with Riggs, then he would have found the gold in his belongings. If he had found that, Jim Harris was in trouble.

Across Cañon Street the Blair banners still spanned the narrow roadway. It seemed drearily symbolic. They had gotten wet in the rain and the colors had run. The Odd Fellows' hall was next to the Hydraulic, and here, as Harris rode in, he saw a throng in the street, listening to a man who stood on the seat of a flat-bed wagon. At once Harris saw that it was Roy Plummer, the newspaperman. At the edge of the crowd, back by the door, stood Big Bill Blair and Harry Wheeler, wearing derbies and listening intently. Old Plummer paced to the tailgate of the wagon and shook his finger at the crowd.

"And I'll tell you something else!" he shouted. "I wouldn't give bar space to a man who'd never made a mistake! Because the only man I ever knew who never made a mistake was an Indian mummy I found in a cave. The reason he didn't make mistakes was that he was dead. And a man has to be dead above the ears to avoid making a mistake once in a while. I made a mistake when I

194

tried to get elected mayor. Not that I wanted to be mayor. But I thought I could wake people up to the perils of a one-crop economy. Well, I couldn't. But maybe this will. Because . . ."

Then Plummer saw Harris sitting on his gray horse, watching him, listening intently, perfectly still. Plummer straightened and stared at him, while the silent crowd kept its gaze on the editor.

"Because this may show you to what lengths Jim Harris will go to protect an investment. Blackmail! What else could you call it?"

Harris rode through the crowd straight up to the wagon. He heard a murmuring arise. He climbed onto the wagon with Plummer. He was still in his work clothes and was glad of it. People had the curious conviction that a man in work clothes had to be a straight shooter. Harris could feel this crowd vibrating like a tuning fork. What he said and did had to be right.

He faced Plummer, the latter-day prophet, and said quietly: "Do you want to retract that accusation, Plummer? Or will you defend it in court?"

"I stand on it," Plummer snarled. "And follow it with another . . . that you milked King dry before you exposed him! You only told us about it after you knew he couldn't be pushed any farther."

"Of course you know you're accusing my board of directors as well as me. I believe we're all rather proud of Mayor Blair and Harry Wheeler."

There was a little spatter of hand clapping.

Harris was encouraged. He saw Plummer frown, and there was less sureness in his voice when he answered.

"I've got nothing against them. You're twisting my words. What I meant . . ."

Harris smiled. "Nothing against Bill Blair? But the day before the election you printed an item that there was an epidemic of hydrophobia among infants of Cañon City who'd been kissed by your rival for the office."

There was a roar of laughter, and Plummer's face reddened. "Well, in an election scrap," he defended, "anything's likely to get said."

"By some people." Harris now turned so that he was facing the crowd below the wagon. He was a good speaker, with an instinct for crowd temper. And this crowd was coming to heel. He spoke to them in a deep, quiet voice. "There's nothing less worthy of a man than informing on another," he said. "Especially when it involves a man of reputation and position. Perhaps Major King hasn't had a tremendous reputation among us, but he is certainly a man of high position. To us he represents law and order. So it would be a less thoughtful man than I who would rush in and say . . . 'But this fellow is a deserter! Throw him out!' Less thoughtful, because my company needs the protection of this little . . ."—he cleared his throat and barely smiled—"this little army of ours. So I gave him every chance. But last night, when I became sure that King had helped vandalize the mine, I knew it was time to expose him. That was why I wrote the letter. That was why I demanded that King be replaced. That is why I still demand it!"

A horse was coming up the steep street. Jim Harris returned his stare to Plummer's face.

Plummer had removed his spectacles as if to think better. "Maybe you can tell me," he challenged, "why King came to me and asked that the whole story be printed . . . before you ever wrote your letter?"

"No," said Harris frankly, "I can't. The man's motives and behavior are entirely beyond me. He masquerades as a sincere and courageous officer . . . then in a single night he tears off the mask, confesses, and destroys the principal source of income of the people of Cañon City."

The steady pacing of hoofs had increased, and now Harris glanced beyond Plummer and saw a rider in a faded Army uniform. He was stricken by a convulsive surprise, a terrible stroke of shock. It was Sergeant Forson, leading a horse that carried an empty cavalry saddle heavy with packs. Men in the crowd were turning to stare, and old Plummer wheeled quickly when he saw the expression on Harris's face. Forson looked very grim, quite tired, and the sleeve of his tunic was stained with blood. He stopped the horse, hauled the led horse in, and gazed at the men on the wagon.

But all Jim Harris could see were the packs on the empty saddle. If that was Riggs's saddle, then there was an incriminating wedge of gold in one of the packs.

XIX

"Son, what in tarnation have you been into now?" exclaimed Roy Plummer.

Forson sighed deeply and slumped in the saddle. "Little brush with a deserter," he said.

"Riggs?" asked the editor.

Forson nodded. He took off his hat and wiped his brow with his sleeve. He did it awkwardly because of a shoulder that was dark with old blood. He replaced his stained and bleached campaign hat and Harris felt the impact of his gaze. "Yes, Riggs, rest his ugly soul. He knifed me."

"My God!" exclaimed Plummer. "Then what?"

"I knifed him. I couldn't stay to load him out. We were in Snake country. Though it sort of seems that anywhere Riggs was, was Snake country."

"What do you mean?" asked Plummer.

"I'm beginning to think he was dynamiting everything we tried to do."

Harris waited, holding his breath. When Forson did not go on, he was compelled to ask: "Now, that's a very mysterious statement, Sergeant. What does it mean?"

"I mean we may have less trouble with the Snakes, now that Riggs has quit. He was more Indian than he was white. I think he was getting some kind of favors from someone to keep him posted on us."

"You wouldn't care to say from whom?" Harris said quickly.

But he saw the sergeant slow down and reflect. *No,* said Forson's expression, *better not accuse him here and take a chance.* "Hard to say," replied Forson. "What's the camp meeting for?" He glanced at the crowd.

Harris's gaze could not leave the saddlebags on Riggs's saddle. He wanted desperately to know whether Forson had opened them; it would make a difference in how he proceeded.

Now Plummer was saying: "Well, son, it involves you, in a way. Mister Harris has just had a letter read in a special city council session. It tells us that your commanding officer was a deserter from the Federal Army."

"That's true," Forson said gravely after a moment.

Harris put his knuckles against his hips. "You knew that, and didn't turn him in? You deliberately protected him?"

"I'd protect you," said the sergeant, "if I thought you were worth it. But I don't. I think you've been holding the threat of exposure over him ever since he came here. He spent every dollar he could raise to buy his commission. He wanted to prove himself again. He claims he was victimized by an officer he replaced in New Mexico."

Harris said angrily: "I resent your implications, Sergeant. I know all of that New Mexico story of his, because I was there to see it happen. He nearly foundered my company. Yet I kept quiet after he came here, hoping he'd gotten himself straightened out. Had he? He settled down to drinking, and gave this country back to the Indians and coyotes. He worked up a grievance against me because I wouldn't loan him some money. Last night he and parties unknown blew up part of my hydraulic equipment."

A slow smile came to Forson's long, tired face. "Is that a fact?"

"It *is* a fact. Here is what I found after the explosion last night." From his pocket Harris drew a little silver match safe Champie had picked up among the splinters of the distributor. "You see"—he smiled, holding it high—"it has an emblem at one end, some sort of regimental insignia, I suppose. And the initial K is at the other end."

"Maybe it was some feller named Krock," suggested Plummer. "Or Klipstein."

"Or King," Harris said harshly into the laughter. "But let's say it was somebody named Kelly, for instance. It doesn't make a damned bit of difference. King is an incompetent and is in the Volunteers through fraud. He's got to go. I'm going to suggest that Sergeant Forson send for a replacement at once."

"I'm going to suggest that you let the Army handle its own squabbles," Forson snapped.

Big Bill Blair's barrel voice bawled: "Not when they're knockin' over my stagecoaches like prairie chickens, mister! That's my squabble, then."

"All right! But give us a chance to straighten things out first."

"How much chance?" demanded Blair.

"Twenty-four hours. That'll give us time to ask some questions of our own. Like . . . what was Riggs's connection with Jim Harris before he slugged the major and deserted for the last time?"

Harris heard the rustle of whispering in the crowd. His jaw toughened. He walked to the edge of the wagon and was about to jump down. But Harry Wheeler's voice piped: "What if Riggs was working with Harris?"

"Well, that's what we need some time to figure out."

"Is anyone interested in asking *me* about Riggs?" Harris shouted. The whispering of the crowd quieted. Wheeler turned to listen. Forson closed his mouth. "He'd found out what I knew all along," Harris went on angrily, "that King is a rakehell and a deserter from the Federal Army!

He tried to sell me the information. I wasn't buying. I told him to get out. He got out, but after he'd left, I checked around and found he'd been in the machine shop, too. He'd taken some expensive tools with him. Unless I'm mistaken, they're in the packs on that saddle. I demand that you leave the packs here for examination before you turn them in."

He saw the pinch of surprise in Forson's face. Then the sergeant smiled. "If everybody's going to keep on demanding things, I'm going on to the fort, where I can demand some things myself."

He rode on. With a jolt of desperation, Harris watched him pass beneath the Big Bill Blair banner and head for Fort Haney. Then he glanced at Roy Plummer who was tugging at his ink-smudged goatee. "Twenty-four hours," Plummer said pensively. "I'm going to hold the press that long and see what they come up with."

Bill Blair had started for the Hydraulic Bar, but paused to send his haw-hawing laugh at the printer. "If they come up with anything besides rings under their eyes," he said, "I'll resign as mayor in your favor and throw in my silk hat."

"Is that the hat with the false bottom for emergency liquor?" Plummer retorted.

Harris mounted his horse and rode out while they were still laughing. He took a side road to a bridge over the wash and crossed. Tree-shaded, the muddy stream below him was a blank red surface. Harris passed through the industrial section of the town—a coal yard, wood yard, feed barn, and some other shabby enterprises. Now he turned left on a poplar-shaded road that soon left the town. Before long he found himself in the willows and juniper along the west bank of the wash. He let the horse lope until he was sure he was ahead of the sergeant, on the regular road on the east side of the wash. Then he descended, crossed in shallow water, and rode to the edge of the wagon road to the fort.

Harris held his horse in the small trees while he studied the moist earth of the road. He put a pencil-thin cigar in his mouth. There were fresh tracks, and he could not be sure whether he had gotten here ahead of the sergeant. Harris swung from his horse and drew the ivory-gripped little Colt he had brought along. The tall, hard-featured man looked at it with a frown. An impulse grew irresistibly in him. His lips dried and he could hardly breathe for the thudding of his pulses. Standing behind a tree, he saw how easily he could take the sergeant by surprise just as he came around a bend. He could not miss. He could have the packs off the horse and be away in a moment.

He did not quite understand himself why he was not ready to go through with it. There was this certainty in him that everything was falling apart. But he was not ready to take a deadly risk like this if he could avoid it. He would give Forson his chance first. Here he came.

Passing the big gray boulder at the bend, Forson rode into view leading the dead man's horse with a short hitch of rope. Both his hands were occupied. He could not try to draw his gun without giving Harris plenty of warning. Jim Harris squared his shoulders under the rough work shirt. He chewed on the cigar as he waited, his eyes narrow. At the last moment he stepped into the road.

Forson jerked the riding horse in and hauled the other horse back. His dark, sober features flashed with an impulse Harris suddenly thought might end in gunfire. The horses sidled and the sergeant yanked the come along of the led horse and stared at Harris, silent and intent.

Harris walked toward him. "Now that you aren't surrounded by friends," he said, "I want those packs."

Forson squinted. "What kind of equipment makes them worth taking a chance like this?"

"Some papers of mine," said Harris. "Cut the horse loose. I'll take him."

Forson's heel went back and touched his horse. It pushed forward into Harris. Harris jumped back and raised the Colt. He settled his feet in the dirt.

"I'm prepared to take them if you aren't prepared to give them up." All at once he knew he could do it. He found himself eager to do it. He hated Forson because the man had put his feet into the middle of all Harris had laid out and probably destroyed everything.

In a moment Ward Forson shrugged and dropped the lead rope. "There's just nothing," he said, "that's worth that much trouble. Help yourself."

Harris moved out and secured the lead rope. He waved the cavalryman on with the gun. "I'll look through them and everything that isn't mine I'll leave right here. You get moving."

"Sure," Forson said. "You bet." He rode on, tall, one shoulder higher than the other, jogging out of sight into the junipers.

Harris waited a few minutes to be sure he was gone. Then he tied the animal to a tree and his hands ripped into the saddlebags. They had a smell of camp grease and smoke. Under the flap of one was lettered in backwoods capitals: W.S. RIGGS. CAÑON CITY, ORE. Riggs's own saddlebags, not Army issue. Harris tore off layers of miscellany—a tintype of a very homely woman in a photograph gallery pose, a twist of smoking tobacco—and he came ultimately to a heavy object wrapped in brown paper.

He wanted to sink down and give thanks. It was still here. God bless the sergeant, he hadn't gone through the packs yet. He ripped the paper off. Then his face fell, while he stared at a small, squarish slab of quartz. It was ordinary rock with some greenish veining. Forson had found the gold.

Harris turned and started for his horse. But with his toe in the stirrup, he realized he could never catch him. Forson was at the edge of the meadow by now. He would be in camp before Harris could catch him. Jim Harris headed back to the mine.

The first thing he did on entering his office was to open a cupboard and take out a bottle of liquor. He drank from the neck of it. He blew out his cheeks and stood there, his feet wide-spaced, frowning, the bottle dangling in his hand. His mind was teeming.

Heavy boots crossed the outer office and Champie came in. Harris did not look up. Champie said heartily: "Those farmers just think they've seen mud. We'll be operating by tomorrow, Jim. Tonight, if you say the word."

"Close the door, John," said Harris.

The latch clicked. Harris heard Champie say: "Kind of early for hard liquor, ain't it?"

"It's never too early when you need it. Have a drink."

"Thanks," Champie said dryly. "I don't need it."

"Don't, eh?" Harris roused himself, glanced sardonically at the big man with the cropped, dark hair and rugged, simple features, and walked to his desk. He sat down and placed the bottle carefully on the dusty oak, precisely where the gold ingot had lain yesterday. His glance rose to pin down Champie.

"We're in trouble, John."

"So?" Champie was holding his cards close, but he looked worried.

"There's part of an ingot in that safe in the corner. The other part's in Forson's hands."

"How come?"

"I gave it to Riggs to get rid of him. He wanted a lot of money to pay his way to California. Otherwise he'd talk about his dealings with us. I was going to melt the rest with some copper and zinc to fill it out. The mint would knock us down a few dollars on that one, but what'd be the difference? But when Forson killed Riggs, he got the gold. Have a drink?" he suggested.

Sighing heavily, Champie drank. He lowered the bottle. "Well, why can't you still do it?"

"Forson's got part of the serial number on his piece."

Champie groaned. He kicked his heel against the desk. "So . . . what're you going to do?"

Harris linked his fingers and frowned at the door. "When they come, I'll tell them they're crazy. That all the ingots are intact. But I'm not going to open the safe for them until they get a court order."

"That gives you a day or two." Champie stared at the safe.

"A day or two is all I want. Do you know how much money there is in the safe?"

Champie's head turned.

"Sixty-eight thousand dollars," said Harris. "It's been piling up since the last raid, when we stopped shipping. And every nickel of it is owed to somebody or other. John," he said angrily, "they've given us the rawest deal a couple of men ever had. If they'd let you operate the workings, and me manage the company, this would be the biggest outfit in Oregon. Now what have we got? A tin can tied to our tails. I'm just a stockholder, and you'll never get another job above boss swamper."

Champie said gloomily: "Hell."

Leaning back, Harris pondered: "You know, gold is funny. Ounce for ounce, it's practically the most valuable metal in the world. But if you've got a barn full of ingots, you're still broke until you figure a way to get it into circulation."

"Can't be done," said Champie gloomily, as if he had considered it before.

"Oh, yes," Harris said. "Where does it come from? Out of the amalgam we float it out with. Where could we get rid of it? Put it back into amalgam."

Champie pushed his thick fingers through his wiry hair. "Maybe I'm tired, Jim. That don't make sense to me. You mean we'd salt a mine or something?"

"No. I mean we'd stake out a gravel-mining claim somewhere . . . maybe California. We'd build a little concentrate rig for a few hundred dollars so that we don't have to go through a big outfit. We're mining nothing but gravel, but who's going to know that? The ingots we brought there with us get melted, recast, renumbered, and we sell them to the bank. After we've got rid of them all, we close up the mine and drift along."

Getting it finally, John Champie paced to the window, glanced down into the cañon, and walked over to the safe. He gave the safe a kick.

"You don't carry out sixty-eight thousand dollars' worth of gold in your hip pockets," he said.

"No. You'd need a couple of pack horses . . . that's all."

The room became tense. Champie stood staring down at his dusty boots.

"In a little while," prophesied Harris, "they're going to come up here and announce that I've been voted out as director. The first man who'll go will be me. The second will be you. As long as you're working for somebody else, it'll always be that way. This is a chance for you to get out on your own."

Again it was silent. Hammers thumped distantly in the cañon, and a mule brayed. "How would you go about it?" Champie asked slowly.

"I'd give them something else to do while I

left. You say the monitors will be set again by tonight?"

The superintendent nodded.

"All right," proposed Harris, "let's turn them on."

"What about Jamie?" asked Champie suddenly.

Harris frowned. Picking up the whiskey bottle again, he said: "There's a stage out of here this afternoon. She'll be on it. I'll give her an address in Sacramento. We'll use it as a hollow tree for a while. After we get through, I expect I'll go East and try for an Army contract. Lots of money to be made there if you've got a little capital."

They discussed what they would need by way of provisions, the best route to take, where to leave the horses, and so forth. Champie left to take care of these things.

Harris had been right about how Wheeler and Blair would proceed. At 3:00 that afternoon, they came to the mine office. They were very formal and were dressed as though they had come from a funeral. Spidery little Harry Wheeler did the talking.

"Jim," he said, "I'm afraid we've got bad news for you. Because of a number of things, we think it wisest that you be replaced as director."

Harris, nodding solemnly, did not argue. "I suppose that's up to you boys, Harry."

"Among other things," Wheeler went on,

"Sergeant Forson sent a note to me a while ago asking me to come to the post. He had in his possession part of a gold bar from our mill. He says he took it from Trooper Riggs's saddlebag. Where did Riggs get it?"

"Harry," said Jim Harris, "you're the man with the answers now. You tell me where he got it."

"Open the safe," blurted Big Bill Blair.

Harris shook his head. "I have some things of my own in there . . . personal things. I want today to clean them up and prepare my final report. Is that asking too much?"

Wheeler's bright little hawk eyes scrutinized him. He knew Harris had the key to the safe and he was not a man who liked force. But his mouth became firm and he said: "Yes, Jim, it's asking too damned much, on top of everything else. Open the safe."

Harris gazed at him a moment, then rose and walked to the safe. After searching his pockets, he turned to face them.

"Now, that's queer. I seem to have left the key at the house. Do you want to send down for it?"

"And have your girl tell us it's up here after all?" said Blair. "Come on, Harry, it's in the desk. I've seen him put it there."

Blair walked around the desk and tried to open the top drawer. But it was locked. He looked up at Harris, his face contorting. "Make an issue of it, Bill," suggested Harris. And he sauntered toward the stage man. Blair seemed to recall the day when Jim Harris almost put his eye out with a cigar. He glanced at Harry Wheeler, and Wheeler made the decision.

"Have it your way, Jim. Until tomorrow morning. Then we'll be up to take over. With a warrant."

Harris shrugged. "Fine. Now tell me how you're going to make money on by-your-leave mining when I couldn't satisfy you by highballing?"

"We think poor management had a lot to do with it. Other mines in this area are getting by. We think, too, that we've been selling Cañon City short by discouraging enterprise in any line but mining or catering to the mines."

"I wish you luck," said Harris sardonically.

"Damn you!" Blair suddenly shouted. "If I knew for sure you'd had anything to do with my passengers being murdered by the Snakes . . . !" He came toward Harris with both fists clenched and his flat moon-face choked with color.

"Come, Bill," Wheeler said harshly. "Lots to do."

Blair halted, chewed on his anger for a moment, and then turned and went out with Wheeler.

Things to do, thought Harris. Yes, by heaven! He had things to do himself. And when Harry Wheeler came up to hatch his golden egg tomorrow, he would find it long cold.

XX

The doctor finished cleaning the knife wound in Forson's shoulder, bandaged it, and left some instructions. "You ought to keep your arm in a sling as much as you can. Keep a bandage on it, at least, and if the suppuration becomes too heavy, let me look at it again. A little suppuration, of course, is good. I'll look in on the major as I leave."

Ward thanked him, and the doctor left. He had not seen Jess since he returned. She had been with her father, who Corporal Collins said was in bed with fever, and Ward's impatience to talk to her was growing. He remembered that feeling he had had a week ago that he had passed the summit in his grieving for his wife. Now he felt that in a sense he was done with grieving; he no longer carried that compulsion to keep himself occupied at all times to keep his mind from his loss. And he knew that Jess was very close to this change in him. Was it because he had been in this mood of change when he first met her?

As soon as the doctor drove out of the post, he stepped from the squad room. He found Collins in the orderly room, slaving over copies of reports. Wearily he shoved back in his chair. "Eight copies of everything," Collins explained. "I'm still

213

working on last month's report to the District. What the devil do they care that a spring vise broke and cut a man's hand?"

"They don't, but it's the custom. The system I used was not to let anything less critical than an amputation get into the sick book. That held down the number of reports, and they couldn't very well send a demand through channels that we have more sickness."

Collins grinned. "That's how it's done, eh?"

"Another way is to get promoted to line sergeant and make somebody else do the clerking. Make up a special order for your promotion. I'll talk to King about it."

As he was leaving, Collins spoke quickly: "Say, Blair was asking for an escort for the stage this afternoon. Can we give him one?"

Ward figured. "As far as Cross Hollows. While the major's down, I'll have to stay here, though. Want to take five men and try it?"

Collins thought a moment and said he thought he could make it. "I'll put Brough on these everlasting reports."

Ward walked down to the commanding officer's cottage. Jess let him in. Her grave eyes inspected him, and she said severely: "The doctor said you were to carry your arm in a sling."

So he knew she must have asked about him. "It was optional," he said. "How's the major?"

"He's asleep just now. Will you sit down? I

214

think he's better, more rested, at least. He had quite a night."

"I've been getting rumors about this night of his," Ward said seriously.

She smiled, but seeming to feel it best to be discreet, she said nothing about it. "I want to thank you for what you did for him. I mean leaving him on his own."

Ward shrugged. "I knew he'd either sit down and cry himself to sleep or fight his way out."

"Well, he fought his way out. And he's back safe. And you're back safe . . . but I'm years older for worrying."

He looked at her with a sigh in him. As she sat in an armchair with one hand resting on the arm of it, she was slender and graceful. Her fair hair glistened with brushing, and tiny blue stones sparkled in the lobes of her ears. After the rough male years of leather and horses and gunsmoke she seemed to him a miracle of daintiness and femininity. He could not take his eyes from her. "Miss Jessamin," he said softly, "did you say your father was asleep?"

"He was a moment ago." She let her hand slip into her lap and glanced at him with a shadow of a smile as he rose. As he walked to her, he heard a clock ticking noisily in the kitchen. He put one hand on the back of her chair and bent over her. A delicious perfume rose from her hair. He put his hand on her cheek and kissed her hair, and then her brow, and finally her lips. She did not move, but she sighed, and at last she reached up to touch his face.

"Jessamin, did someone come in?" asked the major from another room.

Jess started and Ward straightened fast. The girl rose, smiled quickly, and tapped his lips with her finger. She walked with unhurried grace to the door of the bedroom.

"Why, yes . . . Sergeant Forson is here to pay his respects."

"Well, send him in."

Ward found him propped up with two pillows. He was flushed with fever and his face looked gaunt. "Close the door," King said. "Did you hear what happened up at the mine?"

Ward stood by his bed. "Terrible thing," he said gravely. "Somebody might have been killed."

"Liable to set them back a week," said King.

"It looked like it for a while," Ward agreed. "But John Champie worked around the clock to fix up some sort of jerry rig. They'd have been back in business, if Wheeler and Blair hadn't moved in on Harris. He'll be replaced as director. I talked with them, and they came pretty close to admitting Harris's liability in the Indian trouble."

"Well, well," said King, relaxing. Then he said with slow satisfaction: "This time around it seems to go better, Sergeant. It might even give me grounds for asking that my case be reviewed.

Have my copy of the A.R.s covering such matters sent over."

He talked better, Ward thought, with what seemed more bite to him.

"Have you looked at the bulletin board?" King asked.

"No, sir, I just . . ."

King glanced sharply at him. "You passed it on the way here. Always look at the bulletin board, Sergeant. If you had, you'd know that a class in map reading starts tonight. You'll instruct. In the morning there'll be inspection of all equipment."

"Yes, sir. Is that all?"

"No. Bed check at eleven. No passes. That equipment had better be clean. I think that's all."

Jess was waiting by the door when he came out of the room. He captured her with an arm around her waist and pressed a quick, silent kiss on her lips.

"Was there anything on the bulletin board about that?" she whispered.

"No," Ward said. "That's the whole trouble with bulletin boards. They never go far enough."

"A trouble some sergeants never have."

She opened the door finally, and he went out. "Do come back, Sergeant," she said, mostly for her father.

"I will, Miss King," Ward replied, also speaking for the major. "On the slightest excuse," he added, and that was for Jess.

He walked along the parade toward his barracks.

Beyond the walls of the post rose the dark shape of the Strawberry Range. The breeze came up Cañon Creek, scented with grass and balsam. The afternoon was beautiful, and he thought that if he were ranching, this would be a day to take his wife and drive up to cut winter wood and picnic on a hillside.

When the escort was ready, with Collins self-consciously stern and exceptionally neat, Ward took them down to Cañon City. The coach was in the stage yard when they came jingling through the gate. Washed and polished, it had already been loaded with baggage and the leather flap of the boot was buckled down. Blair was talking to the driver. The conductor was calling the names of the passengers from a list. One by one they stepped into the coach. As Ward dismounted, he heard the conductor call: "Miss Jameson Harris! Any hand baggage, ma'am?"

"No," murmured a young woman.

Ward looked around with his boot still in the stirrup. Jameson—funny name for a girl. But it was Jamie Harris's given name, because here she was hastily boarding the coach without a glance at him. Ward walked over to Blair.

"Corporal Collins will escort the coach as far as Cross Hollows," he told him.

Blair grinned. "Thanks, General," he said. With his back to the coach, he slipped a bottle from his coat. "Hair of the varmint?"

"Wish I could. I'm on duty. I don't think there'll be any trouble with this trip," he added. "If there is, it'll be accidental. Harris's daughter is going along."

"So I noticed," said Blair grimly.

Ward was trying to comprehend why the girl was leaving town so suddenly. "Is Harris on the passenger list?" he asked.

"No. He's got a date with us in the morning. He'd better not be on any passenger list."

The conductor closed the door and called: "All set, Mister Blair! Sun ain't getting any higher."

The stage rolled into the street and swung away behind the team.

Ward went back to the fort. He could not forget about Jamie. He did some routine work, but something that had been started in his mind kept nagging at him. It was strange that Jim Harris, who did things so lustily, should submit to being eased out of control of Applejack. Still, what kind of an answer could he make to the testimony of Riggs's gold? Blair had said they had a date with him in the morning. That gave Harris all night to come up with something. The reflection made him uneasy, for Harris was like a rattlesnake—he didn't die until sunset.

After "Retreat", Ward signed out for the evening. It would pay to look in on the Applejack offices, perhaps. He jogged up the lower road through the willows along Cañon Creek. It was late dusk when he reached the workings. He saw that repairs on the hydraulic equipment had been finished. The workmen had left. He rode up the mine road to the big sheet-metal buildings. In the early night everything looked quiet; behind the dusty windows he could see no one in the bookkeeper's office. He rapped, tried the door, and found it locked. Then he shaded his eyes to peer into Harris's office, but it was empty, also. He was all at once ill at ease. With a sensation of being observed, he turned and searched the brush across the road, and then gazed at the dark concentrate mill a hundred yards beyond.

Riding to the mill, he looked around it. It looked like a place where the boss had said: "You might as well all go home for the rest of the day. . . ." He found a place in some trees where he could leave his horse. Then he walked back to the mine buildings.

It was now completely dark. The sky was blue-black with bright chips of stars overhead. Across the road from the office building was a pile of timbers. Ward went behind them and sat on the ground at a spot from which he could see the buildings.

Trying to ease his restlessness, he took out his knife, whittled a while, and finally looked at his watch. It was 9:00 p.m.

There seemed to be no point in staying any longer. Harris probably was down in the big white house, packing, and undoubtedly still scrounging around in his mind for a means of salvaging something. He started back to the horse. Then he heard a low, wind-like roaring in the cañon. At first he thought it was a high wind rising in the trees, but it was too still for that. Suddenly he knew with a shock that what he heard was water.

He started for his horse, but decided it was quicker to run across lots down the hillside. He passed the concentrate mill and began breaking through the brush down the steep hillside. Below him there rose from the cañon that hoarse, earth-shaking roar of the monitors throwing those tons of white water across the cañon. He could feel a cool mist rising against his face as he hit the road farther down.

Finally he could discern the long plumes arching gracefully through the darkness, gauzy as smoke. There was a hollow clatter of stones jostling under water, a muted thunder of tons of earth sliding into the cañon. Then his foot hit a stone and he fell hard. For an instant he lay stunned. He groped for his rifle. As he stood up, he noticed something about those arching sprays from the monitors. They were not directed toward the cliffs. They were hammering at the dam itself.

He stood there, trying numbly to understand what was happening. The monitors were turned upstream. Landing against the rocky hillside, the tons of water were pulling away the earth and rocks to which the dam was anchored. The dark, swirling water flowed under the flume and coursed downstream into the darkness.

Ward ran on down the road. At the bottom he hesitated. The only way to cut the monitors off was to close the sluice gates on the dam. He did not know where the trail was to the top of the dam, and in the darkness he might blunder around among timbering and brush and rocks until the dam went out. As he stood there, he felt a tremendous damp wind from the nozzles fluttering his clothing. He started for the monitors to turn them before tackling the gates. At once he was knee-deep in mud and water. Cobblestones tripped him as he floundered along. At his side something cut the water with a sharp sound; a jet of water broke upward. He heard a loud crack. Then a second spurt of water leaped up and he stopped and looked around. This time the crack of the gun was distinct above the roar of the monitors.

The man who stood under the flume was hardly discernible among the timbers. He stood in the familiar stance of a rifleman, his head bent to the gunsights and his elbow extended as he aimed. Ward threw himself into the water. As he went under, he tried to hold the carbine clear. He heard the impact of a bullet in the water near him. He rose to his knees. In a moment he saw the gunman standing half visible among the timbers. The slim, erect body was reminiscent of Jim Harris. Ward hesitated, afraid to try to make it to the monitors, but convinced it had to be done. There was the other way of stopping them—to close the sluice gates—and he decided that it was the only way, because Harris would pick him off the monitor platform if he ever reached it. He started back, moving in a crouch and keeping the bulkhead and distributor between him and the miner. Harris fired twice again, but he was firing with more anger than accuracy. Suddenly from atop the dam another gun flashed and the bullet hit the iron pipe above the sergeant's head. So now he knew John Champie was guarding the big iron wheel that opened and closed the sluice gates.

Still, there was more cover on the slopes, and he waded on. Soon he was aware of another man among the rocks and junipers on the slope that mounted to the dam. He halted again, his hands moving over the rifle in numb desperation. Then, seeing the man beside a boulder, he decided it was Jim Harris, that he was fading back to block him from the catwalk onto the dam. The sergeant pulled the rifle to his shoulder and took a snap shot at him. But the shot died with a wail among the boulders. Harris fired back. As the bullet hit the sand, Ward lunged up the slope. He sprawled behind a small, conical tree. He heard the big, echoing boom of Champie's gun and that bullet, too, was lost. The accuracy would come when he closed in. Meantime the monitors were eating away at the cliffs, and there was no time for generalship. He made another rush, and crouched behind a slant of rock. Harris did not fire; he was waiting. He had nothing to lose by waiting, for he was forted up like a badger among the rocks. Ward leaned his head on his arm, his eyes shut. He opened them to gaze down at the swirling water below. He thought of the huge, rock-studded wall of water that would soon hurl itself down Cañon Creek to the John Day, sweeping out bridges and lowland farms. Then he remembered the stage-coach, making its endless fords back and forth across the John Day below the confluence of Cañon Creek.

"Harris!" he shouted.

Harris sounded tensely reluctant to answer. "Back off, Sergeant!" he said. "Be a smart lad and know when you're licked."

"Oh, you can stop me, all right. But I'll stop you, too."

"Well, come on then."

"Thing of it is," Ward said, "what about your daughter? Such a pretty little thing to drown in a flash flood."

"I'm not crazy, Sergeant. They're laying over at Cayuse Creek tonight. I thought of that, too."

"No, sir, they're driving all night. I told them there was less danger of Indian trouble. Indians don't like the night air. Maybe the water will catch them at Jack Rabbit Crossing . . . maybe at

Muddy Creek. But that coach is going over like a match box."

Harris let a small wedge of silence drive in. Ward suddenly thought: *He's taking the hook.* But what Harris said was: "You're a better soldier than you are salesman, Forson. I'll take my chances just the way I planned."

While he was still saying that, Ward was leaving his shelter and driving up the slope. Once Harris's gun flashed and the big echoing roar of it came down like an avalanche, and then there was a little brassy click that had in Ward's ears the happy chiming of Christmas bells. It was a hammer hitting an empty chamber. Ward gathered everything into a running, sprawling attack, driving for the scatter of boulders where the miner was forted up, trying to reach him before he drew his Colt.

Harris suddenly rose before him, lean and dark, swinging his rifle by the barrel, at Ward's head. Ward flung up his own rifle and felt it crack as Harris's rifle smashed into it. He plowed into Harris and they went down. He found a stone and struck Harris with it once, and the miner ceased struggling.

Champie was bawling: "What the hell, Jim? What goes on? Jim!"

Ward steadied his Colt across his arm and tried to aim at that dark, bearish form crouching above the ratchet wheel in the middle of the dam. The shot went with a flash and a wide-open roar into the gloom. Then he ran forward, making for the approach to the dam. He made the path and reached the catwalk. There he hesitated long enough to warn Champie.

"Get moving. Harris is out of it. The road still runs both ways, Champie."

Champie did not reply. He stood like a tree behind the ratchet wheel. The roar of the monitors was downcañon; the cold, wet air fluttered Ward's shirt as he waited. Ward dropped to his knees to take steady aim and make a smaller target. Champie broke then. He turned from the wheel and went at a crouching run toward the far bank. It had been Harris's war. Harris was gone; Champie was only a foot soldier in that army.

Ward ran cautiously between the dark water on one side and the roaring emptiness on the other. He gained the big, cold wheel and began turning it. The ratchets snapped and rusty gears squalled somewhere. At last the gates were closed, the wheel would not turn any farther, and downcañon the great cannon-like nozzles faded out with a dying whistle.

Near the dam, Ward found Harris's pack animals. He took them to town and left them at the stage station. Bill Blair was at the Hydraulic Bar, and Ward made his report and went on to the post.

Clear and golden, "Taps" was sounding as he

crossed the dark parade. He stopped and waited while the call was finished, a tall, tired man with his hat in his hand. All the things he felt were in that call. The sadness and sweetness of living. The men he had known who were now dead; the woman he had loved, who was dead. He had the thought that by his grief he had held her somewhere between life and death, but now he had released her, and if there were any happiness beyond life, she could have it.

Was there a beginning on that side? he wondered. As for this side, there were many endings and beginnings, and he knew that for him something fine had already started.

FURNACE FLAT

I

It was dusk when Ryan came down from the mines. He drew his pay, the last he would ever receive from Furnace Flat Borax Company, and hurried to the Miners' Bar. All day he had been thinking that the old boraxer called Mysterious Smith would become suspicious at the last minute and pull out without him. But when he stepped into the saloon, still in his dusty work clothes, miner's cap on the side of his head, and pipe in his teeth, he saw Smith at the table in back near the mechanical piano.

Ryan bought a beer and carried it over. A big, black-jowled man of thirty-two, he looked rough and sober. He sat down and sprinkled salt in the beer.

Mysterious Smith kept his eyes on Ryan's face. Smith looked no different from a score of other wanderers of Death Valley and the Panamint, a bearded apostle of the pick and shovel. He was dark as mahogany and had a chest like a wine-barrel. "Well?" he said.

Grady Ryan nodded. "Did it. Turned my single-jack for the last time. Drew my pay. Thirty-six dollars for us to sink in chuck. Still taking off tonight?"

"The burros are loaded, all but the grub. Got

231

any girls you'll be mooning over, better say good bye to them and get it out of your system. Maybe you ain't coming back so soon."

"No girls," said Ryan. "I only mine the ore that pays."

Smith said: "You don't look like you'd been mining anything too rich. If we don't hit it this time, you better marry a rich widow."

He had a realistic, tart sort of humor that had a sting. Ryan perceived that he had dug down through his tough hide to the thing that had been disturbing him more and more the last few years. The fact that at thirty-two he was precisely where he had been at twenty, still knocking around the desert turning over rocks, hunting the lodestone that kept them coming back all their lives.

You did it so long, and then you couldn't quit. You did a hitch in the mines for an outfit, spent six months living on beans and saleratus biscuits in a box cañon, sinking test shafts and tunnels, and stumbled back disillusioned and sick of it. But after a few months you were ready to go again, your guts knotted up with eagerness, your eyes raving over a story about a strike at Skidoo or Mahogany Flat. This expedition with Mysterious Smith was merely the latest, certainly not the last, of a long series of failures entitled "The Life of Grady Ryan".

It was between shifts. They had the saloon almost to themselves. "Look," Ryan said suddenly.

"Just how much chance have we really got to sink our picks into something?"

"Purty good, purty good." It was the least mysterious thing Mysterious Smith had said yet. It was spoken with a glint in eyes bleached like old denim.

Ryan put a question that was like the probing tap of a geologist's hammer. "Then I don't see why the hell you're letting me in on it, if you think there's something in the bag."

"Fellers all got different talents," said Smith, getting mysterious again.

The saloon door opened and a gang of borax muckers came in, men Ryan had worked with off and on for a couple of years. Among them were Tom Lund, his drift boss, and Pat Hoagland. Hoagland was mine superintendent, a sturdy, affable, double-dealing roughneck who knew more about mining than a company president ever would. Hoagland had instituted the practice of charging miners for the candles and carbide they used. A man had better keep his own time card, Ryan knew, or he would come out owing the company.

Hoagland came over and laid a hand on his shoulder. He wore a canvas-brown mustache and let his long hair curl above his collar. "Good luck, Grady," he said. "Maybe it's the right thing you're doing . . . though I doubt it."

"Smith and I," Ryan said, "are going to find the

Lost Gunsight. Next time you see me I'll be buying cigars, instead of candles."

Hoagland's laugh resembled the grunt of a wild boar. He glanced at Smith. "I'll bet you know where all the gold in Death Valley is, come to that."

Smith said: "All that glitters is not gold."

Hoagland looked pained. He started for the bar, but turned back to Grady. "Kane would like to talk to you before you go. He'll be in his office for an hour tonight, if you've got time."

"Hell, I haven't even got a dress suit. I can't go up there looking like a mucker."

"Kane," said Hoagland, "was a mucker before he was a millionaire." He went over and found his special bottle waiting for him.

Grady winked at the prospector. "And he's going to be a mucker again, or I don't know a sick mine when I see it. Suppose you buy the groceries," he said. "I'll go up to the boarding house for my stuff. See you at Maggie Conway's for supper."

Smith grunted. " 'Tain't safe."

Ryan chuckled. "Who's Maggie Conway? Just another Cousin Jack's daughter. The girl I'm looking for has her picture on the double eagle."

But he thought of Margaret Conway as he walked up the steep, straight road between the lava-stone buildings. If she were just another Cousin Jack's daughter, it was because he had kept her that way in his mind. She had the warmth and ingenuousness of her Cornish womenfolk, with a little bit of their quickness in her speech and a lot of their good humor.

Ryan had become so practiced at self-deception that he was not sure whether it was because of her that he hungered so for a real strike, or simply for himself. But he did know that it shamed him to be in debt to her for meals and, the few times he had asked leave to call on her, that he could not even afford a turnout to take her riding. And that gnawed at him.

It was early January, the air thin and sharp as chilled wine. Night cold was invading the ugly mining town in the parched hills east of Death Valley. Above Furnace Flat's sheet-metal hives, the hills were stark and colorful, birthmarked with patches of strawberry, stained with green stone, rotted with slanting ledges of rimrock like outcrops of rusting iron.

It was a capricious country, ready to dump gold in your lap or burn you to cracklings beside a spring it had whimsically sucked dry. Or ready simply to wear you down from vainglorious manhood into premature senescence.

Kane's office was in a big two-story head-quarters building against a hillside. The boom and clatter of the mill was a discreet distance away, but the dust of it was like talcum powder all over the building and its windows. Ryan arrived in the office of Borax Kane.

He had seen Kane frequently, but had never spoken to him. The president of Furnace Flats Borax Company was a broad-shouldered man of fifty, several inches under six feet. He sat at a rough pine desk with a clutter of papers and three brimming ashtrays. He was smoking cigarettes, which seemed to Ryan a rather effeminate gesture.

He failed to acknowledge the mucker for a few moments, then he said without looking up: "Take a chair."

He went on signing papers while Ryan stood there with fury mounting in him, staring down at the red-veined face with its turgid eyes and slack whiskey mouth. Finally Kane sat back. He looked surprised at the scowl in the other's eyes—it had the effect of bringing him to his feet with an affectation of pleasure. "Sorry to make you wait, mister. Pretty busy this time of year."

"So am I," Ryan told him.

Kane fumbled a box of cigars, almost spilled them, and held them out to Ryan. Ryan took three. He kept his slow, gray-eyed gaze on the man, wondering what the hell was wrong with him. He was like a speaker who had forgotten his lines. Kane kept dodging the cigarette smoke, blinking, moving his head as though he hated the stuff but couldn't remove the cigarette from his lips. Ryan bit the end off one of the cigars.

"Why the hell don't you throw that thing away and have a cigar?"

Kane grunted: "Nothing I'd like better. The doctor took me off cigars last year. Kidneys. Damned nuisance." His flabby, rutted face annoyed the miner, somehow. "Ryan," he said, "Hoagland tells me you're quitting us. Why?"

"If I could eat the candles I have to buy," Grady said, "I might see the sense in staying."

"You can't eat desert holly, either." Borax Kane smiled. "You must feel fairly sure of yourself to give up a good job. We've let off twenty percent of our workers, you know."

Ryan said: "Yep." He saw through Kane like polished glass now.

Kane dropped the cigarette on the floor and stepped carefully on it. The racket of the mill was a muffled booming in the room. "What are you and Smith looking for?"

"I think he's got a popcorn mine staked out."

Kane sat down, two displeased lines between his eyes. "Why are you taking this attitude?" he demanded. "I asked Hoagland to send you up so I could wish you well, and . . . well, I'm interested in all our employees. Hoagland's mentioned you several times as being one of his best men. Frankly I have a feeling that a man as determined and as thorough as you are may have some luck. I think I can make it a little easier for you on this trip. Whatever you're looking for." He handed Ryan a check. It was for $200.

Ryan looked at both sides of it. "I was reading in

a Mojave paper where the stockholders were climbing all over you because they didn't get any dividends last year. Sure you can spare this?"

There was color under Kane's heavy jowls. The essential nature of the man surfaced in his eyes. "It isn't that the borax is running any less high-grade," he retorted. "I had my own reasons for building up the surplus fund. Which naturally wouldn't be clear to stockholders."

Ryan flapped the check. "This buys you how much of what we find?"

"I thought of a forty percent interest. Fifty would be customary, but since there are two of you . . ."

Ryan let the check flutter to the floor. "Maybe you ought to go prospecting, too. I don't have to get my news about the mines from the newspapers, you know. I'm one of the boys that digs the stuff you sell. It ain't running so sweet these days. Unless you hit a new ledge, I'd say your stockholders were going to be auctioning off some equipment in a couple of years."

Kane snapped: "Forget the whole thing! Men have been licked before you because they were under-capitalized. You could hit a mountain of solid gold and still lose your shirt because it costs too much for you to get it out. But once you leave here, you won't come back to anything as good as I'm prepared to offer."

"I don't know where the idea got started that

Smith and I own a mine"—Ryan shrugged—"but I hope it's true. If we do, we'll damned well not sell it to a scrounging rock merchant."

He went out. Below him, lights gleamed in the early darkness. *I've done it now!* he thought. Whatever he did, he would never be able to return to Furnace Flat. Yet it was pleasant to reflect that Borax Kane was in a more uncomfortable spot than any of his workers.

All they had was a wife and a few kids to ride them for not making any more money. Kane had a few thousand stockholders to apologize to each time he skipped a dividend.

II

It was 8:00 p.m. when he left the company rooming house with his belongings. A remembered feeling as of a hairspring jiggling inside him began. A man his age ought to be rid of illusions of big strikes. But there was always the chance. Just this one last trip. One more pull at the bottle, bartender, before you cork it. But suddenly the bottle was empty, the visions old, the drinker disillusioned of his drink, but betrothed to it forever.

Ryan started down the hill with his old rattan suitcase on his shoulder. It was amusing, the way even Kane credited Mysterious Smith with having a hidden claim. Rot. Smith wouldn't be letting other men in on it if he had. Put a beard on a man, fill his mouth with secret gibberish, and they whispered of buried treasure and divining rods.

Smith was not at the café. Grady had kept a single dollar of his pay; he could eat sparingly on this. Margaret Conway placed steel knife, fork, and spoon before him with efficient, slender fingers. She gave him what seemed a special smile; it puzzled him.

A light-limbed, blonde girl, she wore her hair up, a pencil thrust into it. She wore a starched blue-and-white blouse that made her look like an illustration for a James Whitcomb Riley poem. Her skirt was long and dark, snug about the hips and full below; she seemed to Ryan something entirely too fragile and feminine for this country.

He had mulligan, pie, and coffee. All through the meal, as she passed near him going to and from the kitchen, he kept wanting to say something to her, something significant but not too significant. *Well, Mysterious Smith and I are going out prospecting together. I'll be coming back rich and full of ideas in a couple of months.* No good. He'd be coming back broke and hungry. But one of these days he would see a ring on her hand when she set out the silver, and soon after that she would be merely another miner's wife, just a woman to tip his hat to on the street.

Ryan ended by saying nothing. He laid the

dollar on the counter, took his hat from a nail, and walked out. He had the feeling that he was walking out of her life and, though he knew he had never really been in it, it took some of the shine off the trip.

Suddenly he heard the door open again as he moved away. He turned. She stood in the doorway, hands on hips, slim with the light behind her, the dream a man saw on lonely trails.

"Grady," she said, "they tell me you're leaving. Is that the only good bye you've got for me . . . a silver dollar?"

He went back. "Chloriders come, and chloriders go, but Ryan goes more than anybody." He grinned. "I'll be back one day, do another hitch for Kane, and take off again."

"You aren't a man to stay with a thing, are you?"

"I've stayed with the valley fourteen winters and one summer."

Maggie Conway tucked the pencil in her hair. It made him think of a schoolteacher, a young and pretty schoolteacher, but one trying to get a point across.

"Staying with the valley is just a way of not staying with anything," she said. "You're a young and stout one, Grady Ryan, but you won't always be. Why don't you stay with Furnace Flat?"

"I'll be stout longer following a jackass than I will be digging widow makers."

"I was watching to see you make drift boss,

superintendent, and then go after old Kane's job. You don't have to stay in the mine, you know."

"Those things make good reading, Maggie. But I've yet to see it happen. For me, the caper is to hunt the lodestone. Aaron Winters found it, One-Eye Thompson and some others. Maybe it's in the cards for me. If it is . . ." His tongue ran down. Thin ice crackled under him. "Well, the first thing I'll do"—he smiled—"is to pay my grub bill at Maggie Conway's."

She made an impatient gesture. For a long time the violet-gray eyes speculated on him with something of the same look she had given him in the restaurant. "There's something . . . Grady," she said suddenly. "You're going to strike it this time. It's on you. The look is on you. That's what I saw when I was putting out your silver."

Ryan laughed. "So the Cousin Jane broke her needle last night, and now she looks everywhere for omens. Have the tommyknockers hung a halo over my ear?"

"It wouldn't hurt some people I know to keep right with the little people." She continued to stare at him in a kind of awe.

"No," he told her. "It isn't the little people . . . it's the big people who make our luck. Men like Kane and the Mojave bankers. What can the tommyknockers do for a chlorider who has to sneak out of town to beat an eleven-dollar restaurant bill?"

Suddenly the inhibitions lost their grip on him. Banter and bitterness both fled from him. He was reaching out to hold her waist between his hands, pulling her close to him and saying roughly: "Maggie, I'm nearly out of brags, but here's my last. I'm going to lick this God-forsaken valley. I'm going to find something so rich the bankers will climb over each other to invest in me. When I do . . . though it may take twenty years . . . I'm coming back to Furnace Flat. That was the big thing you saw on me, my wanting you. Nothing else. But it's enough to make me shine like a gilt Indian."

She pulled him out of the light of the café window. Her lips laughed up at him. "You don't even stay with a brag all the way, do you?"

Ryan's arm crushed her body against him, his fingers dug into the golden tangle of her hair, his mouth pressing hers hard. When he let her go, he felt wrung-out, burned down to the core, exalted, and yet sorry.

"And now I'm wanting to ask you to wait," he said bitterly. "I'm full to the ears of promises. But all I'm saying is . . . I'm coming back. Rich or poor I'm coming back. I hope you're still here, but I'm not asking you to be."

"I'll be here," she whispered. "I'll be here till April, and we're going out on the parlor car of the Tonopah and Tidewater in style. Because you're on your way."

Ryan clung hard to his convictions. "I'm a burned-out chlorider at thirty-two. I believe an assay when I run it myself. I believe in a gold piece after I've bitten it. You don't go off glory holing with a cañon rat like Mysterious Smith if you're any more than a cañon rat yourself. We're putting our stake on the double zero, but the odds haven't changed any."

Margaret put her finger on his lips. "You are going to hit it," she said slowly. "That's as sure as the sun's coming up tomorrow. Name it after them, will you? The Tommyknocker Mine. They'd like it."

Ryan kissed her again. "I'll build a home for aged tommyknockers, if I hit it. And one for you. On top of Nob Hill, in San Francisco. That's no cheap brag."

They traveled that night until sunup, making dry camp in a region of twisting, painted mole burrows. After a few hours' rest they went on. Mysterious Smith was a taciturn traveler. A grunt was a full speech.

It seemed to Ryan that he knew where he was going, but it was a back-and-switching route he took to get there. He had thought he knew the valley, but Smith led him into cañons he had never seen, under an eroded rim of green rocks he did not know at all, and on the fourth evening he threw off on a high ridge between two cañons. The cañons were narrow slots of burned ochre, gouged with caves. The ridge was like a dinosaur's backbone, hairless and bony, supporting a few desert holly.

Ryan scratched his head. "Seems like we've passed a dozen campsites better than this."

Smith snapped: "Seems like it suits me."

Grady shrugged and started breaking up pieces of greasewood with which he had festooned his gear during the last hour. Smith stopped him. "Not yet." He led him down to one of the caves they had passed on the switchbacking climb from one of the cañons. He walked into it and sat down.

In Ryan's mind, a dark suspicion lurched up. The old man was crazy. Camp above and then come down to roost in a cave. But he carried it off casually, stooping to enter the cave and sitting down, cross-legged.

"Damnedest spot I was ever in," Ryan confessed. "I keep hoping you've already got a ledge spotted, but I know dang' well you haven't, or you wouldn't be letting anybody else come along."

Smith slipped out his upper plate, removed a shred of chewed wood fiber from between two teeth, and slipped the pink horseshoe back into his mouth. "'Tis so, I reckon. For both of us. First time I ever went prospecting with anybody. You'll do, though. Talk too much, but you'll do."

Ryan cleared his throat. "I keep wondering why you asked me to come along."

Smith peered down the cañon. "I've got some rocks staked out, all right. Nothing much. Fellers got to get their sights down. They look for borax like they'd look for a field of cut diamonds. It don't come that way any more. But this sorta suited me, and I riz a couple of monuments. Took a little sack of ore samples to town with me. Damned if I didn't misput them. Knew right where they were, but when I come back to camp from town they were gone. I got the idea somebody else liked them."

Ryan's mind shot with the clarity of a carbide beam to the session in Borax Kane's office. It was all plain, now. Mysterious Smith was a long way from being crazy. But somebody else was crazy to think he could be gotten around.

"That was two months ago. I've been kinda watching you. I like you, Ryan. You don't kid yourself nor try to kid the next man. You know the desert can't be licked, but you like it for what it is. So when I knew I had to have a pardner, I began thinking about you. I ain't so tarnal old, not what you call downright decrepit, but I ain't fit for a real battle. We're going to have a battle before we get our test shafts sunk, and another one keeping the rocks for ourselves. And I'd like a young 'un to help me make it. Is it worth half a borax mine . . . I ain't guessing what kind . . . to risk having your behind shot off?"

Up the twisting little cañon drifted the scuff of

mule shoes. Grady smiled. "They didn't lose much time, did they . . . ? Sure, it's worth it. You cover me. I'll go down and talk to them. When'd you spot them?"

"Yesterday. We're a long way from the borax, you understand, but I wanted them to catch up to us where we could handle 'em. Wonder if Kane had the guts to come hisself?"

III

First came the burros, a pair of strong, mouse-gray animals carrying light packs. Pat Hoagland came after them, peering upward along the ridge. The mine boss was dusty and flushed; he wore a winter Army shirt and geologist's breeches terminating in laced boots.

Close behind him strode another man, younger than Hoagland and taller, hatless, his hair blond and his skin dark. This man was familiar to Ryan, too. He was one of the geologists, a man named Fisher, with the distrust of the comparatively uneducated for the overly educated, Ryan had never cottoned to him. He was one of the whiz boys who would spend five minutes in a drift, announce that shoring would be necessary, and get out before the hanging wall fell.

Fisher said suddenly, stopping to thrust at the ground with a stick: "Look here!"

Hoagland went back. Fisher was examining a clutch of fresh burro sign. "Can't be an hour old."

"We'd better throw off here. We don't want to run into them tonight. They've run the legs off us," he said, "but we're closing in."

Ryan walked from behind a pitted lava buttress. "You're doing better than that," he told Hoagland. "You're there."

Both men turned with a quick rustling of gravel under their feet. They looked so tense, so guilty, that Ryan began to chuckle. "You fellows look like you were about to break into somebody's bank."

"We have as much right . . . ," Fisher began hotly, but Hoagland cut in angrily: "Sure we're following you. That's our privilege, isn't it?"

Ryan shrugged. He carried no gun, and suspected that Hoagland might be filling with a false confidence because of the Colt at his hip. "If you want to play it all the way out," he declared.

"Play it out? We'll play it any way we want. We're curious to know why you sneaked out of town in the middle of the night. I say we'll find out." He was an odd combination of saloon roughneck and professional man. About all the gloss engineering school had put on him was to teach him how to frame a threat in parlor language.

Fisher came in impulsively. "What's the matter with you valley men? You came out here with a little homemade geology and a pick, starve for six months digging in a spot a trained geologist could tell you was barren, and then refuse the help of someone like Borax Kane who wants to set you up."

Ryan could taste temper on his tongue like salt. "Kane," he said, "has been setting me up for quite a spell. I could almost eat on his set-up. If you want to take your burros back with you, start now."

Hoagland shook his head, a grin tucked in the corners of his mouth. "Don't mind us. We'll just trail along. We're not claim-jumpers. But the law only allows you so many feet anyway. We'll take the leavings."

"Right. But not until we know what's leavings and what isn't. If we strike anything, we'll run some honest-to-God tests before we decide what's for us and what's for the rest of you."

Hoagland looked back at Fisher with a grin, then started past Ryan. Grady brought a fist from his hip in a short, decisive uppercut. Hoagland tried to sway out of line; the blow landed on the edge of his jaw, sent him reeling against the cañon wall, and sliding down at the base of it. He was coming up immediately, getting to his knees before he thought of the Colt.

Fisher was ahead of him there. He carried a small .32 revolver in a hip pocket. He had it halfway out of his pocket when the cañon shook under the dynamiting roar of a rifle a hundred feet above. A slug howled off the pocked lava wall. Fisher stood paralyzed.

Ryan said: "Take it out, but throw it where it won't tempt you. Same for you, Hoagland. And then come up fighting, if you've the guts for using your fists any more."

Both men rid themselves of their weapons. Hoagland looked steady enough when he got on his feet. He started slowly toward Ryan, but Grady suddenly launched a drive that smashed him back against the cañon wall. They went down together, Hoagland's hands groping at Ryan's throat.

Ryan threw him off, but, as they scrambled up, Hoagland began slinging long punches from his shoulders. He was a strong and zealous opponent, surprisingly solid, an executive whose impatient energy carried him into every activity his mind entered. The miner suddenly found himself on the defensive.

A fist smashed his mouth. Another crashed against his ear and filled his head with a dark roaring. Hoagland's face seemed to balloon and devour him, hard and eager, betraying a sort of surprised pleasure, as if the man were thinking: *This mucker isn't so tough! Why don't I do more of this?*

Ryan stood up to him, but Hoagland was on the march, taking a stride after each swing, and not many of the thrashing blows missed.

Suddenly Ryan found himself looking at the gritty earth from an all-fours position. He rose to his knees, started swaying at the rugged, unmarked face of the mine boss. He lumbered up thickly. Pat Hoagland stepped forward with his left foot and drove his right hand into Grady's face.

He was on his back. He was licked. He was tasting blood and thinking that he was glad it was over. Yet that small and ill-natured monitor that dwells in some men's minds was frantically trying to whip him up, like a testy mule-whacker. *I'd rather die than be licked by a college man,* he thought.

Through a blanket-thickness he heard Fisher exclaim enthusiastically: "My God, Mister Hoagland!"

Up there on the cliff, Mysterious Smith must be indulging in some profane thinking. He had mistaken a cut-proud capon for a fighting cock.

Grady Ryan took a shuddering breath and propped himself up with a hand outstretched behind him. He was a bloody, dirt-smeared relic of the overly ambitious fighter who had swung at Hoagland a few minutes ago. He drew one foot up, rolled over onto all fours, and stood up. Pat Hoagland shook his head.

"You've had enough, you damned fool." But as the miner started for him, he fired a long blow at Grady's head. It rocked the dark, battered head but did not slow him. He came on, shoulders hunched, face tipped down, eyes glaring up at Hoagland. Again the mine boss stabbed, but Grady knocked this one aside and abruptly seized him by the shirt and swung a haymaker. It landed on the side of Hoagland's head.

He reeled aside, pivoted, and lurched back, an intemperate fury on him. He closed with Grady and pumped one to his belly. Grady took it and snapped his head down, striking Hoagland on the nose. Hoagland blurted something and tried to back away. Ryan had a hand behind his neck and held him while he slugged at this jaw. It jolted him. Another punch cut the hard skin under his eye.

Ryan saw him foggily. The blow to the belly had robbed him of the strength he needed to finish it. A cold greenness flowed through him, but he continued to stand there. He saw Pat Hoagland coming forward, gathering everything into a single blow that started slowly and gained momentum.

Ryan tipped his head. The punch tore his ear. Grady brought his fist up like a miner ramming a stull home under a timber, not with an explosion of speed, but with a dogged force that kept moving. It took Hoagland under the chin and stood him up as stiffly as a hung hide.

When he sank down, he sank all the way. He sat heavily on the gravel, slowly fell over on his side, and lay, twisted, with his cheek against the earth.

Mysterious Smith had come down from the rocks. He was there to give Ryan a drink from a pint bottle and to strike him once on the shoulder. Then he left Grady to sit on a rock with a gun on Fisher while he brought back the burros. He cut the lashings and dumped all their gear on the ground. Throwing out a few cans of beans, he set fire to the oiled tarps and burned everything but the beans and the burros.

When Pat Hoagland came around, Smith told him: "There's easier ways of mining than this. Easier places to travel than where we're going, too. So long, boys."

The secret map in the head of Mysterious Smith led them both down more barren washes, across rocky hogbacks, winding in and out along the gaudy bluffs of the Funeral Mountains. On a clear, crisp morning, as Ryan threw a hitch over his pack saddle, he glanced up and saw Smith regarding him.

"Got any secret vices a future pardner ought to know about?" Smith asked.

"One. My guts growl when I'm hungry."

Smith walked up and down, a perplexed, barrel-chested old chlorider. "I'm seventy-four years old, and I gotten two dollars to my name. But I'm going to die in the damnedest mansion *this* valley ever seen. I'd kill the man that tried to do me out a dollar of this fortune. I've lost two others when my pardner's ree-lations set the lawyers on me. It ain't a-going to happen to me again. *Look!*" he yelled suddenly.

He ran up the slope. They were camped at the bottom of a wide wash from which rusty ridges ran up in rimrock steps. Smith was tugging at a clump of creosote brush. He pulled it away and revealed a hole not much larger than a coyote hole. "Get yer lamp!" he screeched. "Show you sumpthing, pardner!"

A kind of excitement he had thought buried with his youth fountained up in Grady Ryan. Lamp fizzing, he crawled through the adit after Smith. Just inside, the tunnel flared to regulation dimensions, about six feet wide and seven feet high. Mysterious Smith had said borax did not come high-grade any more. But the drift had been cut through a vein of borax as pure as diamond. In the shrill carbide light, a galaxy of stubby borax crystals gleamed all about them. It was the purest borax Grady Ryan had ever seen. It was bonanza borax.

IV

The drift was already nearly a hundred feet deep. They brought the burros inside after enlarging the adit, screened it again as best they could, and made the drift their camp. They spent two weeks probing around the cañon for new outcrops. They never found another like the first, but a narrower ledge of the same clear mineral was opened down along the dry wash.

"You name this 'un," Smith invited. "I called the first the Bellyache Number One, because I had the grip the day I struck that chimney."

Ryan thought of a blonde girl who looked like a picture in a poetry book and who surely had the vision of the Cornishmen. "What about the Tommyknocker?"

"Suit yourself." Smith packed his burro, and again checked the monuments about the Bellyache. Ryan was ready to travel. "Sure you ain't got any kin?" Smith asked suspiciously.

"I've got an aunt somewhere. Haven't seen her in years."

Ryan did not look at him when he spoke. As he heard Smith's pipe strike the ground, he looked about. Blood choked the prospector's features. His eyes were small blue marbles in a stricken face. He backed off a pace.

255

"So you ain't got any kinfolk . . . but you've got an aunt!"

"I told you I haven't seen her since . . ."

"You'll see her soon enough after she hears you're rich! It's off!" he yelled. "It's all off!"

"It's too late to call it off," Ryan snapped. "I grubstaked you. I took a licking for you. We're pardners, now, like it or not."

Smith made a sobbing sound and leaped on him. He was heavy and compact; they fell and rolled. Ryan pinned him flat and sat on his chest.

"Now, you old catamount! You'll not have any kin trouble with me, but you'll have every other kind if you try to deal me the split card!"

Smith squeezed his eyes shut. After a moment Ryan got off him. Smith got up, panting.

"You get your cut, don't squall so. But I keep the Bellyache. You got no more share in it than I have in yours. That pays you off. I'll have no part of you. Kinfolk lousy!"

"It's going to take two separate outfits to work them if we split up. Two freight outfits to reach the T. and T., too."

Smith's salmon-pink plates showed in a laugh. "Freight outfits? And you call yourself a valley man. Ryan, you're only four miles from Furnace Flat."

Yelling with idiot glee, he drove his burro up the cañon.

Ryan hurried after him. Four miles. A mine was

valued in this country in direct ratio to its nearness to a railroad. He savored it. The T.&T. would build a spur. It was the warp and woof of luck. The tommyknockers were in this one for sure.

Grady Ryan spent a month in the grip of a misconception. He was green enough at good fortune to think that certain benefits were automatic—good clothes, a rig to take your girl out in, pale-green cigars. As it worked out, he spent a month in the direst poverty.

He could sell the mine for $10,000 cash, but he couldn't borrow a dime on it. He must sink new drifts before anyone would risk money on him. He took Margaret Conway for a walk one night.

"I haven't forgotten that house on Nob Hill, Maggie. But that and the fine clothes will have to wait. Could you carry me another month on that grub bill?"

"All your life." She laughed. "The gilt is still on you."

Miners settled like locusts upon the Cinnabar Flat area. Every unfiled claim was taken overnight. Most of them were middling chimneys of mixed tuff and borax. Grady had his eye on them. He would buy them at a dime a dozen after he made his peace with the banks.

He borrowed $200 from Tom Lund, his old drift boss, and hired Tom and a few other boys away from Borax Kane. They achieved enough footage in the first month to start Ryan and a sack of samples across the valley to Mojave to try to dig up cash to go on.

The bank did not want his paper. They turned him over to a fat Swiss in a back room, who extracted a deed and the first installment of twelve percent on $20,000 before Grady ever saw the money. $20,000 would barely buy some second-hand machinery and get him started. In the meantime, the Swiss would drink his beer and think fondly on the mine he expected to own.

It was warm when he returned. Cinnabar Flat was two thousand feet below Furnace Flat; summer would strike like a bronze gong. A Tonapah & Tidewater spur was already building to the mines. Smith was pulling out tons of borax and even Kane had some gopher holes producing.

Ryan was just in time for an auction of mine machinery at the Blue Gravel diggings. He rented a turnout and joined the caravan streaming over the hills one morning. Maggie rode with him, starched and cool in blue and white. She opened her handbag to take out a sheaf of yellow backs.

"There's why I could carry you," she said. "There's more money in filling miners' stomachs than in digging ore. Fifteen hundred dollars, Grady. How much Tommyknocker stock will that buy me?"

Ryan shook his head. A gang of worries chased

about his mind. "Stick to filling their stomachs. If I go under, it'll be alone."

She sat back indignantly. "You'd turn me down for my share, after I called the turn for you?"

"Your share," said Ryan, "is half of everything I make. But God knows how I'll squeeze out the money I already owe, with the mines shut down for five months this summer and the interest still snowballing."

The Blue Gravel Mine was on a hillside sage-tufted like a candlewick spread. In a junkyard of rusting equipment, a flat spring wagon had been parked as an auctioneer's platform. Grady saw Borax Kane with the auctioneer.

The day was savagely hot. The auctioneer, a corpulent big man wearing a black suit and stock and too dignified to remove his coat, looked as though he were strangling. He took a drink from Kane's pint. His lips were flaccid and his face purple as he pressed a handkerchief repeatedly to the glistening crown of his head.

Yonder was Mysterious Smith, with his super-intendent. He looked no different, a man too old and withdrawn to change—suspicious, close, and wistful.

Brannigan, the auctioneer, climbed the wagon and pounded on a box with a wrench. He went through the wherefores and put a selection of office furniture on the block. Ryan took it from a disinterested rival for $200. Other small lots went cheaply. Then the heavy equipment went up. It would go as a single lot if a bidder could be found.

"The entire operating equipment of the United Metals Corporation," Brannigan panted. The heat had his face blooming; his eyes were choked in moist red flesh. "Equipment used and unused, as she stands . . . strap-iron railway supplies, timbering, and head frames. Gentlemen, what am I bid?"

Down to the dollar, Ryan knew what he could afford to bid. $12,000 would leave his blood white as milk. "Eight thousand," he said.

Smith said: "Nine."

Brannigan tapped the box. "Do I hear ten?"

On a long chance, Ryan made a jump bid: "Eleven!"

Smith turned slowly and stared at him. The small blue eyes were steady and venomous. He turned back, cleared his throat—and said nothing. Joy surged up in Ryan, another thousand to get it down to Cinnabar Flat. He was set.

Suddenly Margaret was whispering: "I'm not just going to watch this game, Grady Ryan. I'm going to be in it. Either you sell me stock, or I loan it to Smith."

"I told you why I can't take your money. If you want to wreck me, this is as good a way as any."

"I don't want to wreck you. But I practically helped find that mine. And I want to take any risk there is along the way, and not have people saying

Maggie Conway married the Tommyknocker Mine, not Grady Ryan. Do I get my stock?"

Brannigan struck the box. "Eleven thousand once!"

Ryan was a man who led more easily than he pushed. He was also a man with old-fashioned ideas about widows and orphans. He thought of how far that fifteen hundred would take her if she ever really needed it. He called to Brannigan: "Get on with it!"

The auctioneer pounded the box a second time. Maggie's chin went up. She ran over to Mysterious Smith and put an arm about his shoulders. She whispered to him. Smith's head did not turn, but suddenly he called out: "Twelve!"

Ryan stood like a man on a rock. "Thirteen," he said.

Maggie stared her fury at him. Ryan felt relief softening his joints; he let out his breath. Smith was boxed for fair.

"Thirteen thousand once. Thirteen thousand twice!"

Someone was moving through the crowd. Borax Kane reached Smith's side and began to talk in a confidential, smiling way to him. Ryan bawled: "Pound it out!"

"Just a moment!" Kane said. "Smith, I'd like to . . ."

"Pound it out!" Ryan roared. He started for the wagon.

Brannigan raised the wrench. Then his face acquired a foolish, slack-mouth look. He reached blindly before him; someone was there to catch him just as he collapsed.

In the shade of the wagon, a canteen dumped over his head. With his coat and stock pulled off, he began to come around. Outlanders did damned-fool things in the valley. All this time, Ryan had to listen to the bland chicanery of Borax Kane while they waited for Brannigan to come to.

"I'll back you up to three thousand, Smith. You've got a real mine down there."

"Going to keep it for myself, too," said Smith doggedly.

"What good is a mine without any machinery?"

Maggie counseled vociferously, but Smith's sandbagged features admitted he had to have machinery; he was licked without it. At last he agreed. As they hoisted Brannigan to the wagon again, sodden and mauve-featured, Mysterious Smith cracked: "Fifteen thousand! Now, by . . . !" He wheeled and gave Grady Ryan a triumphant stare.

"Fifteen-five," Ryan said. *I can raise the money to operate from the Swiss. Might as well go down in a cloud of smoke.*

Smith did not react. He was beyond it. He had a shirt-tail partner, no machinery, and owed money he probably could not pay. Brannigan hammered the deal down. Grady went forward to pay up. He stopped near Kane. Kane's big, drink-pocked face was pleased. A red smile wreathed his face.

"Good luck with that machinery, Ryan. You don't need to feel sorry for Smith, because there is all the machinery he needs right at Furnace Flat . . . for a consideration."

V

Kane and Hoagland moved their men and their methods to Cinnabar Flat like a couple of cavalry generals taking a town. Overnight, Mysterious Smith became merely an old chlorider who visited his mines like a man bringing flowers to a sick friend. He collected a few dollars a week for food and beer.

Grady went ahead doggedly. He had Tom Lund steal a gang of hard rockers from Kane. Short of cash, he sold them on a deal by which he retained half their pay for a year, paying six percent. He and Kane sweated each other's games. Knowing each other's finances, knowing neither could weather a summer on interest without production.

On a hot evening in late May, Grady walked down the street of Furnace Flat to the café. It was after the dinner hour. The café was closed, but through the window he could see Margaret with her fat Irish cook, packing heavy restaurant china in newspapers as carefully as though it were bone.

Margaret let him in with prim coolness. Ryan had got over his pique, but women had the faculty of nursing a grudge as they might a child. She tried to serve him pie and coffee without recognizing him, but Grady caught her hands and pulled her down to him. He gave her a peck on the cheek.

"As a millionaire customer," he said, "I'm entitled to service."

"You'll get the same service they all get."

Ryan watched the women place china ceremoniously in a crate. It came to him that packing china was an odd occupation for this time of night. Margaret flipped up an arch glance when he asked about it.

"I don't know about miners, but restaurant people have enough sense to get out of the valley in summer. I'm leaving on the First of June. We were going out in April, before . . . remember? When are you going to let your men pull out?"

Sooner or later, someone had to ask it. Ryan had kept hoping it would be Borax Kane who made the decision, so that Kane would be the black dog of Furnace Flat, the first man to condemn his men to the valley heat.

"Haven't decided," he said.

Margaret crossed the floor and looked into his eyes. "You're not shutting down at all," she declared.

Ryan stirred uncomfortably. "I didn't say that. . . ."

"But I can read it on you. Grady, it will hit a hundred and twenty-five down there."

"Not in the mines. If I can get them underground, they won't be any hotter below than they would be in winter. At worst, I'll operate the night shift alone."

Afterward, Grady remembered the way she had looked at him. "Get out of it, Grady," she said slowly. "Get out of it while you can. They've taken off their blessing. I can see it on you."

"If they've had their blessing on me so far, I may do better after they take it off," Ryan said. He got up to leave. Someone else entered the restaurant. It was Tom Lund.

"I tried to catch you before you left," Lund said. He was a strapping redhead with a face like something carved artlessly from rock, his cheek bones jutting, mouth wide, and jaw square. He carried his worries in his eyes, hazel under bleached, thorny brows. He had a miner's hands and thick, strong wrists. Lund was a man without artifices. Where another might have broken his news carefully, Lund blurted: "Hoagland's driven into one of our ledges. He's been high-grading our rock for two weeks."

Ryan strode past Lund. Margaret ran after him to get between him and the door.

"Don't go down there, Grady. Talk to Kane . . . but don't go down. I tell you they've taken off the blessing."

265

Grady moved her aside. "The trouble is underground. The ironing out of it will be, too. And the only blessing I'll need is these two fists."

"I couldn't get the notion of rock like that coming out of the coyote hole it did," Lund told him. They were on a hand car coasting down to the mines, the air rushing past them, hot and dry. "It was pure colemanite, but the drift it came out of was the old Slab Bacon claim . . . not worth the powder to blow it up. But I had it from one of their men today that Fisher's drove a shoo-fly into our own main ledge."

"What have you done about it?"

"Jawed with Hoagland and that fool, Fisher. They claim there ain't any such cut . . . but they're not welcoming visitors."

"They'll welcome me." Ryan took a sullen joy in the development.

Flares lit the night operations in the broken rimrock cañon. Borax rattled and roared down the hurries into T.&T. ore cars. A dull hammer stroke marked the bursting of dynamite in a deep mine. Ryan picked up an armload of dynamite at one of his own mines, some fuse and caps, and started up the hill. Tom Lund carried a six-foot drill and sledge. They had donned lamps and caps.

At the foot of the Slab Bacon chute, ore cars on a precarious hillside trestle were receiving clattering loads of borax. The dust was heavy and stifling. They climbed the slope through a rubbish of spilled rock, broken timbers, and boxes. A short line of tiny mule cars was backed out to the grizzly, where workmen in dust-chalked clothing, their faces pallid in a greasy dusk of oil flares, were tending them.

Grady halted, set down his load of dynamite, and lit his lamp. "Sure about this?" he asked Lund.

Lund's lamp spat into life. "This guy had all the directions and footage. It checks out that they're only using this as a portal." Abruptly he said: "Here they come."

Grady saw the pair coming down from a shed. They were Pat Hoagland and Borax Kane's blond whiz-boy, Fisher. Hoagland carried an oil lantern, setting it down when they had reached the others. The mine boss rocked on his feet with his hands on his hips.

There was still a fat wad of cartilage above his right eye, where Ryan had hit him that day. It gave his face a slightly lop-sided look and, knowing Hoagland's compulsion to exert his will on others, rather than to have it exerted on him, Ryan knew that he must be conscious of that scar whenever he talked to any man.

"You boys going to do a little mining?"

"A little unmining," Ryan told him. "That's good-looking rock out there. I looked this hole over when it was sold. I wouldn't have guessed it would give anything but cotton ball."

Fisher's face was clamped in an expression of nervous determination. "You can't always *guess* what's in a mine by the kind of surface rock it shows."

"That's right. If there's ore in there, I've learned something about mining. I'd like to see just how you opened up this seam."

Hoagland rubbed his hands together, still pleased, still poised like a boulder on a cliff. "We have a mine tour about once every six months for the stockholders. Why don't you sit on your hands until then? We'll show you how to make a borax mine pay."

"You'll show me how to make somebody else's mine pay, you mean."

Hoagland's eyes picked up the harsh gleam of the lamps. "That's too subtle for me."

Grady was aware that the white carbide light was dulling Hoagland's vision. "Too subtle?" he said. "Try this."

He had picked up the sledge as the others came down the tracks. He held it by the head with one hand and swung the handle in a short arc to the side of the miner's head. Hoagland stumbled forward. He was not out, but he was not quite capable of co-ordinating thoughts and actions. He fell and lay on the tracks with a thick-tongued moan.

Fisher was coming in with a strangled curse. As he passed Lund, the redhead slammed one into the side of the head. Fisher staggered and went to his knees.

They picked up their tools and walked quickly into the tunnel. They followed on down the tracks. The timbering stretched away from them in a geometrical diminuendo of angles. The trace of borax seam on the wall began to fade. It died in a cavern where every ounce of worthwhile rock had been chipped away. Off to the left, a new drift opened up. The polished strap-iron rails caught the carbide lights as they followed them. There was no sign of borax anywhere but along the tracks, where it had spilled from laden cars.

The tunnel was heavily timbered; seams and faults made the whole section dangerous. The tunnel ran in defiance of geological formations—in defiance of mining law, too, boring through the mountain toward Tommyknocker Number 3.

Suddenly they were in borax again. The clink of a sledge became audible. Past a turn they saw in the distance a miner holding a six-foot drill while another man swung a double-jack. These men turned suddenly.

Ryan jerked his thumb. "Out."

The men got out. They knew they had been in Tommyknocker rock for two weeks. This was no concern of theirs, but they knew it was Ryan's.

Ryan walked after them until he had left the

borax deposit behind, reaching the area rotten with faults. It took little work with the drill to open a hole he could load with a charge of dynamite sufficient almost to lift off the top of the hill. Then they walked another hundred feet and opened a second seam.

Grady measured fuse. "Go on," he told Lund. "I can take it from here."

"Hell with that. I'll run down and light that first fuse. You start this one when you hear me coming."

A toothed edge seemed to be at Ryan's nerves. He had never felt mine fear before. "I said get out!"

Tom Lund hesitated. Then he shrugged and started off.

Ryan touched the first fuse with his lamp and sprinted. He lit the second, and legged it so hard that he bumped solidly into the man coming the other way before he saw him. He fell and rolled, lost his lamp, and had a glimpse of a lean, wild-eyed man rising out of the dust ten feet beyond him. Fisher had gotten past Tom Lund.

A coal-oil lantern burned on its side near him, chimney shattered. Fisher's hand snatched up a rock, his arm drew back, and he hurled it at Ryan's head before Ryan had time to duck.

VI

In the darkness he ran on. Ryan pressed his hand against his ear. The rock had gouged it as it whirled by. For one moment he hovered in a humming darkness, then, his head clearing, he came up on his knees and shouted: *"Fisher!"*

Fisher was out of sight around the bend. His footfalls ran brokenly down the drift. Ryan's act was not humanitarian. They would call it manslaughter if the engineer died in an unauthorized blast.

Fisher lurched along a hundred feet ahead of him as Ryan followed. Fisher reached the first fuse, yanked it from the charge, and stood uncertainly. Ryan could feel the clammy fright that had suddenly come home to the man. Was that another fuse burning down there?

Fisher started back, hesitated, and looked once more at the sparkling hole in the blackness. Even he knew what a blast could do to this kind of formation. He pulled his fears into one last impulse and his long stork legs carried him toward the dynamite.

Ryan hurled the rock. It caught Fisher on the leg. He sprawled. Ryan got him by the back of the neck and rushed him back down the drift. Fisher was not fighting Ryan, but stumbling helplessly.

They were at the turn where they had collided when the vast, paralyzing explosion of gases shook the mine.

Ryan was down on hands and knees in the blackness, hearing nothing but a roar of giant waters, feeling the thud of rocks against his body. He let himself slump against the mine wall. It was too big to fear. He was a tiny black speck of life against a sky, not worth reaching for, but death was impartial.

Then there was a crumpling roar ahead of him, and afterward it seemed as though a cork had been twisted into a bottle. Sound ceased. You couldn't call that pattering of small stones up and down the drift genuine sound, not in this place of massive concussion.

He heard his lamp fizzing like a beer bottle getting ready to let loose. His hand encountered the warm metal and he flicked the flint wheel. Fisher sat against the side wall opposite with blood streaming down his face. Ryan had forgotten him. Terror was microscopic in its effect, excluding everything but selfish thoughts.

Fisher leaped to his feet. Ryan's eyes went with old training to the hanging wall above. He saw the great slab of gneiss suspended over their heads, sinking gently toward them.

He came to his feet and started Fisher along the tunnel. Shortly he heard the brief, crumpling sound of the rock falling. They kept walking until they saw the mass of stone clogging the shattered tunnel, its jagged shoulder veiled in gray rock dust. Fisher pivoted suddenly and swung a blow wildly at Ryan's jaw. It hit Ryan on the side of the head and jarred him.

"Crazy bull-headed boraxer! Dynamite us both to hell, will you? Die like drowned-out gophers!"

Ryan swerved into the geologist. He turned the man's jaw with a short, chopping punch. It hurled Fisher back against a stull and dropped him in a loose, gangling huddle, and he began to sob.

Grady went to work. There was not a foot of the drift he would care to spend five minutes in. He examined the slide. They were sealed in. He told Fisher gruffly: "This isn't a coal mine. Nobody's going to die of black damp or poison gas. After we get used to it, we'll start moving rocks around."

By Ryan's watch, it was twenty hours later when they paused in a spell of careful work on the slide to listen. Fisher had been docile ever since the fight. Now he started tearing rocks aside with a wild yell.

"They're coming!"

Half the town of Furnace Flat was waiting to see them stagger out of the Slab Bacon. Tom Lund was the first man to seize Grady, tears in his Irish-blue eyes.

"The damn' fool was laying for me. Hit me with a rock and I never come around for an hour."

Borax Kane was there to receive his geologist like a lost son. But Fisher's eyes, striking Ryan's for an instant, were ashamed. *This man,* they said, *has seen the core of me . . . the sawdust where there should be courage.* Shame like Fisher's, Grady knew, could turn a man like him into an enemy more dangerous than two-fisted Pat Hoagland.

Margaret got through the crowd to Grady. Ryan held her, filled with an aching relief. "You will defy every omen under the sun," she told him. "Do you believe me, now?"

Ryan hesitated, moved through gratitude to admit he had been wrong about everything, but a man's convictions were hard to shake. "I believe that college geologists should stay where they belong . . . in offices."

Margaret regarded him steadily. "I've bought two tickets to Tonopah. It was a deal I made with them . . . if they brought you out, I'd get you away from Cinnabar Flat for the summer."

Ryan shook his head. "You give the little people credit for knowing everything. Will they tell me how to keep the mines if I close them?"

"Perhaps if you'd go, they would. I'm using my ticket on the First of June. You can use yours when you feel like it. But you won't find Maggie Conway waiting long in Tonopah."

Margaret ran off to the railroad. There was a sharpness in the heart of Grady Ryan, but he was still standing there when she took a seat on the little car with its row of benches. He and Tom Lund drifted over to a flat car and sat on the edge of it while it filled. Lund seemed waiting for him to say something. At last he asked Grady: "What'll I tell the boys?"

"Tell 'em I'm alive, if you think they'd be interested."

"No I mean . . . well, there's enough Cousin Jacks among them to keep the old superstitions alive. This looks bad to them. The owner of a mine nearly dying underground. What shall I tell them?"

"Tell them," Ryan said, "that we're going to work all summer. Extra pay. They'll bunk at Furnace Flat. I don't see why it should be so different from any other time of year."

Lund was silent a while. "Kind of forgot what summer's like, ain't you?"

"I know better than most. But we're going to try it, anyhow."

Though Grady Ryan did not know it, that was the night before summer. By 10:00 a.m. the following day, every miner and mucker in Cinnabar Flat knew it would be a day to remember. The thermometer just inside the big Tommyknocker Number One registered one hundred and thirteen. It was one hundred and seventeen by noon.

A wind roused off the desert, rushing up the

cañon with its kiln-like breath to carry gray clouds of dust into the mines. At 2:00 it was a hundred and twenty, and Grady had the good sense to dismiss all outside workers.

The heat continued to roast Cinnabar Flat all week. Suddenly it was apparent that it would not let up until winter. Five months of skull-cracking heat ahead. Ryan went on summer schedule, put out water barrels, and raised wages.

Kane posted a notice on his bulletin board.

> Owing to unfair competition by the Ryan mines, we are forced to continue mining operations beyond our regular closing date.

And also, Grady speculated, owing to some unpaid notes and failing mines. The rich Belly-ache ledge was not living up to expectations. Ryan's Number One, after a slow start, was expanding and becoming purer. Despite the heat, he was almost optimistic by the night Lund came shame-facedly with a miner's delegation to the small sheet-metal office building.

"I tried to talk these stiffs out of it," he explained, "but they will say their piece. They say they're quittin'. They want the wages you've held back."

Ryan had been working with a desk that had come apart. Furniture had to be made in the valley, without glue, to endure the heat. He stood in the doorway, shirtless, sweating, a dark, blunt-chinned man with temper in his face.

"What's the matter?" he demanded. "Tired of waiting for that spree?"

"Tired of the heat!" a miner shot back.

"What heat? It averages sixty in the mines. That's cool enough for anybody."

"It don't average sixty after you come out at seven a.m. Better'n a hundred, and you can have my share of sleeping in a sheet-metal shack, even at Furnace Flat."

"Where do you think I sleep? You can bunk in one of the mines, if you want."

Someone laughed. "Work, sleep, and eat underground! We ain't gophers, Ryan."

Lund put in an apologetic complaint. "The watermen don't keep the barrels full, either, Grady. They're always dryin' out and fallin' apart. And the chuck at Maggie's is gettin' worse. Meat spoils so fast she's serving nothing but salt-cured bull hide."

"All right," Ryan said. "If you're bound to quit, you'll quit. But I can't pay your back wages. The agreement was that I kept them for a year. In a year, you'll get the money with interest."

There was a muttering of displeasure. "That was the promise," Lund reminded them. "Take it or leave it. But if you quit, you'll probably wander off to the gold mines or God knows where and lose out on it. Take a hitch in your belts and stay."

In the end, they decided to stay. Lund remained after they left. "There's something else," he said. "Did you specify seasoned lumber when you bought your timbering?"

Something in Ryan slowed up and held its breath. "I picked it out myself."

"Maybe you'd better let me pick it out next time," Lund growled. "There's a lot of sags showing up. Some places the stulls and timbers are beginning to separate. The boys are grousin' about snow in every damned drift we're working."

"I'll look 'em over," Ryan promised.

He said it casually enough, but it had the impact of a rock between the eyes. Snow. Catastrophe dust—the gentle sift of earth that preceded a cave-in. It meant faulty or inadequate timbering, and to replace timbering would mean the finish.

He spent the better part of one night examining the stulls and timbers of the main drifts. Lund was right. Almost imperceptibly, the overheads were bowing. In other spots, the stulls had developed bad cracks.

Ryan closeted himself with his books and did some figuring. New timbering at $6,000. Labor at about half that. Lost time . . . He was scared. He wanted to tell everyone to keep his voice down, to walk softly, not to drop anything heavy. It was not immediately serious. But if the settling process continued, it would soon be serious enough to close the Tommyknocker mines for good.

He had a heretical thought, one at variance with his nature, that no matter how much he made, it could never make up to him for the things he had lost. Maggie. Mysterious Smith. Some cherished illusions. Happiness and the struggle for money were incompatible.

When they touched, one was quick to tarnish. In this case, both had tarnished.

VII

On the 1st of June, Margaret Conway closed her café and moved over to Tonopah. For Ryan, the edge was off everything. He ate at a third-rate beanery and thought of Maggie's cherry pie. He rode home from work through amber dawns and dreamed of her hair.

The stark beauty of the winter season had burned out in dust and heat. Sand and salt storms raging down in the furnace called Death Valley invaded the cañons, fouling machinery with grit. At night, the ninety-degree heat was bearable. But by day, Cinnabar Flat was a ghost camp.

Yet the ore coming out of Ryan's mines was clear as rock candy. Mill checks began to flutter back to him. Some of the pressure eased off. He'd lick them with this summer club of his. He could meet his first interest payment handily, get the Swiss to set the installment on the principal over till fall, and catch up then.

He was thinking this the night Borax Kane came to call. Beyond him in the flare-lit darkness, Grady made out the barrel-shaped form of Mysterious Smith. Grady let them in. In the lamplight, Kane's face was a harsh pattern of impatience and anger bottled up until they soured. He wore a neckband shirt without the boiled collar, and his pants were dusty and creaseless.

Smith, the patriarch of all prospectors, carried a large volume that Ryan discovered was a Bible. There was something withdrawn about his eyes. Ryan thought: *The old son's going to make a speech.*

Kane shot a glance at the heat-curled wall calendar. "June Sixteenth. Hell of a time to be in the valley. How much longer are we going to pussyfoot around this way?"

"I'm not pussyfooting. I'm mining borax with both hands."

"And losing money every day."

"A *good* mine will always pay itself off."

Kane let the mark slide off. Mysterious Smith stood by the door, gazing down the dim cañon.

"Look here," Kane suddenly blurted. "We're a couple of strong mules, you and I, but we're pulling in the wrong directions. Now, Smith and I . . ."—he glanced with some uncertainty at the

280

boraxer—"we've been talking about a merger."

Smith said: "Two wrongs do not make a right."

Kane looked disgusted. Grady laughed. "Nor two bad mines a good. What's the matter, Mysterious . . . the Bellyache mines gone bad?"

Smith shook his head slowly. "It's not that. It's the hatred and strife that are wrong."

"They didn't used to disagree with you."

Kane's temper suddenly ripped out at the seams. He strode to Grady's reeling desk and began to pound on it. "I've had enough of backing and filling over this. I've got you in a corner, Ryan, and you'll come out of it on my terms. We're going to merge, whether you like it or not, and the terms will be a lot more to your interest if you co-operate."

Grady said stonily: "So you've got *me* in a corner, now!"

Borax Kane was taking a paper from an envelope. He unfolded it and let the miner have a brief glimpse of it before he replaced it. Grady felt a cold finger trace his spine. "That looked like my signature."

"It should. That piece of paper was signed in Mojave. It was for a loan made by a man named Zeelendorf. It cost me a cut of the Bellyache mines, but the point is . . ."

Ryan could read the page entire. "The point is, I owe you instead of the Swiss, now."

"You may find me a less co-operative creditor,"

Kane remarked. "I see that you've got an install-ment of interest and principal due next week. I'll want it all in cash, unless we work out something else before then."

All at once Kane went stumbling backward out the door. The ledger Ryan had flung had struck him in the chest. He rolled down the slope a short distance and got up, shouting obscenities. Ryan heard him stumbling away in the darkness. He slumped into a chair, breathing hard, glaring at Smith. Smith shook his head.

"You shouldn't have done that, boy."

"I didn't have a gun. It was all I could grab."

"You didn't used to be so buttish. Used to be slow-going and smiling. Money's changed you."

"Not money. Lack of money, Mysterious."

Smith deposited the twenty-pound Bible on a table and opened it to a place marked with a bartender's suds knife. "I think I got this all figgered out. It's all right here in the Book." He read: "'Vanity of vanities, saith the Preacher. Behold all is vanity.'"

As he read, Ryan perceived that he had found the irrefutable apology for failure: the Lord wanted it that way. He said wearily: "That's OK. That's good stuff, Smith. But . . . damn it," he said wryly, "don't you wish we could've cut the mustard? You and I should never have busted up. We'd have stood this valley on its ear. We'd have had buckets of money by now. Remember that house you were going to build?"

Smith's eyes filled. He closed the Bible slowly, stood looking down at it, and declared plaintively: "Now you've went and took that away from me. What's the matter with you, man? You're bitter to the core."

"Just about." Ryan sighed. "And if I don't find . . ." Suddenly he sat up straight.

Smith's face, too, acquired a curious look. He appeared to listen. "You hear sumpthing?"

Ryan did. He had heard the sound several times in his life. Californians were bound to. It was a distant, shaking rumble. Then the shack began to rock. It was like being in a boxcar taking a turn, giving itself a shake, and then straightening out. It went on for a full half minute, dust sifting down to them, the hanging lamp swinging, sheet-metal siding chattering. It was over, then. It might be the last, or it might be the beginning or end. It was an earthquake.

Smith grunted. "Glad I ain't in a mine tonight. But we're purty well timbered. Not like when I was a young feller. Your legs for stulls and shoulders for timbers. Better come up with me and have a shot of holy water, Grady."

Ryan got the words through the dust in his mouth. "No, I think I'll stick around a while yet. See you in town, Smith."

As the old man went out, Ryan thought: *You*

missed a bet, old-timer! The Lord has just spoken, and you didn't even hear his voice. It was practically supernatural. One minute he was saying the Bible was all right, if you believed that sort of thing. The next . . . came catastrophe. Rigidly he kept his mind from plunging into conjecture. Falling rocks, broken timbers, crushed bodies of miners—these things were swirling in the darkness just beyond the shores of consciousness.

Smith's Bible lay on the desk. He turned it. The stuff the prospector had found so comforting was, he decided, downright level-headed. This preaching had come out of a wise head.

He looked up, his eyes softening. *Maggie, girl, I wish I'd turned an ear to you. You had something to tell me, if I'd been able to hear you. If I'd closed up, I wouldn't have had those boys in the mines tonight.*

He read on for a half hour. And by this device Grady Ryan killed the half hour before they came for him.

Tom Lund came alone, blundering up the path like a blind man. He stopped in the doorway, gripping both jambs, dirty, sweating, and scared. "Cave-in in Number One! Haven't checked all the rest. Did you feel it?"

Grady got his cap and lamp and went with him. Up and down the cañon, men were scampering like ants. Inside the main Tommyknocker drift, they squeezed along between the walls and a line of ore cars carrying out tons of cleared rock. Shattered timbers thrust up from the flotsam. Grady worked through a gang of muckers. Jury timbering had been thrown up. Slabs of rock the size of an ore car had fallen. They were being laboriously dragged back to where they could be handled. Ryan took his place with the men.

It was 3:00 in the morning when they cleared a snake hole. Shouts came to them from beyond, and presently a face showed in the aperture as a miner crawled through. Four men came out. They told of two more trapped under the rocks.

At 5:00, they recovered the bodies. A pearly daylight suffused the hot morning sky when they reached the grass. Ryan watched them carry the tarpaulin-draped bodies down to the railroad. He had an impulse to explain that it wasn't his fault, that an earthquake could catch anybody napping.

Yet he knew the best defense he could make was to keep his mouth shut and try to salvage enough out of the wreckage of the Ryan mines to help out the widows. It was all cut and dried, the whole heartbreaking business closed. The fight that had begun one night over a table in a saloon was ended. There was nothing to do now but purge the soul with whiskey in that same saloon. Something holy about whiskey, too. Holy water, saloon variety. Beyond this point cares dared not tread.

He rode up to Furnace Flat with a carload of weary muckers. In the saloon, they left him alone, a hulking, haunt-eyed man frowning into a whiskey glass, as if words of wisdom might be written there. Certainly he had found them nowhere else.

Presently Pat Hoagland, Fisher, and some of the Furnace Flat men came in. Hoagland wore a look of sanctimonious gravity. But inside he must have been ready to erupt with glee.

Grady drank for an hour. He sat listening to the senseless hammering dissonance of the mechanical piano, taking his liquor with beer chasers. It was like pouring whiskey down a drain. It muddled without touching his grief. He kept seeing the broken forms of two miners who, but for him, would have been alive now. And yet he would have taken a miner's oath that those timbers would hold.

Hoagland stopped by to lay a hand on his shoulder and say: "Sorry old man." He jumped as Grady started up, but Grady let himself sullenly back into the chair and merely watched as the Kane crowd departed.

It was not long after this that red-headed Tom Lund barged into the saloon. Lund carried a short length of shattered twelve-by-twelve. His cap was off; he was filthy with rock dust, but there was a kind of shine to him. He walked across the floor straight to where Ryan sat swaying on his chair.

VIII

Lund put the timber down on the table so heavily the legs creaked. He scrubbed dirt away from the wood with a muddy handkerchief. "Look there! What do you call that?"

Ryan looked at the timber, with its splintered end and deep saw marks, without comprehending. "I call that a busted timber," he told Lund thickly.

Lund said: "I call it shenanigans!" The broken nail of his forefinger indicated four deep, blade-thick ruts across the wood. It was at the fourth that the tough grain of wood had broken. "I found a dozen of these doctored jobs in Number One alone. Don't know how many in the other mines."

"Saws slip," Ryan said obtusely.

"Four on one timber? Four inches deep? The hell they do!"

Ryan frowned. He discerned suddenly that it had been one of the cuts that caused the timber to break. Slowly he pushed his chair back. He stared at Lund. "Who set this thing up?"

Lund's tawny eyes pinched. "That's what I've been trying to find out. I knew it was a gang of company busters I hired away from Hoagland. Thought they came along kind of easy. You won't find any of them on the payroll now. They've quit, a man at a time, not even squawking about leaving half their wages. Why not? I'd reckon they were drawing pay up the line. I've talked to some boys who swear those busters practically locked them out of the mine while they done the timbering."

The whiskey finally caught fire. It warmed, fountained up darkly inside Ryan, turned loose something that had been a long time bound. He started across the room, lurched against a table, and tipped it over. He had to grope his way. Lund grabbed an arm and steered him to the bar.

"Get Mister Ryan some coffee. Grady, I'm going to make a speech. Soak up about a gallon of coffee while I talk."

Ryan never knew what Lund said, but he was conscious of loud voices in the saloon and men swarming about him, and someone yelling in a high, old-man's voice: "Bring that stick along. We're going to nail Kane and Hoagland up for everybody in Furnace Flat to see."

Ryan turned and saw Mysterious Smith near him. Smith came over and gripped his arm. "Forty years in the valley, and I never seen a thing like this before. Won't again, neither."

"Tell you a better stunt," Lund declared. "Re-timbering is going to wreck the Tommy-knocker. Kane knew that when he sent his hunkies in to high-grade us. I'll work for beans until we get them all tore out and replaced. Anybody going to help me?"

It seemed that nearly everyone was. But Ryan himself cooled the idea.

"That's great. But what are we going to use for timbers?"

Lund laughed. "Excuse the boss, boys. He's drunk. Kane's got a whole timber camp down there. All the twelve-by-twelves we'll need and, if we run short, we'll take them out of his mines. Why don't we start now, before it gets too hot?"

Ryan, beginning to sober, was carried out with them.

Hell was a great place to be from. You could not evaluate the things you had until you'd spent a few weeks there. This was his conviction as they rattled along on the flat car. The heat seemed wonderful, the gaunt walls of calico stone beautiful. But the finest thing of all was to have been the black dog of Cinnabar Flat, and to be accepted again by the sort of men you understood and respected.

At 6:00, the heat already pouring down into the cañon, the mines were deserted. *Fine,* thought Ryan. No one to object when they took the timbers. But he'd be having a talk with Kane and Hoagland one day. A moment later, scanning the sheet-metal building that was the local Furnace Flat office, he saw that the mines were not entirely deserted. Someone stood at a window, watching the work train coast in.

He waved the donkey man on when the train

began to slow. "We'll pick up granny bars before we go on up!" he called.

Lund was not deceived. "Sure granny bars will do the job?"

"I've got a couple of hollow crowbars with Forty-Five caliber ammunition in the office," Ryan told him.

While the workmen swarmed up the slope to the tool crib, he and Tom secured guns from the office and started up the tracks to the Bellyache. Mysterious Smith had, mysteriously, disappeared. There were just the two of them walking up the tracks to the main hoppers, climbing along the hurry chute toward the gleaming corrugated shed leaning on stilts against the flank of the mountain. Two men without much shelter.

The heat rose up sulphurously from the cañon as if from a river of molten iron. *It must be hell in the shack,* Ryan thought. The men in there must have good reason to stay inside.

They were within a hundred feet. A rough mule trail led from the chutes to the office. When they had gone a short distance along it, someone shouted. Hoagland stood in the doorway with a rifle.

"Leave the guns if you're coming in!"

Ryan stopped, his eyes taking inventory of the closest boulders. "The guns," he said, "are the reasons we're coming in."

He took two strides more when Hoagland

snapped the gun up. A bullet slashed through a gray holly at the side of the trail. Grady dived for a rock. He heard Lund digging in behind him.

Lining the Colt out across the rock, he sent a slug crashing into the wall. It opened a small perforation in the metal, and perhaps in someone inside. With the echoes still pouring down the cañon, he sprinted another twenty feet up the trail. Kane's ill-tempered voice reached him.

"I'll kill you both quicker than I would a chuckwalla if you try to break in here. But I'm willing to dicker."

"So am I. Here's my second offer." The bullet passed through the wall.

"So help us God, Ryan!" shouted Hoagland. "We mean business. If you're coming here with any notion that we were responsible for your cave-in, leave it behind. We can adjust this."

"One way," said Ryan.

Lund's gun crashed, the report striking Ryan heavily as he crouched ahead of him. He heard Hoagland yell again: "Let the damned fools have it!"

At the adit of a mine above them, a gun roared. Grit exploded at Grady's side. He began to crawl, but Hoagland took a snap shot that struck in front of him and forced him to flatten against the ground. He wriggled around into a shallow depression, hearing Lund grunt and swear as he, too, sought shelter from both points. Another shot

291

screamed down at him. It passed so close that the sound on the gravel was like a cap crack.

Hoagland or Kane fired once more from the building. Lund cried out, gripping his forearm the way a man did with more than a scratch. In a moment he picked up his Colt and fired wildly at the shack, but dropped the gun immediately and tried to stanch the blood gouting from his arm.

Ryan turned back. He could lie here and be picked off like carrion, or he could make a run for it. He took shells from his pocket and reloaded the gun. He pulled his legs up under him, and braced himself.

Someone called to him. It was the pink-gummed voice of Mysterious Smith. "I figger to fire a stick o' dynamite over thataway directly, Ryan. I'd lay still if I was you."

Ryan froze. From the sound, he figured Smith must be below the shed, somewhere between it and the railroad. For an instant Hoagland was exposed at a window.

Up in the mine, Fisher began wildly pumping shots down the slope. But Smith appeared to be well hidden. A moment later something tan and cylindrical arched from the rocks, struck the tin roof, and rolled off, to lie closely beside the shack.

Fisher was screaming: "It's a trick! Stay inside!"

But the men inside would not gamble. They lurched into the brassy sunlight, Hoagland firing as he came. He ran up the slope toward the mine,

Kane sprinting for a rock and flopping beside it. Grady took cool aim at his former boss's running figure. He pressed the trigger and felt the good, solid buck of the gun. Hoagland broke stride and went down hard.

Mysterious Smith took Kane from the back. Ethics, when dealing with men whose ethics were those of a sand rattler, seemed foolish. Kane bleated like a sheep.

Fisher, not a man to stick by a partner any more than a principle, came out of the mine with his hands up.

A moment later there was a concussive blast close against the side of the shack. One wall was crushed inward as dust rose about the building. Smith, it seemed, had not been bluffing.

Grady Ryan left Furnace Flat on the narrow-gauge train for Tonopah that night, after seeing Tom Lund taken care of in the company infirmary. He and Smith had had a brief talk about the possibility of a merger. In a new burst of religion, Smith wanted to call the outfit the Golden Rule mines. "Credit where credit's due," Ryan argued. "You name yours whatever you want. I'll keep on calling mine the Tommyknocker."

He thought Maggie would like that. It was a lot of foolishness, of course. But if you had to believe in superstitions, the little people were good ones to stick with.

About the Author

Frank Bonham in a career that spanned five decades achieved excellence as a noted author of young adult fiction and detective and mystery fiction, as well as making significant contributions to Western fiction. By 1941 his fiction was already headlining Street and Smith's *Western Story* and by the end of the decade his Western novels were being serialized in *The Saturday Evening Post*. His first Western, *Lost Stage Valley* (1948), was purchased as the basis for the motion picture, *Stage to Tucson* (Columbia, 1951) with Rod Cameron as Grif Holbrook and Sally Eilers as Annie Benson. "I have tried to avoid," Bonham once confessed, "the conventional cowboy story, but I think it was probably a mistake. That is like trying to avoid crime in writing a mystery book. I just happened to be more interested in stagecoaching, mining, railroading. . . ." Yet, notwithstanding, it is precisely the interesting— and by comparison with the majority of Western novels—exotic backgrounds of Bonham's novels that give them an added dimension. He was highly knowledgeable in the technical aspects of transportation and communication in the 19th-Century American West. In introducing these backgrounds into his narratives, especially when combined with his firm grasp of idiomatic Spanish spoken by many of his Mexican characters, his stories and novels are elevated to a higher plane in which the historical sense of the period is always very much in the forefront. This historical aspect of his Western fiction early drew accolades from reviewers so that on one occasion the *Long Beach Press Telegram* predicted that "when the time comes to find an author who can best fill the gap in Western fiction left by Ernest Haycox, it may be that Frank Bonham will serve well." Among his best Western novels are *Snaketrack* (1952), *Night Raid* (1954), and *Last Stage West* (1959).

Center Point Large Print
600 Brooks Road / PO Box 1
Thorndike, ME 04986-0001 USA

(207) 568-3717

US & Canada:
1 800 929-9108
www.centerpointlargeprint.com

11/15
lefm